INTIMATE PORTRAITS

INTIMATE PORTRAITS

by

Cheryl B. Dale

J&H Press

Other Fiction by Cheryl B. Dale

Romantic Suspense

Treacherous Beauties
The Man in the Boat
Set Up

Paranormal Romance

The Warwicks of Slumber Mountain

Light Mystery

Taxed to the Max
Overtaxed and Underappreciated

Copyright Information

Copyright 2013 by Cheryl B. Dale
Published by J&H Press
Cover Art by coversbycali.com
Edited by B.L. Wilson

ISBN: 978-0-9853910-2-7

INTIMATE PORTRAITS

www.cherylbdale.com
cherylbdale.blogspot.com
cherylbdale@hotmail.com

Chapter One

"*NO-O-O!*" THE TODDLER threw his sippy cup at Autumn Merriwell.

She sidestepped. It clipped her collar bone but missed her camera and tripod.

"Okay," she soothed him, thankful that the bruise would get better. A broken Nikon wouldn't. "It's okay, Dalton."

While the doting mother clucked over her son, Autumn swept up the sippy cup, whipped out a tissue, and wiped juice dribbles off the hardwood floor. "I think he's tired, Mrs. Jenovese, but I've got some good shots you can choose from."

She'd better have.

If she didn't, after thirty minutes of the kid's kicking and tantrums, she'd scream, too.

After assuring Mrs. Jenovese the proofs would be ready by the middle of the next week, a relieved Autumn waved goodbye.

The little imp was so photogenic, the shots should have been a breeze. A shame he felt so rotten today. A bigger shame his mother hadn't cancelled till his cold got better.

As Autumn took her next client—a high school junior wanting a better senior portrait—back to the studio, her receptionist caught her. Excitement made the rotund Iris bounce like a rubber ball. "The *lady* you shot before Thanksgiving is on line one."

The lady…? Sarita! Autumn had given up on hearing anything.

"Be right with you." She rushed off to the teen's "Hey! I need to get done here before—"

Over the phone, Sarita sounded gravelly, like she lounged in bed after a late night. "I needed a break, and couldn't wait for Mom to get back next week so I sneaked out of LA early. I'm dying to see those proofs. Can you be a doll and bring them over?"

"Sure." Like Autumn would turn down Sarita Sartowe, Atlanta's homegrown living legend? No way. Especially after pretty much writing off Sarita's photo shoot.

Not that this was a request. The international celebrity expected people to drop everything and jump when she snapped her fingers.

Autumn obliged. "When would you like to see them?"

Sarita's distinctive gurgle filtered over the line. "Now."

"Okay." And it was definitely okay. Nothing mattered except that Sarita was still interested in the photographs taken three weeks back: not the rushed senior picture for the impatient teen, not the four remaining appointments that had to be reshuffled, not the forty-minute drive in heavy lunch traffic. Nothing.

Sarita wanted to see the proofs!

At the entrance gate to the North Atlanta mansion where Sarita waited, Autumn spoke into the box, pleased at how calm she sounded. Like she met with celebrities every day.

But butterflies skimmed her stomach. So much depended on this. If Sarita liked her photographs, the studio's reputation would be made. People from all over would come to Private Portraits by Merriwell.

She could…

No, don't even go there. Wait to see what Sarita says. She may hate them.

The wrought iron gate swung open, allowing access up the winding drive to the neo-eclectic mansion, a wedding present from Sarita to her mother and stepfather two years back.

At the double front doors, Autumn took a big breath and pushed the bell. Chimes died away before one door cracked to reveal Sarita in designer jeans and tee. Her eyes looked sleepy but her trademark tiny braids were neat. "Come on in."

Autumn stepped inside. In the empty foyer, silence hung heavy. A lot different from the October shoot amid an entourage of assistants, hairdressers, maids, and a bunch of other people Sarita hadn't bothered to introduce. "Are you all by yourself?"

"Yep. Just li'l old me." Sarita made a face. "I told you, girl, I sneaked off. I'm tired of those fools hanging on all the time. Now let me see the pix. Sit." The curved sofa faced a glass coffee table. "Put them on the table here." Sarita sank down on an ottoman by the side.

Autumn laid proofs out as commanded. She started to point out lighting and texture, but Sarita, intent on the proofs, ignored her explanations. She hushed and tried not to fidget.

Occasionally, Sarita commented on a hairdo or piece of jewelry but mostly she looked. What was she thinking? No matter how Autumn studied her, her expression didn't give a clue.

At last, Sarita sat back on the sofa. Her arms stretched up, pulling the tee tight over perfect breasts. Sultry lips pushed out in a bored pout. "Nice." Her arms fell down. She let out a disappointed sigh, cocked her head to one side, straightened a crooked proof. Sighed again. "Very nice."

Bummer. Sarita didn't like the proofs.

So why should she? The woman had the best photographers from all over the world panting to shoot her. She'd only tried out Autumn because Reseda, who cleaned house for Sarita's mother as well as for Autumn, had asked her to.

Then Sarita's indifference melted and she hopped up. "I love them!" She squealed and did a victory dance. "They're effing unbelievable!"

She likes them!

Before Autumn could take it in, Sarita grabbed her and whirled her around the glass coffee table where the proofs lay.

Gushing the entire time.

She totally, absolutely, positively adored the proofs. She had to have at least one eight by ten of each, more of the fab shots she absolutely truly positively loved, definitely one full length life-size pose. Or two. Or three.

"Oh, girl, when these get released, every woman in LA is gonna be clamoring for you to take their pictures!" She stopped, frowned and cursed. "You have to sign an agreement. My stuff comes first, before you take on anybody else. We'll put you on retainer or something. You'll have to move to LA."

Retainer? Move to LA? Autumn, dazed, recovered enough to say, "Let me get my order sheet and fill—"

Sarita waved a hand. "Later. Leave the proofs and I'll have my PR man get back to you with how many we need and all that. I can't believe how super effing great these are! Reseda and Momma kept telling me you were something else, but I thought they were blowing smoke. The only reason I posed for you was to shut them up."

Not that Autumn cared why Sarita had agreed.

An hour after she entered, Autumn floated out of the half-timbered mansion, hopped into the studio minivan and wheeled down the driveway. The day might have been gloomy, but not anymore, no matter how gray the clouds. And wasn't the sky lighter on the horizon? It was going to be a beautiful weekend.

"Sarita liked them," Autumn sang as she exited into the tree-lined neighborhood. "Sarita liked them, she liked them."

Going around a curve in the middle of the quiet street, she almost ran into a florist's van. A quick swerve, a tap of the brake, and she was back in her lane. Her luck held out.

Not that her pounding heart proved it. "Cool it, idiot. All you need is a wreck killing you before you can deliver the biggest job of your career."

Lucky she didn't meet any other traffic till she hit busy West Paces Ferry. By then she'd settled down, thinking of what Sarita had said about putting her on retainer but mostly...

Sarita liked the proofs. After sweating it for weeks, deciding the diva had forgotten her, mentally writing off her big chance… The waiting was over.

Autumn thumped the wheel in triumph, giggled again. No need to worry any longer. She might as well go by Perimeter Square since she was so close, and pick up a holiday top for the weekend. A mountain weekend with the Degardoveras after this morning's coup would top everything off. Kind of a celebration.

Retainer…move to LA…Degardoveras…

And then the lurking thought came out into the open, unbidden, unwanted.

Rennie's in LA. I can see him again.

Rennie.

****

AN EASY JOB, BERNIE had told Sam Bogatti. Get in, do her, collect the stuff, and get out.

Blah, blah, blah.

Easy. Yeah, sure. He'd found the stuff all right, but Sarita had bolted LA for Atlanta. So as quick as he'd handed the package off to the courier, he'd had to haul ass across country.

Huh. Everything was always easy for Bernie, snug in his law office, drawing up wills or contracts or whatever the shit he did to earn his twenty percent. Bernie's ass wasn't on the line.

I could've gone to school. Sam chewed gum and wheeled the van off the Perimeter. *Been a high-priced lawyer like Bernie. Took my cut off the top and never got my hands dirty.*

Yeah. Right. Stuck at a desk, choking in a tie, dealing with assholes like Bernie every stinking day.

Not hardly.

Nah, he couldn't complain. Over the years he'd made a lot of money and traveled all over. Like the west coast Tuesday, the sunny south today. Never got to see much of the countryside, but the pay made up for it.

Entering the exclusive neighborhood that sheltered Sarita, he came around a curve and met a minivan half over the center.

It swerved.

He swerved.

They missed each other by inches, so close he could see the shocked, circled mouth under big sunglasses.

Blonde hair. Woman driver. It figured.

Sam wasn't an excitable guy so he didn't overreact. But he did slow to a crawl. The GPS positioned the house a block away, and he needed to check addresses anyway.

Mansions stood like isolated castles among hardwood branches clawing at the sky, but thick evergreen stands of pines, cedars, and hollies barred passers-by from seeing into yards even in December. The owners of the castles valued their privacy.

Like Sam.

A pedestrian appeared. On this crisp December afternoon, the lone out-of-shape jogger gasped for breath as he bounced his way back to health.

More like a heart attack.

Sam, snug inside the van with its stick-on vinyl panels advertising Betty and Lulu's Flower Boutique, grunted. A man could die trying to lose twenty years' worth of fat in a week.

Not him. He might be pushing forty, but he had the body of a man ten years younger. His skinny frame might fool people into thinking he was a wimp, but he kept himself in tiptop shape.

Had to for his job.

By the time he turned into the winding driveway of the massive half-timbered Tudor dwelling sited across a creek, the jogger had long since staggered out of sight.

Halfway to the house, a closed gate met the van.

No *prob-lem-o*. He punched in the code. *Thanks, Bernie boy.*

He drove through, parked in back at the delivery door.

Mother and stepfather gone. Nobody'll be home but her, Bernie'd said. Piece of cake.

Like Bernie knew shit.

Not many things in life that simple.

After Sam took out his gum, he wrapped it in its saved paper and stuffed it in his litter bag. Then he got out with the floral box.

It even held roses in case she wanted to see them before opening the door.

Little extras like that had saved him grief more times than he liked to remember.

Double patio doors lay adjacent to the delivery entrance, so he stepped over the edging blocks onto bark mulch that wouldn't take footprints and leaned over small shrubs for a quick peek.

The house's open design gave a clear view across an open interior to large windows framing trees. Nice. He liked that.

What he saw inside he liked even better.

Sarita Sartowe, this year's flavor of superstardom, sat by herself on an ottoman with her back to him. He could tell it was her by the mass of tiny braids tumbling forward as she bent over something in front of her. Her arm occasionally moved.

Thumbing through a magazine? Searching for articles about herself? Sure were lots of them out there.

He tried a door. Unlocked. No need to ring the bell. Maybe Bernie would be right for once.

Inside, notes from a sultry trumpet flowed from surround sound speakers and masked the door click. Louis Armstrong. Sweet. Not what he'd expect from a trending gal like Sarita.

Retrieving the silenced .22 Ruger, he laid the floral box on a cozy dining table. Four chintz place mats and bright red napkins circled a fern centerpiece.

Cheerful. Homey. A lot different from Sarita's LA digs.

Sam noticed stuff like that. His wife said he had a sensitive soul, but his eye helped in his work. Like he spotted right off there was no bodyguard tucked in the corner of the great room.

Yeah, she was alone like Bernie the prick had promised.

Nice layout, too. Like a scene from an old *noir* film where the director posed his leading lady in silhouette against ceiling high windows while the bad guy sneaked up behind her.

And Sarita was oblivious as any *noir* heroine.

When the trumpet's suggestive tones gave way to the

raspy croon of Satchmo, she began to sway and hum with the music. Her voice was husky, delicious, unmistakable.

Mesmerizing.

Sarita Sartowe, performing for herself and an uninvited fan. Glorious. One of those rare unforgettable moments.

A bullet in her head seemed out of place. Blasphemous.

He stuffed the Ruger into his belt and pulled out a thin blade six and a half inches long from its utilitarian hilt to its tip. Its edges were honed razor sharp, an instrument designed to his specifications and fabricated for a single purpose.

Weighing it, he hesitated. All that blood. Messy as a bullet.

Eyes on her back, he retreated to a window where he slashed the cord of a Roman shade and looped an end around either hand.

There. The cord felt right. More appropriate.

Go with the gut. It's never wrong.

When he glided toward the sofa, when he was three feet away, she stopped humming.

He froze.

She gave one long luxuriant sigh and stretched both arms up.

The braids must have been hot because she caught and held them away from her neck for a moment, then bent back to whatever kept her so rapt.

Sam relaxed. Not a clue.

The big windows to her front trapped his shadow behind him. The thick carpet muffled his sneakers.

Not until he threw the cord over her head in one lightning quick stroke did she realize she wasn't alone.

Too late.

"Ahhhh—" What would have been a scream died.

She struggled, but he held firm.

She half rose and clawed at the cord.

He didn't let go.

She tried for his face.

He pulled his head out of reach.

All the time the cord's pressure choked her windpipe. He

sweated, but held on tight long after she slumped against his chest. His heartbeat thrummed in his ears.

Kind of eerie holding her so close. Almost like he was one of her lovers.

She was still, not breathing, but he kept her there for three minutes, four minutes, five.

Trembling from the effort—how come movies make strangling somebody seem so frigging easy?—Sam released the cord and lowered her to the ottoman.

No pulse, but his own heart thudded so he could have missed any thread of life.

Wait till you can tell. He did his stress exercises, counted his pulse rate, settled down. Okay. He checked again.

She was dead. The sensual lips were slack, never again to curve invitingly. Nor would that dainty ear hear any more whispered endearments from besotted lovers.

Shit, he hated this part of his job.

Don't look at her.

He couldn't help it. Her complexion, once vibrant as mellowed oak, had dulled to grayish brown. Her tongue lolled to one side. Dark eyes popped out, opaque and staring.

She was ugly now as she'd never been in life.

He'd seen violent death lots of times, but this…

The familiar queasiness surged.

Don't get sick. Look away, dumbass. Think of something else.

What had engrossed her so much she hadn't heard him?

Pictures. His latex-clad finger fanned them out. Photographs of her. Lovely, every one. Like her.

He could imagine her, pointing with a long magenta nail, saying, "This is good," and her soft hand that in a different time, a different place, could drive a man wild, shifting that proof into a stack to keep.

Two years ago he and his wife had attended Sarita's United Center concert. If that night had left any doubts of her charisma, these photos dispelled them. She was unique.

In one lounging shot, a snowy sheet emerged from between her thighs to cover most of the dark triangle and one golden hip. A hand cupped a breast, not protectively but like she relived a lover's caress. Tiny black braids fanned to one side. An amulet lay on the hollow of her collarbone. A lacy earring traced a pattern on the white pillow. Huge eyes wore sex's aftermath.

Jeez, that picture was something else.

There were others, all seductive, all with her looking like an angel. Sam shuffled through them. She'd been a damn fine singer, a damn splendid woman. A shame he'd had to do her.

It's my job. No reason to feel guilty. And she was no angel, that was for sure. A wonder someone hadn't offed her before now.

The familiar mantra didn't work, but at least he'd quit trying to puke.

Stealing a proof, he had it halfway to his pocket when another caught his eye.

Sarita leaned dreamily against a mirror. Her gown, frothy and light, fell off smooth shoulders. One erect nipple touched its reflection. A large collar of beads, vivid blue and purple beads primitive as the woman herself, fanned out from her neck.

That necklace. He recognized it from the stuff taken from her LA safe.

No way. She wouldn't have…

He bent closer.

Shit.

He thumbed back through the proofs and cursed.

Another telltale shot of ivory. And one of turquoise.

The dumb son of a bitch.

If whoever had diddled Sarita hadn't let his pecker rule his head, Sam would never have had to silence that glorious voice.

Now he was caught in the middle.

Because nobody, least of all him, could afford this snafu.

He swept all the photos up, noted the studio name.

Lucky he had sharp eyes and a sharper mind.

Why did people make his job so complicated?

Chapter Two

IN THE MIDDLE of the afternoon, Autumn skipped up her condo walk, swinging her shopping bag.

She still couldn't believe it.

When word got out Sarita Sartowe was a client, studio business would double. Maybe triple. No more pictures for school yearbooks. No more dodging sippy cups. No more scratches from cats whose fond owners mouthed empty apologies or strained muscles from chasing runaway dogs through the studio.

Her key turned in the knob effortlessly.

Same for the dead bolt.

Both unlocked.

Had she forgotten to lock up this morning when she left?

No way. Not *Miss Caution* personified. Besides, she distinctly remembered hearing the bolt clunk into place.

Cell. Where was it? She pulled it out of her purse, and then turned the doorknob. Yep, open.

Tinny applause crackled from the TV.

She froze, heartbeat ratcheting up. When she'd gone off that morning, she certainly hadn't left the TV blaring.

Someone was here.

Reseda? No, Reseda cleaned on Tuesdays, not Fridays. But hadn't she mentioned taking off next week? Something about relatives from Mexico City? Maybe she was making up for it today.

That was logical, wasn't it? Stepping inside, Autumn

looked for Reseda Degardovera. No plump figure bustled through with dust-rags or vacuum, but could be, she was upstairs.

Or maybe she gave Fran her key.

Oh sure, that was it. Lowering her cell, Autumn breathed again. Fran was driving her to Helen for the getaway weekend with his sisters.

Then she frowned. Fran with a key to her condo?

Fran did *not* need her key. Not even to pick her up. She was wary of jumping into anything she might regret, and joining Francisco Degardovera's string of women was definitely something she'd regret.

Better make sure he gave Reseda her key back.

Autumn set down the Brooks Brothers shopping bag containing a new snowman sweater. A talk show featured two skinny wild-haired kids confronting two older wild-eyed women. A down jacket hung over a chair. A sofa cushion bore a head's imprint. A pair of battered men's loafers rested on the area rug in front of the sofa.

Fran had stretched out to watch the tube except...

Those loafers. Persnickety Fran wouldn't take out the garbage in such dilapidated shoes. Someone had made himself at home, but not Fran.

A whiff of cologne lingered, tantalizingly familiar.

She sniffed. Too subtle. Fran wore strong scents, something that announced his presence and attracted women's attention.

Okay. Not Fran, but someone comfortable in her home.

Few people were. Work left little time for cultivating close friends, especially for introverts like her.

Who then? Eddie, Reseda's youngest and a high school senior? The shoes would fit him, and he wasn't a clothes hound like Fran. But why would Eddie be here?

A creak came from the kitchen, from the cabinet door housing the glasses.

Clutching her cell, she slid her purse off her shoulder. She ought to run or call for help, but a casual burglar wouldn't settle in as if he belonged. And that cologne...

Had to be Eddie, but no sense taking chances. She dialed

911 but didn't press *CALL*. Instead, she picked up a fireplace poker and crept round the corner to the bar.

A sock-footed man, back to her, stood at the gaping refrigerator door. Squeaky, between his feet, wrapped her tail around his calf like she was his cat instead of Autumn's.

A loose T-shirt hung from wide shoulders. Worn jeans hugged slim hips and long legs. The afternoon sun streamed through window panes and turned dark curls into a frenzy of mahogany sparks. As some people have an unconscious habit of humming, he whistled softly between his teeth; a thin reedy, tuneless sound.

Radiant, body-tingling happiness cut through Autumn. She didn't need an exposed profile to recognize him.

Rennie. Lorenzo Tomas Degardovera. Friend of her childhood, counselor of her youth, object of her desire since before she knew what desire meant. Rennie, who'd left home years ago.

Happiness vanished. Gut-wrenching longing didn't.

Autumn swallowed. All right, so Rennie was back. Here in her kitchen. So what? She squared her shoulders.

The studio was going great guns, and Sarita Sartowe *loved loved loved* her photographs. She had taken control of her life. She didn't need Rennie's approval or anyone else's.

He turned, jug in hand. Like his body, his face was lean and bronze, with clean, strong bones. The hair was longer while the dark eyes had new lines around them, but he was still Rennie.

His eyes went to the poker she held. "Planning to start a fire or should I be concerned?"

Like she was one of his sisters he'd seen the day before.

She clicked off her cell and tried for breezy, too. "I didn't know who was here. You scared the stew out of me."

Thick brows lifted. "But you knew Francisco was coming."

"No. Yes. Not this early. You know Fran. I figured it would be five or six o'clock before he got here. Where is he, anyway?"

"Working. Okay, cat, I hear you but milk's not on your diet." He grinned at Autumn. "His boss was invited to replace an indisposed speaker Sunday for some shindig at the High Museum. Our Francisco's busy dealing with the schedule switch."

How like Fran. Not even a phone call to warn he was sending Rennie in his place. If she'd known, she could've been prepared.

She rallied. "The High Museum? That's great. Their supporters have money. Gobs of it. And I guess more exposure means more publicity for Gus's campaign."

Rennie pretended to think. "I believe little brother mentioned that. Along with more donations to keep the workers paid. Like the campaign manager."

"Who happens to be Fran." She focused on the milk tumbling from jug into glass to keep from ogling him. "Gus's wife must have finagled it. She's assistant director at the High."

"Whatever. Anyway, Fran can't get loose till tomorrow and then just for the day. He wanted Laney to wait and take you up to Helen with her and John. You can guess how that went over."

Her pulse settled. "Yeah. Laney tried to leave last night, she's so anxious. She's planned this trip for months. I'd be about as welcome as a case of mumps."

"Uh huh. So I told her to go on with John, that I'd cover." He headed for the sink with the empty jug. "The kid's growing up. A year ago, he'd have told his boss to forget it."

"He can't. He's in charge of everything. You ought to see him, trying to make sure Gus looks and acts like a gubernatorial candidate. Poor Fran's on call twenty-four hours a day."

"I know. But little brother's gung ho. If Huertole wins, Francisco has visions of being named press secretary or assistant governor or king of Atlanta or something. Anyway, I got in yesterday and Mom gave me her key and volunteered me to pick you up." He stopped in front of the sink. "You don't mind, do you? If you'd rather wait for—"

"Of course not." Darn those sharp eyes. He could pick up on the slightest sign. "Without a ride, I'd have to stay here. My car's in the shop so I'm using the studio minivan, which, sad to say, is on its last legs. Thanks for filling in."

"You're welcome." He looked at the poker she still clutched. "Didn't mean to scare you."

"Don't be silly. You know what a coward I am. If I'd been scared deep down, I'd have run screaming bloody murder when I found the door unlocked. I'll put this back."

"I think it's safe. No burglars here. I haven't even come across a cockroach."

"And you'd better not. Reseda would be outraged."

Again the unhurried grin. "Once Mom spotted him, any intelligent roach would roll over and wait to be stomped dead."

She snapped her fingers. "So *that's* why I haven't seen any around. They've wised up."

His cologne had changed, but the new choice still smelled of cedars and pines. She should have known who was here. Maybe subconsciously she hadn't wanted to be disappointed.

After sticking her cell in her purse and putting away the poker, she returned to find him rinsing the jug. Squeaky— the little traitor—was rubbing against his denimed legs. She said, "Guess I'll eat my cereal dry in the morning."

"You won't be here for breakfast tomorrow."

"True. I won't need milk, will I?"

"Nope." He turned the force of his personality on her briefly, indulgently, in a gesture unique to Rennie, where his head didn't move but the eyes flicked up, hit their target, and returned to the task at hand. Her heart swelled.

Still… His narrow face, with its lash pattern against flat cheeks and delineated bones, revealed a difference.

Maybe he was tired. Or it might be the light.

Don't stare. She fastened on his hands. Like the rest of him, they were quick and sure, slim and brown.

He held up the jug. "Recycle or trash?"

"Recycle. There's a bin in the utility room."

Those creases radiating from his mouth and corners of his eyes hadn't been so pronounced the last time she'd seen him, but that was two years ago.

When he returned, he took the glass of milk and held it up. "Want half of this?" Despite her refusal, he didn't drink. "Your cat seems glad to see me, but I figured I'd get at least a hug. Tell me, is it my breath or has my antiperspirant failed?"

She was, after all, caught staring. "Oh, Rennie, how thoughtless I am. Welcome home. You took me by surprise."

Going over, she put her arm around his waist and squeezed as if he was a dear friend she hadn't seen in a long time.

Which he was.

Too bad the faint cologne didn't hide his body scent, his Rennie-odor that made her stomach churn and her nose want to nuzzle into his chest.

Better let him go before she embarrassed herself.

She gave him a final pat on the back. "Squeaky, I'm sad to inform you, isn't discriminating so don't think she's fond of you. She'll take up with anybody she hopes might feed her. I really am glad to see you. I just wasn't expecting you."

"Certainly not raiding your refrigerator. Depleted as it is."

He lifted his glass to her and drank, throat muscles rippling.

"Yeah, raiding my depleted refrigerator." She'd better put some distance between them. "Are you home for Christmas?"

"I'm home for good."

"For good?" She stopped mid-step. "You mean it?"

"Yep. Well, not here in Atlanta. Athens. I signed a contract with the University this morning. The first of the year, I'll be teaching two classes for the AI Department along with doing some research and development stuff."

He'd be home. Close by. "That's wonderful. Does Reseda know?"

"Mom does *not* know. In fact, nobody at home knows. You're the first one I've seen since it happened." He checked his cell. "Approximately three hours ten minutes ago. If you don't mind, keep it to yourself. I don't want to tell the others before Mom. She left for her trip before dawn, but I'll talk to her tonight."

"Reseda will be beside herself. She'll be more excited than when you got your doctorate."

"Probably. She's always hated me being so far away."

What about Jane? She wanted to ask whether Jane was moving to Athens with him, if they were getting married.

She didn't.

The other Degardoveras blurted out everything, never caring if they pried or hurt feelings. Not Rennie. He was the quiet one, the private one.

Your secrets were safe with him, but he never shared his.

She pushed the bowl of oranges on the bar an inch to the left. "I'm not packed." Her hoarseness came from longing. She cleared her throat. "That's why I took the rest of the day off. Well, I knew Fran wouldn't be here so I went by Perimeter first, but... And I meant to get home early so I'd have plenty of time to pack, except... Let me run upstairs and get my stuff together and we can leave. I'm excited about going to Helen with the gang. I don't get many weekends off and I haven't seen Norma in ages."

Great. *Really coherent there, Autumn.*

She'd finally got a handle on life and now this. Why did he turn her into a babbling idiot? He was an old friend, that's all.

Keep saying that and maybe she'd believe it.

Rennie, being Rennie, politely ignored her blather. "Take your time. Please. We've got the entire weekend to be interrogated by my sisters and entertained by Francisco. Not to mention being cooped up in an isolated mountain cabin where we can't escape any of them no matter how hard we try."

She dredged up a chuckle. "Come on, celebrating Laney's anniversary will be fun. Think of the family togetherness."

"I prefer quality time over quantity time when it comes to my siblings. A little of them goes a long way."

"Liar. You love them. Be ready in a jiffy."

Confronting him so unexpectedly had put her out of

sorts. Safe in her upstairs bedroom, she busied herself to calm down.

Concentrate.

This duffel bag would do. For the anniversary dinner, her navy slacks would go with the new holiday sweater. Then some jeans and a sweatshirt for walking around town. She'd also need underwear, jammies, maybe a robe and house slippers. Toothbrush, toothpaste, shampoo and makeup.

Mustn't forget makeup. Not if she wanted to be presentable tomorrow and the next day.

The stairs creaked before Rennie appeared. "Autumn?"

His voice, like him, was low-pitched and reassuring. He never raised it, not toward parents or siblings or anyone else.

Never. He met every situation in the same easygoing way.

That was another thing she liked about him.

Growing up with her aunt and uncle, she'd had to pick up on each intonation, each change of posture, each shifting expression. Failure meant reprimands or punishment.

But Rennie was always kind, never judgmental.

"Be right with you, Rennie. Won't take a sec."

He wandered into her bedroom. "You don't mind that I'm taking you up to Helen instead of Francisco, do you? Sure you wouldn't rather wait and go with him tomorrow?"

Darn. He'd noticed her agitation.

She looked over her shoulder and gave him a smile that had to be brilliant because her mouth stretched so wide her face felt like it was cracking into tiny pieces.

"Don't be silly. Knowing Fran, he may miss the weekend entirely. You wouldn't believe what a workaholic he's become. Without a ride I'd have to hang out here with the TV for company. Say, that reminds me. My car might be ready. Would you call the garage and check? Maybe we can pick it up before we leave town. The number's on a card by the phone at the bar."

Great. Keep up the jabber, and he wouldn't want to drive her anywhere.

"Consider it done."

When he turned, the poster-sized photograph of Fran hanging on the wall confronted him. His foot checked, but he didn't comment on his brother's nudity or the provocative pose.

She opened her mouth to explain.

His step resumed. "I'll check on your car."

Her words of explanation never materialized. Rennie wasn't curious, didn't think it strange she kept a sexy photograph of Fran in her bedroom.

No need to justify its presence because Rennie didn't care.

Let down, she took out a scarf and jingle bell earrings to pack, then found walking shoes and thick socks.

Spending two nights with the Degardoveras in a cabin near the north Georgia resort town of Helen had sounded like fun when Laney invited her. She couldn't think of anything she'd rather do than celebrate her friend's second wedding anniversary. But with Rennie in the party…

"He's not going to spoil my weekend," she muttered.

Besides, her stupid outburst when he went away to UCLA was old news. Her neck heated at the way she'd begged to go with him, at how she'd sniveled when he ever-so-kindly turned her down.

Afterward, he never mentioned her breakdown. He'd treated her the same way as before. Like a friend.

Might as well accept it. That's all she'd ever be.

Tail high in a question mark, Squeaky strolled in. She leaped onto the bed and began to lick her paws, aiming a knowledgeable stare toward Autumn.

"All in the past, my dear," she told the cat. "No more wearing my heart on my sleeve for some stupid cupid to shoot down. You see before you a woman in control."

Squeaky stopped with one paw upraised. She cocked her head to one side as if she didn't believe it.

"I am too in control!"

Squeaky plopped down and rolled over on her back, sticking all four legs up into the air as if laughing.

Silly cat. What did Squeaky know?

She raked a brush through her hair in front of the mirror. There. Her usual face looked back at her. The same face she always wore.

Unlike the difference in Rennie's that her photographer's eye had picked up on.

She frowned, then shrugged. Not like she could do anything about it anyway.

Chapter Three

WAITING FOR AUTUMN, Rennie idly clicked through the TV menu.

Hadn't his mother emphasized Autumn specialized in sexy photographs of women? So why was that explicit picture of Francisco in her bedroom? Arrogance? No, she was too modest.

If she'd taken it, she was as good as everyone said. The photo projected the smoldering carnality that intrigued any female foolish enough to venture within ten feet of Francisco.

Autumn should be too smart to fall for his overbearing brother, but that picture was too intimate, too revealing.

Nope, he had to be wrong. Francisco and Autumn didn't belong together.

Like he and Jane hadn't belonged together.

Disgusted, he switched off the TV and lay back into the squishy sofa.

Seemed he was good at choosing women wedded to their careers. Maybe this time he'd learned his lesson. He laid his head back, clasped his hands on his stomach, and stared up at the ceiling.

Pointless to dwell on the past. The future would keep him busy enough. He'd have to find a place to live in Athens, put down utility deposits, give notice at his job, sublease his LA place, get his things packed and shipped…

Not today. All that could wait. He had a whole week off to relax, get his head together.

He stretched, edgy in the condo despite its soothing blues and greens, its precise placement of furniture.

Such tidiness contrasted with the Degardoveras' constant state of chaos. His mother, who cleaned for other people, kept her own carpets vacuumed and floors mopped, but with nine children, nothing got put away. He was used to clutter.

Face it, man, you're thirty-five years old. Time to admit you aren't going to change. Once a slob, always a slob.

Unlike Autumn.

The first time he'd seen her, she was five. She wore a pink dress with a matching hair bow and shiny black shoes, and looked like a child model. When later, the kids ate snacks, her place at the table was, unlike everyone else's, free of crumbs.

She'd been fastidious then. From what he could see, she still was. Everything out of place here belonged to him.

And that was why her being with Francisco irked him. She was too structured, too trusting. Francisco would break her heart.

Not that Autumn's love life was his affair.

And wasn't there some compulsive disorder associated with excessive neatness?

He snorted. "Your envy's showing." Getting up, he slipped on his scuffed loafers that needed replacing. One of these days, he'd get around to it.

Over the fireplace, a Richmond Stubbs watercolor, full of peaceful blues, graced one side of the mantel. On the other stood candlesticks he'd given Autumn for her seventeenth birthday, his last spring at home. Mom had asked him to take her to an estate sale where he'd spotted them. Graceful, on marble bases with curving pewter tops, they reminded him of Autumn.

They'd been buds back then. No stand-offishness like today.

What was up with that? She was reserved even as a child, but after that warm welcome today, she'd cooled noticeably.

Because she was disappointed? Maybe. Unlike him, his brother fascinated women, in particular standoffish women like Autumn. Those types fell all over themselves for Francisco.

He'd hate for Autumn to be one more conquest.

Light quick steps flew down the stairs.

The slacks and knit blouse showed she was still willowy, but she'd changed her hairstyle. Close on the back and one side, but long and clinging to the other jaw in a trendy cut that accentuated gold highlights and set off delicate bones.

"I like your hair like that."

"Thanks. It's easy to take care of."

Like she was easy to look at. Autumn had always been pretty and still was.

She dropped a duffel on the varnished foyer floor, barely missing the skulking cat. "What did the garage say about my car?"

"Not ready yet. A belt hasn't come in. Maybe Tuesday."

"Drat. They sent for that belt a week ago. I guess it can't be helped. Good thing I have a ride." She smiled at him, a natural smile but not radiant like earlier.

What made the difference? Emotion. Or its absence. Perhaps spontaneity. Sure, that was it. Autumn hid her feelings, but for one brief instant on seeing him, delight had won out.

She was happy to see him.

Not that you could tell now. She was as restrained as ever.

"I'd hate to miss Laney and John's party." She opened a closet door and pulled out a Dresden blue jacket which, when slipped on, turned out to be a swingy cape-like affair.

A lot different from the tailored blazers she used to wear. This coat was flamboyant enough for one of his sisters. It didn't look like Autumn, but what did he know?

"Nice jacket."

She started to close the closet door as the big orange cat streaked inside, left it cracked. "A little dashing, maybe." She flipped the cape sides and twirled. "But Aunt Laura bought it for me after my uncle died, when we went to Europe to recuperate. It's wool, warm. The weatherman says Helen will be cold this weekend."

"Cold, but we'll enjoy it."

"Uh huh. Helen's a fun place." Her fingers, ringless with short nails, fastened buttons with unhurried efficiency.

No longer plump and dimpled, her hands were thin and agile. A woman's hands. He'd been thinking of her as a girl. "I haven't been up to Helen in years. I might not recognize it."

She was, what, twenty-seven, twenty-eight? No. She was between Laney and Norma. Laney was thirty-one and Norma had turned twenty-nine last February so she'd be...

Thirty? Could that be right? Yeah, when he'd left home she'd been barely seventeen. He'd sure changed in the intervening years so how could he expect Autumn to stay the same?

She set a camera bag down beside the duffel.

He walked over. "Want me to get those?"

"I'd rather you pull the minivan inside my garage. I don't want to leave it out while I'm gone and there's no need to take it back to the studio since my car isn't ready."

"Sure."

One hand threw her key to him as the other brought out a cell phone. A confident woman used to coping with any and all situations. "While you do that, I'll check in with the studio and then make sure Squeaky's got enough dry food and litter. Oh, and watch her. She'll dart outside if you aren't careful."

He wasn't sure he liked this poised stranger as well as the shy girl.

When he moved the van inside her garage, a memory stick fell from an open dash pocket marked with an *SS* and today's date.

Inside, he said, "A thumb drive fell out of the dash, but I put it back."

"Thanks. I'll take it to the studio Monday."

He couldn't resist teasing. "Celebrity shots, by any chance? Like maybe of the notorious Sarita Sartowe?"

Her blue eyes widened. "How did you—? Oh. Fran, I suppose. He blabs everything."

"The boy can't help himself."

Not that his brother would confide anything to Rennie about Sarita.

Not after last year's full-fledged quarrel. A quarrel that had nothing to do with Sarita but everything to do with Francisco's deep-seated, mystifying envy that made him try to outdo his big brother in every way.

Rennie would never understand Francisco.

Fair was fair though. "Actually, the kid was the soul of discretion. Mom couldn't help crowing about how she got you the commission through Kaneka."

Kaneka, Sarita's mother, was another of his mother's housecleaning customers.

Autumn made a *moue*. "It doesn't matter, except I wanted to tell you myself and impress you."

"Hey, I'm impressed, believe me. Mom said you were taking the proofs to Sarita today. I gather she liked them."

"I think so."

"You think? You couldn't tell? Knowing Sarita, I'm sure she gave you some pretty heavy hints. She's not the reticent type."

Not in the least.

If only he could forget the days of hysterics and quarrels and laughter. The nights of biting and scratching and name-calling. The screaming, shattering orgasms after making up.

Sarita could never be called reticent.

Not that Autumn would ever know anything about Sarita's proclivities or his long-ago part in them.

One whole summer in thrall. He'd been young but still… How could he have been so naïve? Those memories could belong to another person.

He'd give anything if they did.

"Actually, Sarita was very outspoken." Autumn glowed. "She said she liked them, loved them, *adored* them. She's going through the proofs right now to see which ones she wants."

"Then why aren't you excited? Aren't you happy?"

The glow vanished. "Sure. I've never been one to jump up and down."

He'd hurt her feelings. "Of course not. You never get

wound up about stuff. Are you going to do more pictures for her?"

A tiny line creased her brow. "She wants me to shoot publicity shots for her concert tour next summer. She says if I move out there, I'll have no trouble getting clients."

"Move? To LA?" She'd never make it in Sarita's world. She'd be broken in six months.

He couldn't say that. What Autumn did was none of his business. "Big decision."

She ran fingers brusquely through her hair, a gesture that would have signaled nerves in anyone else. Her pacing, true to form, was slow and dignified. "I thought I could fly back and forth at first, see how it goes. Then later I might move. I don't know. Fran says California's terribly expensive. Is it?"

Candid blue eyes fastened on him. Maybe she was nervous.

"Yeah, it is pretty expensive."

"Fran says that's why he came back, that the cost of living was so high he couldn't stay. Is that why you came back, too?"

Fran says. Autumn couldn't be so naive as to fall for a womanizer like Francisco.

He chose his words. "Money was part of the reason. But this opening at the University came up and I was sick of—" No need to broadcast his failures. "Sick of working eighty hours a week."

"I see."

"Besides, California's too weird for me. I'm a straitlaced conservative at heart."

"I thought you were a liberal Democrat."

"No, ma'am. Not me. I'm one of the dissatisfied, disenfranchised, disinterested independents."

Thick lashes narrowed and nearly converged into one black line. He'd forgotten the way her eyelashes bunched together when she laughed. Autumn was a nice kid, even if she was a neat freak.

No, not a kid. A nice *woman.* "Ready to go?"

"Soon as I get the groceries I'm taking up to the cabin."

When she passed by, her perfume wafted by, the same rose scent she'd worn in high school.

It had clung to his shirt after she cried on his shoulder the night before he left for graduate school, when she'd begged him to take her with him. The poor kid was miserable at home, but he'd pointed out that the next year she'd be leaving for college herself. He'd hated leaving her with her aunt and uncle, but he'd persuaded her she could hack one more year.

That was all he could do. And they'd never again mentioned her lapse nor his inadequate response.

"Hey!" he called after her. "I wouldn't mind a preview of Sarita's photos. Or any of your work. Mom and the girls have been bragging like crazy about you, but I'd like to see samples."

Over her shoulder, she made a wry face. "The kinds of pictures I take don't lend themselves very well to viewing by third parties."

"Oh, come on. I'm a good critic of naked women. I've seen at least five in the flesh, counting my sisters and Tia Alejandra."

"When you were six? Sorry. Confidentiality is something my clients insist upon."

She disappeared into the kitchen without sounding the least bit sorry. Instead, she sounded like the successful photographer his family claimed she was.

Oh, yes, the Degardoveras had been delighted to fill Rennie in on Autumn's mushrooming career.

When her uncle had died and she'd dropped out of Ringling Brothers College of Art to join her aunt at the studio, its trade had consisted of the usual family, business, and school shots. Autumn had begun experimenting with intimate photographs, staged in the comfort of women's homes among familiar surroundings. According to Laney, the shots sexed up the plainest female.

And Sarita's photos, Reseda had prophesied, would make Private Portraits by Merriwell known worldwide.

It'd be nice if his mom was right. But Autumn ought to stay in Georgia. California might be touted as a place where dreams came true, but far more dreams died there. He'd hate to see that happen to Autumn.

She reappeared. "Besides," she said, taking up their previous conversation, "I don't photograph naked women. Most of the time, the vital spots are covered."

"That can't be fun for their boyfriends."

"You'd be surprised. I haven't had any complaints. Ready?"

After loading her groceries and bags in the trunk, he got behind the wheel. "I noticed Francisco's picture in your bedroom upstairs. Did you do it?"

Damn, why did he bring that up?

"Yes." Her crinkling eyes hinted at agreeable recollections. "Did you like it?"

"It was great. You captured everything about him in that one shot. Everything."

So she *did* have something going with Francisco. Mom, zealous in policing her children's romantic interests, had hinted that Francisco was serious, but Rennie had heard that before. Autumn, elegant and refined as she was, should have been proof against his brother's volatile charm. Couldn't she see that Francisco was all surface and no substance?

From the looks of that photograph, no.

She'd shot Francisco nude, sprawled in a squashy armchair with his legs stretched out before him. Concessions to modesty were the angle of one half-bent knee and a religious medal hanging around his neck. An unidentifiable but unmistakably feminine garment lay in a frothy pile at his feet. While one hand held a cell phone, the other held a condom foil. His dark curls hugged an old-fashioned, wired telephone receiver, caught between ear and shoulder. Sultry eyes challenged the camera.

The picture implied that Francisco murmured enticements on the phone to one lover while simultaneously seducing a second with his eyes and texting still another on his cell.

Autumn had to be the lover in the room.

He turned the ignition key. It was none of his business,

but he couldn't help himself. "I didn't think you photographed men."

"I don't. Just Fran."

The indifferent words emphasized her life separate from his, a life he had to guess at. Sunglasses covered her eyes, further distancing her.

Rennie couldn't imagine her flailing beneath Francisco in passionate abandonment. Someone like Autumn shouldn't be with anyone remotely resembling his brother.

How the hell could she fall for Francisco?

He pulled the Lexus away from the curb slowly, smoothly, with no jerk or screech of tires.

Madre de Dios, he hated seeing a fine girl—woman!—like Autumn fall victim to Francisco's charm.

****

As RENNIE AND Autumn started their journey toward Helen in northeast Georgia, Sam Bogatti sat in a car parked at a hamburger place. Cars whizzed by on the busy side street, several entering and exiting beside where Sam dialed a throwaway cell phone.

"Yes?" came the tentative voice over the phone lines.

"Me."

"What's wrong?"

Sam didn't take the rudeness personally. His call hadn't been expected and wouldn't be welcome. "We gotta problem."

A pause came, like Bernie was searching his memory. "What kind of problem?"

A gray-haired couple got out of a sedan and went inside, walking side by side without speaking to each other, complacent like two people who've lived together for so long that each knows the other's thoughts.

He and his old lady would look like that in fifteen or twenty years.

"I *said*, what kind of problem."

Sam dragged himself back to the present. "Like some pictures."

Silence, then: "What kind of pictures?"

"Like of the stuff."

"You're shitting me."

"No."

"You mean she took pictures of the stuff?"

Bernie might be a high-powered lawyer, but he was dumb, dumb, dumb. Dumb enough to get on Sam's nerves. "No, asshole. Somebody else took pictures of her wearing it."

A hiss came over the line, a long-drawn exhalation. "You get the pictures?"

"Yeah, but somebody took 'em, saw the stuff. Somebody here in town."

"Do you know who?"

Bernie was scared. About time.

"Yeah. So here's the thing. Do I recover any originals and the camera? Or let it all slide and hope the photographer's got a bad memory?"

Sam knew what he'd do if it was up to him, but he wasn't about to call the play. Decision-making wasn't his job.

The line went silent.

Sam pictured Bernie chewing on his bottom lip like he did every time he got nervous.

Dumb ass. What was there to think about?

"We can't let it slide," came at last. "If anybody sees, puts two and two together... We can't risk somebody... And if the guy who made the pictures remembers... I don't know."

A sturdy teenager in leggings and tee shirt emerged from the hamburger place with a super-sized drink and paper bag.

Kids. Eating that kind of stuff and no exercise would make her sloppy-fat in five years. Good thing his boys liked sports. They had to work out and watch their diet. His wife was good about cooking lots of vegetables and fish, too. And that chicken broccoli casserole she made...

Bernie was still thinking out loud. "Probably on the computer, too. Damn digital cameras. You'll have to, you know, take care of it. Him, too. The photographer, I mean. We can't risk him recognizing the stuff."

About time Bernie figured it out.

"Okay." He'd already recalculated his fee. "Two cleanings, double comp plus extra expenses."

"Double? That seems kind of… How about fifty percent more? You're already there."

"Double."

"My clients may not wanna pay that much."

Lying weasel. Bernie's clients didn't give a shit. They paid through the nose expecting Bernie to deal with whatever. Bernie was trying to keep his own cut intact, that's what Bernie was trying to do.

I ain't gonna be stiffed. "Gotta go. I'll call back in a coupla hours. See what they say."

"Wait!"

Sam put the phone back to his ear.

Bernie sighed. "Okay. Do it ASAP."

Without goodbyes, Sam disconnected and rolled his head around to ease the bunched-up neck muscles.

Guess this screwed his getting back for the hockey game tomorrow. His older boy would be disappointed, but it couldn't be helped. Maybe he could make it home by Sunday. His wife got pissed when he missed church.

Like he got pissed when plans didn't work out.

All because of a few lousy photographs.

Chapter Four

AS THE OUTSKIRTS of Atlanta rushed by, Autumn settled back against the plush leather of Rennie's Lexus.

Thirteen years before, a raw adolescent, she had flung herself on his neck and told him she loved him, couldn't live without him, and begged him to take her to California with him. He must have thought her an idiot and maybe she had been.

No, just out of her mind at his going away.

Rennie had assumed her hysterics stemmed from problems with the aunt and uncle who'd taken her in after her parents died. He had pointed out his leaving Georgia wasn't the same as dying and told her she'd feel better once she went off to college the next year. Then he'd dried her tears, promised they'd be lifelong friends, and promptly forgot her meltdown.

Time she forgot it, too. She was a woman in control, remember?

"A Lexus," she said. "I'm impressed."

"You're supposed to be. After having to drive that old clunker through high school, I swore I'd start driving nice cars as soon as I was able."

"There was nothing wrong with Amy Jean. After you left, she took Elena and Norma and Fran all through school before she went to that big junkyard in the sky."

He chuckled, deep in his throat. "Yeah. Amy Jean was dependable in her day. I guess that's one mark in her favor."

"Dependability is important."

"In people more than cars." Something dusted his features.

Pain? Had Jane hurt him?

Autumn couldn't ask. Instead, she talked about the traffic, a nice safe topic.

A montage of gray tree trunks and green pines pasted against bunches of brown leaves and mottled blue skies slid past. Once the congestion and tall buildings of Atlanta's northern suburbs fell behind, the rural setting of wintry forests and pastures provided a welcome contrast for jaded city-dwellers.

Her cramped muscles refused to unwind. What could she say in their two more hours together that wouldn't sound flat-out thick?

See if you can't reconnect. "So. Tell me about this new job."

He did, for several minutes, until they were past Lake Lanier and well up Georgia Highway 400. "The opening at UGA came at the right time," he ended. "Jane had left, and there was no reason for me to stay."

Her breath caught. "Jane left? Is she not coming back with you then?"

On the wheel, his hands tightened.

Darn, he would think she was prying. Why couldn't she keep her mouth shut?

But he answered evenly. "No. We decided to go our separate ways. Actually, Jane decided. She got a big promotion last March that meant her moving to New York."

So that explained the change in him. "I'm sorry."

"Don't be."

"I didn't mean to bring up anything painful."

"You didn't. I'm okay now. I've never been up to Helen in the winter. What's it like?"

Okay, so Jane was off-limits. She plunged in, offering up facts about the Alpenlights, Helen's holiday festival currently running through the first of the year. Drivel, maybe, but anything was better than offending him.

Not that her chatter kept her from thinking about olive-skinned, energetic Jane.

During her one visit to Atlanta for Laney's wedding two years ago, tiny Jane had bossed Rennie around and charmed the Degardoveras. She'd enthusiastically joined in every activity and made Rennie take her on frenzied sightseeing excursions.

Autumn had seen Rennie, Jane in tow, exactly three times the entire week.

Her well of conversation slowed. How much could she say about Christmas in Helen?

Not that it mattered. Rennie hadn't heard a word. "I don't think of Jane too much anymore."

Forget the Alpenlights. "Of course not."

"We'd talked about getting married, but... When she moved, we tried commuting. Didn't work. She loved New York and her job. I didn't want to live there. She didn't want to leave."

"Her loss." Foolish Jane. There were things far more essential than ambition or location. "You'll be at a new place with new people now. That'll help, Rennie."

"Huh. Ya think?"

She'd offended him. "I'm sorry. You know me. I say whatever comes into my mind."

At least she always had to Rennie. He was easy to talk to.

The upbeat Rennie she remembered resurfaced. "That's one of the nice things about you, Autumn. You do say what you mean. As for Jane, that's past. I'm okay with it. And I kind of like where I am right now. In a nice car with a beautiful blonde. Who could ask for anything more?"

The chagrin from blurting out the wrong thing faded. "The nice car I'll give you, and I may be blonde. But beautiful? Careful. I'll get a swelled head."

"No danger of that. You're one of the most beautiful people I know, Autumn. Inside and out."

She didn't miss the underlying sadness.

He went on, "Inner beauty's way more important than outer."

Jane had hurt him, and hurt him dreadfully.

"Oh, Rennie." She wanted to lay her hand over his on the wheel, let him know she understood. If she were Reseda or Laney or any of the voluble, empathetic Degardoveras, she would know instinctively how to banter and draw him out of this uncharacteristic mood.

But she wasn't. She was herself, awkward and shy and inarticulate. Pitifully inadequate at reaching out. "People sometimes aren't what we want them to be," was so lame.

"No, they aren't. Lots of people aren't what we want them to be, but I guess you've found that out."

"Sure. Every month when I send out invoices."

That chased away his frown. "Tell me about you and Francisco."

"There's nothing to tell."

"You've been dating him since last summer, Mom says."

"I don't know that I'd call it dating. After he got back from California, he had a pretty hot affair going on with someone. He wouldn't talk about her, which as you know is unlike Fran. We figured it was serious." She couldn't gauge his expression. "Then she ditched him."

He watched the road. "Yeah, I know."

"Oh? Do you know who he—?" She was prying again. "Not that it matters. Anyway, Fran isn't used to being ditched."

"No. He isn't."

"He got pretty down for a while. I hung out with him, held his hand, played nursemaid till he recovered."

That unfathomable gaze flicked at her and away. "Thanks to your nursing?"

What was he thinking? "I helped when I could. He's my friend."

"Is that all?"

What did that mean? The brothers teeter-tottered in a complicated relationship, part friends, part competitors.

"Of course that's all." Rennie must be remembering Fran's portrait, wondering if there was anything between them. He and Fran cared for each other. No question about it. But underneath the affection Fran, twenty months younger, was fiercely competitive; he couldn't stand Rennie besting him.

Half-forgotten images returned. Fran going out for the

tennis team because Rennie was on it. Fran hitting on girls Rennie dated and crowing when he took one away. Fran making a higher grade on an English term paper than his brother and waving it in Rennie's face.

Rennie's indifference had infuriated Fran no end.

That adolescent friction should be long dead—so what was going on with Rennie?

"Sure you're just friends?" he pressed.

He *did* think she was involved with Fran.

You can't tie yourself up to a Degardovera, he'd said thirteen years ago as he dried her tears. *There are lots of nice guys around who're in your league. You'll meet one someday.*

That was when she got the picture.

She might be Norma's best friend, but she wasn't a part of the Degardovera family. She'd never be part of it.

And Rennie's opinion hadn't changed, even if another Degardovera might be the one to want her.

"Yes." She kept her voice level. Strange how normal it sounded. "We're definitely just friends."

"That's good." His relief was palpable. "Francisco wouldn't do for you."

She clenched her teeth. Yeah, she could be a buddy but never anything more. To him or Fran.

They came to the end of 400 at Dahlonega where he pulled the car up to the stop light and braked smoothly. "We Degardovera men do seem jinxed in our love life, don't we?"

"Are you?" She didn't miss the plural. "Maybe you Degardovera men need to find yourselves different women."

When he laughed, he sounded like the old Rennie.

****

As RENNIE AND Autumn made their way toward Helen, her one employee printed out appointment reminder postcards.

Iris Cabell, a widow who acted as secretary, receptionist, and bookkeeper for Private Portraits by Merriwell, waited impatiently for six o'clock. She had a long drive to visit grandchildren near Birmingham over the weekend.

The bell hanging on the door clanged.

Oh no, not now! Why does it always happen?

A customer right at closing. She masked irritation at the man indecisively looking around. "May I help you?"

Thick glasses turned away from an inspection of the early Kodak Brownie exhibit. Middle-aged, average height, kind of scrawny. Ordinary features that looked pleasant, maybe shy. He wore a hat and topcoat too heavy for Atlanta's mild December weather, with a red and green holiday muffler wrapped round his neck.

Nothing to provoke alarm.

He said, "I'd like to talk with the photographer, please."

His accent wasn't southern so he could be from up north. Or maybe from the Midwest. On his way home like thousands of other Atlanta transplants, except he *would* have to stop here. What luck.

She hid a sigh. "About an appointment?"

"Yes." He cleared his throat. "I'm interested in having some, um, personal photographs done."

Ugh. One of those. Those nasty pictures Autumn took seemed to be all people wanted nowadays. And ten more minutes before she could lock up. If she could get rid of him that quick.

At least he had on pants under the overcoat, not like that pervert who came in and flashed her last spring.

"Ms. Merriwell is out of the studio till Monday. I'll be happy to answer your questions." Any question she could answer in ten minutes, anyway.

"Great." He plucked a card off her desk and studied it. "This Autumn Merriwell. Does she do all the, er, intimate photography?"

How could she run him off without being downright rude? "Ms. Merriwell does all our photography, period. That includes the Private Portraits line. Shots can be set up in the studio or home or anywhere else the client is most comfortable," she rattled off. "Client poses are private, unless otherwise specified."

At this point, she usually asked if he was here on behalf of his wife or girlfriend, but not today. She looked pointedly at the wall clock.

Busy examining the card, he didn't notice. "Do you use a processor? Anybody else who sees the photographs?"

Hah. Couldn't look her in the eye. "Most of our cameras are digital. All photos are printed on the premises by Ms. Merriwell herself." Her spiel flowed smoothly. "Proofs and selected prints go to the client while the originals are stored on CD-ROMs or negatives that stay here in our files. No one has access except Ms. Merriwell. Not even me. No one else sees the shots at any stage of preparation unless the client so chooses."

He finally looked up. Thick lenses made his eyes murky dark holes, but his mouth smiled. "Ah. That's what I wanted to know. My wife and I wouldn't like other people involved." A hint of apology mingled with a tacit plea for understanding.

Iris thawed. She knew perfectly well a lot of these portraits went to the floozies' married lovers, but this man wasn't an adulterer, just an embarrassed husband. She was an old hand at spotting which were which.

He went on. "Do you use off-site storage in case the CDs are corrupted or lost?"

"Absolutely. We switched to AllSet last year and it's been very satisfactory."

"Good. We wouldn't want to go through all the effort and then lose the images. We might want more prints later."

"No fear of that. You may take this with you." Iris slid a brochure across the counter. "It explains our policies and precautions."

He picked it up, looked at the front and back, held out the inset of Autumn. "Would this be Ms. Merriwell?"

Iris confirmed it was.

"She looks young."

"Her grandfather started this studio fifty-eight years ago. Ms. Merriwell was brought up in the business. She got her first camera when she was six years old, so she's quite experienced. It's all in the brochure."

"I see." He seemed suitably impressed. "My wife's the anxious type. Very modest. She wants to talk to Ms. Merriwell personally. Can she call her at home tonight?"

"We don't give her home number out."

Six o'clock. Praise the Lord!

Polite but firm, Iris held up her watch. "Sorry. Time to close." She pushed her chair back. "Have your wife call here Monday. Ms. Merriwell's in Helen for the weekend but will be—"

"Helen?" He followed her glance toward the pad where she'd written down the restaurant's phone number and time.

Oops. She shouldn't have mentioned Helen. But it didn't matter. This man was no stalker. "A friend's having an anniversary party there tomorrow night. Ms. Merriwell had me make reservations for their dinner so you see, she really isn't available. She'll be back in the studio Monday morning at nine."

"Helen. Is that near here?"

"No." He hadn't lived here long if he had to ask, but she wouldn't be the one to enlighten him. She rose. "If that's all…"

"Oh. Of course." He put the brochure in his pocket. "I'll come back or have my wife call Monday. Thank you so much for your help. Sorry to delay you."

At his prompt retreat, irritation fled. He seemed nice enough and unlike many men, he wanted photographs taken of his wife and not some tramp he was seeing on the side.

Not that Iris understood women posing for Autumn's photographs. Women dressed in those scanty things for one reason and one reason alone: to arouse the lust of decent men.

But she'd worked at Private Portraits for over thirty years, since it had been Merriwell Studio and before Laura and Parnell Merriwell had inherited the business from old Horace Merriwell and changed the name. Iris might not approve of what Autumn was doing—intimate photography indeed! Pornography was more like it—but she didn't have any say-so. Older women not yet eligible for Social Security had hard times finding jobs.

Besides, Autumn was like her grandfather, easy to work

for. Not half as demanding as Laura Merriwell had been, the old witch.

I ought to be counting my blessings.

Iris gathered up purse and coat. She had steady employment, a good boss, and health insurance, even if the premiums were ridiculous. Lots of women her age didn't have that much.

Locking the studio, she checked her watch as she got into her car. Eight minutes past six. Not bad. Good thing she'd brought her suitcase so she could leave from here. Once she got to Birmingham, she'd forget about work. She'd even turn off that blasted cell like Autumn said she was going to do. Nothing urgent ever came up when they were closed.

If she hurried, she could reach her daughter's house in time to help put the baby to bed, the little darling.

The polite man was forgotten.

Chapter Five

As Iris Cabell headed toward Alabama, Autumn and Rennie arrived at Unicoi State Park near Helen. To celebrate her second wedding anniversary, Elena Degardovera Kinsellen had rented a three bedroom cottage and invited several friends to join her and her husband for the weekend.

"This must be it." Rennie pulled the Lexus into a parking space beside a late model Ferrari. "Hey, we have a view of the lake. Sweet."

Autumn stretched. "Even if it is kind of far off and hidden by the trees." One thing had run through her mind the whole way. If Jane was out of the picture, Rennie was available.

Not that she intended to court another humbling rejection from a man who'd told her years ago she was like another sister. Not after he'd all but warned her off Fran today.

Rennie didn't want her in the family.

Darn. She needed to stop thinking of Rennie and the departed Jane who'd personified his ideal woman and who was so opposite to everything Autumn was or could hope to be.

"Still a nice view. Kind of isolated, though." Rennie unbuckled his seatbelt. "Wonder how my party-loving sister decided on it."

"Laney said John needed a restful weekend."

"Looks like he's found the right place."

The modified A-frame cedar was one of four that stood in a secluded cluster between the main part of the park and the camping areas. Several spaces beside the road were laid out for parking. Railroad ties marked steps down to the cabins, rustic and dark to blend in with the surrounding woods.

Autumn nodded toward the Ferrari. "That isn't John's car."

"No, but the porch light's on at the next cabin. It probably belongs to whoever's staying over there."

As if on cue, a woman appeared and started up the steps.

Rennie opened his door. "Look, Autumn, she's wearing your coat."

Autumn got out, too. Sure enough, the newcomer wore a blue swingy jacket. A closer view showed workouts and surgery hiding an age somewhere between thirty and sixty. Blonde like Autumn, her pixie 'do was bleached and toned by a professional.

Nearing, she waved at Rennie. "Don't tell me. You must be one of Elena's brothers. Y'all look so much alike."

The touchier Degardoveras spouted off whenever someone commented on their resemblances.

Not Rennie. "Yep, I'm one of them."

The woman extended a manicured hand, weighted down with green, red, yellow, and white gemstones. "Karalene Ballencer. Call me Kiki." The smoke-hoarse voice assumed they recognized the name. "Happy to meet you." She looked Rennie over. Her grin widened. "Elena told me all about her family. She didn't say her brother was so good-looking, though."

Autumn would have cracked up at Rennie's expression if she hadn't been too busy trying to figure out where she'd seen Kiki.

"I'm next door." Kiki gestured. "I met Elena this morning." Every finger including the thumb wore rings, some of them large. The gems' gaudy sparkle made two big South Sea pearls look cheap.

Too much jewelry. Even more than Sarita wore.

If this woman and Sarita ever met, they'd hit it off. Like

a child playing dress-up, Sarita had flaunted pins and necklaces and earrings for Autumn's photos. When Autumn begged for simpler shots, Sarita had refused. "This is me!" She'd thrown her arms wide and whirled. "Take the bling or leave it."

If Autumn went to California, maybe she could talk Sarita into posing without ornamentation.

If. Now that Rennie was back minus Jane, did she want to go?

Kiki was rattling on. "So I told her to yell like hell if she saw The Hulk trying to get in my cottage. I think the steroids from when he played pro ball baked his brain."

Ah. Now she had it.

Roger Ballencer, a onetime linebacker for the Vikings and Falcons, had married the socialite ex-wife of Atlanta entrepreneur Thomas Woodring Picksten. No wonder Kiki took recognition for granted. Scarcely a month went by that her name or photograph wasn't in the news.

Now Kiki pouted. "Roger's a fricking psychopath. He threatened me with all kinds of shit if I left him, so I didn't tell him where I was going but who knows what he'll do if he finds me. Anyway, Elena said that I shouldn't worry, that y'all would keep an eye out for me. Is this your wife, Rennie?"

Rennie blinked, taken off guard by the abrupt question coming after the stream of artless confidences.

Or by the question itself.

For pity's sake. He didn't want to be linked to Autumn, even in casual conversation.

"No, I'm not his wife," she all but snapped. "I'm Autumn Merriwell, a friend of Elena's."

She reached into the car for her coat to avoid Rennie's eyes, but heard him murmur, "A friend of mine, too, I hope."

Like she'd been the one tromping on feelings.

Autumn closed the car door. His bewilderment brought on guilt. "Well, sure. That goes without saying."

She was too prickly. He hadn't thought a thing about Kiki referring to her as his wife.

Kiki stopped checking Rennie out long enough to stick out her hand. "Hi, Autumn. Hey, your coat looks like mine. Can you imagine two people ending up in this godforsaken place with the same jacket?"

Diamond pendant earrings flashed when she moved closer. "Close to the same color, but yours is lighter, don't you think? I got mine in England a few years ago. I was pulling myself together after catching my second husband doing the maid, the louse. They say third time lucky but, my dears, they are so fricking wrong. Tom may have been unfaithful but he was at least a gentleman. Roger's a stinking SOB. That's why I'm hiding here till after the divorce hearing."

Thin lips turned ugly. "Then we'll see who comes out ahead. After I'm through, he'll be lucky to have a pot to pee in."

Rennie shied away.

Remembering her audience, Kiki batted her eyelashes and tried to look helpless. She didn't succeed. "I'm terrified. My lawyer got a restraining order, but… Husbands!" She shuddered, turned to Autumn. "Wherever did you find yours? Not here, I'll bet, unless it was a specialty shop at Lenox or Phipps."

Find her husband? Autumn blinked. What husband?

Oh. The jacket.

"Harrods." She stroked the bright blue wool.

She and Aunt Laura had gone on a London tour after Uncle Parnell died. Her aunt, spotting the coat, had bought it for Autumn. "Looking at that wonderful color makes me happy." Grief had softened her and temporarily drawn her and Autumn closer. "Blue's never been my color but on you, it's perfect."

Now Kiki crowed. "Harrods. I knew it. Do you mind?" The ringed fingers tugged and turned the lapels out. "Same label as mine. How about that. Isn't it a small world?"

After they agreed it was, Kiki volunteered the information, somewhere in the middle of lamenting the lack of telephone and television and microwave and dishwasher in the cabins, that she had seen Elena and her friends go out about a half hour before. "Can you get inside? You're welcome to stay with me."

Rennie said, too quickly, "Thanks, but we picked up a key at the lodge."

Kiki pulled her jacket close. "Good. You don't want to be stuck outside for hours. It's too fricking cold. And forget taking a long hot shower. The water got so cold so quick, I had to climb out and stand in front of the fire. Speaking of which, I'm heading up to the lodge to buy some of their expensive firewood. My dears, you would think they could give you enough wood to burn for the days you've rented the place, considering the hideous lack of decent amenities. Do come over and see me. I'm having friends up Sunday for dinner and you're more than welcome to join us." She fluttered her lashes at Rennie.

Again Rennie was quick. "Wish we could, but Laney has the weekend all mapped out."

"Oh, too bad." Her face fell. "Well, if your plans change, let me know." Even in the fading sun, her farewell wave spun a rainbow of colors before she climbed into the Ferrari.

"Whew," Rennie said after Kiki had pulled away and they started carting bags and groceries to the cabin. "She sure does chatter, doesn't she?" He opened the door. "And you and she have something in common, Autumn. You're both globe-trotters."

"Yeah, real globe-trotters. She goes to England to get over her husband cheating, and Aunt Laura and I go to get over my uncle dying. And now Aunt Laura's gone, too."

Why'd I say that? Too late to take the whiny words back. His surprised glance flickered. "Sorry. I didn't think."

What had come over her? She never let hurt and disappointment spill out like that. Never.

She set down the groceries on the counter. "I'm the one who's sorry. I didn't mean it the way it sounded."

"It's all right to grieve, Autumn."

"But not to unload my baggage on you."

"You didn't even want to claim me as a friend to the ditz."

Rennie had a knack for making people ashamed. His sisters complained about his underhanded use of embarrassment, sympathy, and forgiveness. At the moment, Autumn heartily agreed. It was unnerving to find herself the focus of his reproach.

On the other hand, he never betrayed a confidence.

He cared because he was a friend.

You're like my sister, he'd said as she sobbed her heart out long ago. *I won't let you do anything foolish like running off.*

"You know you're my friend, Rennie. I didn't want you embarrassed by Kiki lumping us together as a couple."

He raised his brows.

She rushed past the dangerous subject. "I do miss my uncle and aunt. They were hard to live with, but they were all I had."

Parnell and Laura Merriwell had taken her in after her parents' car accident. Childless themselves and unsure what to do with a five-year-old, they tried their best. They might have lacked a warmth and understanding of children, but the Degardoveras had filled the gaps.

Sometimes being with the Degardoveras hurt, to see their easy interplay and understanding and know that, close as she felt to Laney and the rest, she wasn't part of them.

After Rennie's kind but firm rebuff, Autumn had faced the truth: she was an outsider. An outsider in her aunt and uncle's lives, an outsider in the Degardoveras' lives, an outsider in everyone's life.

No matter how much she wanted to belong to someone, somewhere, she would always be odd man out.

But she'd accepted it. After her uncle's death, working with Aunt Laura had helped. Once her aunt died, her last tenuous claim to a family, no matter how dysfunctional, was gone.

Usually she managed not to let it bother her, but here with Rennie, all the old yearnings rushed back.

"Sometimes I feel so alone," she confessed as they put away groceries. "Sometimes I think if I come down with an incurable disease or get murdered or kidnapped, no one would care."

"Not true." He laid his hand on her shoulder. "You have us."

No, she wanted to shout. She didn't have the Degardoveras, and she didn't have Rennie. Not the way she wanted him. Even if she gathered up her courage to try again, it wouldn't do any good.

Rennie liked perky, assertive livewires like Jane. And he thought of Autumn as a sister.

She forced a smile, too aware of his comforting hand. "Thank goodness for the Degardoveras. Wonder where Laney and John went."

"Shopping for groceries, I hope." He squeezed her shoulder before moving away. "This fridge is barer than yours. Want to ride back to town and look for them?"

"Yeah, let's. They're having a live glockenspiel this year. If we hurry, maybe we can catch it."

"Ooooh, man!" Rennie threw up his hands. "Let's hurry then. There's nothing I want to do more in this entire world than catch the live gluckenfeel."

****

RENNIE COULDN'T BELIEVE the kid felt so lonely.

The *woman*.

He had to stop thinking of Autumn as the forlorn little girl his mother had brought home.

"This is Autumn," Reseda had announced to her brood. The child stood apart, bored, clutching an overnight bag. Reseda laid her arm over the skinny shoulders, drawing the girl against one ample hip. "She's come to live with her aunt and uncle, but she's going to stay with us a few days while her aunt has surgery. Laney, take her to your and Norma's room and show her where to put her things."

Panic briefly showed in eyes as blue as his mother's hydrangea flowers.

That's when he realized Autumn hadn't been bored. She'd been scared to death.

Sounded like she still was.

Well, if she wanted to see a live gluckenfeel, whatever a gluckenfeel was, they would find one. Anything to cheer her up.

From the time they met, he'd looked out for Autumn, made sure his rambunctious family didn't swallow her up. Strange how the old protective instincts came back.

After he parked in front of the Alpine Village Shops, they began the walk back up to the heart of the old town.

Decades before, citizens and storeowners had transformed Helen into a copy of an alpine village to attract people visiting the nearby lakes and forests in the north Georgia foothills. A small shopping mall and expanded holiday festivities led to year-round tourist events like balloon races or Octoberfests or river tubing.

The Alpenlights, marked by holiday lights strung on every lamppost, sign and building, ran from the beginning of December into the New Year, but this first part of the celebration found things slow.

Rennie liked not being stuck in throngs of people as they strolled.

Soon the open area of the parking lot gave way to sidewalks lined with wire forms depicting reindeer, French horns, and other symbols of the season. Large balloon figures represented Helen's annual balloon race, but twinkling lights hadn't yet come on to turn the mock alpine village into an evening fairyland.

As dusk neared, Autumn and Rennie, breathless after walking uphill, arrived in the middle of the profuse gables and turrets and gaily painted storefronts.

A familiar red-suited figure sat in a sleigh surrounded by giggling children. When a small tyke in line bolted at the last minute, Autumn stepped up and asked Santa about the live whatever-it-was she wanted to see.

Rennie ambled after her, amused at such single-mindedness. When had she become so intrepid? This Autumn was a far cry from the retiring child he remembered.

"Saturdays and Sundays," Santa told them from under his white beard. A real beard. "At two and four in the afternoon, weather permitting. There's one at Charlemagne's House y'all can see today. It's not live but it's nice. You can make the six o'clock show if you go now."

Autumn's face fell. "No, I've been to it before. I wanted to see the live one."

"Well, then, come back tomorrow."

She turned away. "Drat. Laney's got the hike at Anna Ruby Falls planned for tomorrow. I hate missing the live one."

"Awww. Me, too." He grabbed her arm. "Hey, watch out!"

He scooted her out of the runaway's path as the little boy's parents chased him, protesting loudly, back toward Santa.

Time to cheer her up. "I'll tell you what." He fell into step beside her and leaned over confidentially, breathing in roses. "We'll probably get lost in the wilderness anyway so let's stand up to Laney, demand she let us skip the hike tomorrow and come see this gluckenfeel. If we stick together, we might have a chance against her. She can't take us on a twenty-mile hike if we all boycott it. What d'you say?"

Autumn was suspicious. "Do you know what a glockenspiel is?"

"Sure I do." He widened his eyes innocently. "Kind of. Sort of. One of those musical things they play with hammers?"

"Rennie." Her laugh burst out, bright as sunshine. "How could one of those be live?"

"Isn't it like the floor piano Tom Hanks played with his feet in that movie? Maybe with people doing the part of the hammers. I can see them now, hopping up and down on the notes."

She cocked her head, eyes twinkling. "Rennie."

"No?"

"No." A giggle started, was controlled. "A glockenspiel isn't a musical instrument. Guess again."

"A nativity scene? A German nativity scene? A Swiss nativity scene?"

"No." She took a deep breath and pressed her twitching lips together. "A glockenspiel is… Well, you've seen those clocks where on the hour, instead of a cuckoo, little mechanical people come out of the inside and dance around and then go back inside?"

She was definitely a beautiful woman.

"Oh, little dancing people clocks. Sure." He clapped a hand to his forehead. "Why didn't you say so? Don't I feel like an idiot. Tell me; how did they find people small enough to fit inside one of those clocks?"

"Rennie." She pushed him, gave up her attempt to be serious, and convulsed in laughter.

He'd missed a woman's laughter. Jane hadn't laughed much during their last year together. Come to think of it, Jane'd been pretty damn solemn the whole time they were together.

His heart lifted. "How about a funnel cake?" He tucked her gloved hand under his arm. "It won't make up for missing the gluckenfeel, but they sure smell tempting."

As they followed the smell of hot pastries and confectioners' sugar across the street, contentment swathed him.

It'd be a shame if his brother messed up Autumn's life, but Francisco was a determined bastard. If he'd made up his mind to have Autumn, he'd sweep her off her feet and keep her in the clouds for a while. Then drop her to chase after a new woman more exciting. More exciting women always came along for Fran.

There ought to be some way to keep Autumn safe.

Chapter Six

PRIVATE PORTRAITS BY Merriwell was one of several strip shops that, except for a drug store and run-down bar on one end, closed early. A jewelry store flanked the left of the studio, an embroidery place sat on the right.

When the nondescript beige van, now minus its magnetic side panels that had this morning trumpeted Betty and Lulu's Flower Boutique, pulled up to the back of the shops, no one lurked in the alley to notice the black-clad man who got out.

No need for finesse. Sam Bogatti jimmied open the door to the studio, sliced the silent alarm wire, hopped back into the van, and drove around the block to park among rows of vehicles in another strip mall across the street.

Nice that the jewelry store was next to the studio. Someone would think he picked the wrong door. Leaning back in the seat, he stuffed a stick of gum into his mouth and waited.

Four minutes later, a police car arrived. Sam monitored from his vantage point as the officer checked the front and went around back. Then the man got back in his car and bent over the radio.

After a while, another man in sweat pants and top—the owner?—arrived. He spoke to the policeman working on a report or something in his patrol car. The officer got out, had the man sign something, and then left before a locksmith van arrived.

Sweat Pants let the locksmith into the building. About

ten thirty, both men came out and left. The strip mall was dead on the studio end.

Sam grunted and stretched. Time for food. The restaurant two shops down would work.

No need to hurry. The shop's owner would try to get in touch with Autumn Merriwell, but she wasn't home. She was in Helen, wherever the shit Helen was. He'd let the PD come by a few times, get used to everything being okay.

****

IN HELEN, AUTUMN and Rennie left town without seeing Laney and John, but found the couple already back at the cottage.

Along with a woman. The redhead with flawless skin and photogenic features, Autumn immediately discerned, was meant for Rennie.

Laney, blissful in her own marriage and certain that no unattached single person could possibly be happy, constantly sought to match-make for siblings and friends. So far, none of her matches had worked out, but that didn't stop her trying.

"Victoria Montezela. She works at CNN," Laney introduced her friend to her brother. A side glance gauged Rennie's reaction.

"Hi, Victoria. So Laney suckered you into this trip, too, eh?" Rennie greeted Victoria as if she was one of his sisters. "What did she promise you? Blue skies, snowflakes, hot toddies before a roaring fire? You may as well know the truth. There's no TV, no radio, no microwave, and no telephone. And even cell phones don't work up here."

"Rennie!" Laney hit his biceps.

He flinched. "Ouch."

"Sounds terrible." Victoria's laugh said different.

Rennie rubbed his arm. "For that, sister, I'll tell her the rest. We have to pay for every log we burn. Worse, we have one tiny bathroom with limited hot water to be allocated at intervals among the smelliest. Oh, and some nut whose husband's a homicidal maniac is hiding out next door. If he gets the address wrong, we could be in trouble."

"Kiki isn't a nut." Laney glared. "She has problems. And

there's nothing wrong with doing without some of the things we take for granted every day."

"Right. Being away from the luxuries of civilization lets us get in touch with our inner selves." Victoria's appraisal said she wouldn't mind getting in touch with Rennie.

"Ho-o-kay. If you say so." Rennie raised a thick brow. "Sounds like Laney's been doing some brainwashing here."

Laney preened herself for bringing two unsuspecting people together. When John came in with some logs, she slipped her arm around her husband's waist and wrinkled her nose. "And you said it would never work."

Autumn tried to stop gritting her teeth. Pooh on Laney. Victoria had a gorgeous face, a toned body, and was doubtless intelligent to boot.

Perfect for Rennie.

Even her name. Victoria. Old-fashioned. Solid.

All the Degardoveras liked people with those kinds of names: Elena with John, and Norma with Paul, and Rennie with Jane. Why couldn't she have been named Kate or Sarah or Mary? A good plain dependable name.

But no. She was stuck with Autumn.

Laney pulled her forward. "And this is Autumn," she said to Victoria. "She's the great photographer I told you about."

"Victoria." Autumn held out a hand. "Good to meet you."

What business of hers was it as to who did or didn't attract Rennie? Hadn't she promised herself this very afternoon she would control her life from now on? She was tired of being on the outside looking in, tired of letting the insiders have all the fun. She was going to have a good time this weekend and to heck with Rennie and Victoria.

"This is the first time Victoria's been up to Helen," Laney was saying. "She went to school in Indiana and worked several other places before she came to CNN last summer."

John dropped into an easy chair. "I see Victoria on TV every day. Gus watches CNN religiously."

Gus was Agustin Huertole, the personable state senator

hoping to become Georgia's first Hispanic governor. John, his chief aide, had brought in Fran to manage the campaign.

Laney seconded her husband's praise of CNN and perched on the chair arm beside him. "Victoria's been great about giving Gus favorable coverage."

The newscaster's laughter tinkled as she sat down "So far Huertole's earned favorable coverage. But if he screws up, don't think we won't be right there." She wore the same wrinkle-avoiding smile as models and actresses, the one that touched the corners of the lips and stayed away from the eyes.

Knowledgeable, assertive, and capable. Exactly the type of woman to appeal to a man like Rennie.

Autumn exhaled as Rennie aimed his sexy hit-the-target-without-moving-the-head glance at Victoria. "I don't think you need worry about screw-ups," he drawled. "I heard Fran makes Huertole brush his teeth three times a day, they're so eager to keep his image clean. Also something about shaves and showers on the hour."

Laney threw up her hands. "Totally unfounded. Gus bathes no more than twice a day. I have it from his wife."

"Now there's an asset no candidate should be without." Victoria, ensconced on the loveseat, straightened her sweater over boobs doubtless as perfect as she.

C cup at least. Maybe D. Likely pure silicone.

Slap yourself, girl. You're being catty and you don't even know the woman.

Crossing booted feet, Victoria leaned back. "Danielle Huertole is the savviest woman I've ever met. She single-handedly persuaded the Louvre to loan this ornament exhibit to the High Museum. It's the first time some of the things have ever been outside France."

"I can't wait to see it." Laney wriggled eagerly. "They've been setting up for weeks, but admission for the first two months sold out ages ago. I heard they plan to extend their hours to accommodate everyone. Fran's going to the reception Sunday night for an advance viewing, lucky dog."

"Because of his job." Pragmatic John was the perfect complement for exuberant Laney. "He's got to look out for the candidate, hon. Don't worry, we'll go in January or February. After the rush is over, but before the campaign heats up."

"Do you think Huertole has a chance to be elected governor?" Rennie raised his brows. "This is a pretty conservative state. Unless things have changed considerably, voters will go with their good old boys and to hell with anyone who speaks a different language."

"Bite your tongue." Laney threw a handy box of tissues at her brother. "Fran and John wouldn't be working for Gus if they didn't think he had a chance. Of course he has a chance."

"A good one, according to the polls," Victoria said. "And things *have* changed while you were gone, Rennie." She patted the cushion beside her. "Elena says you've been in California. I was outside San Diego for a while at a little station where…"

When Laney started toward the kitchen, Autumn followed.

Tangerines in a bowl and a festive pine wreath smelled like holidays. Too bad she didn't feel like celebrating.

Washing her hands, Laney said, "Isn't Victoria adorable? Beautiful and brainy. Mom and I think she's perfect for Rennie."

A scream threatened. Autumn slapped a dish towel across Laney's arm. *Change the subject.* "Have you heard from Fran? Is he coming up?"

Laney dried her hands before she took a foil-wrapped ham from the fridge. "Missing him already?" Her smug look wasn't lost on Autumn.

"Come on, Laney." The Degardoveras assumed she and Fran were a twosome, no matter how often she told them otherwise. They weren't, and she said so again as she washed her hands with unnecessary vigor. "For the umpteenth time, Fran and I hang out together. We're buddies."

"Sure. That's why you have that wonderful nude of him in your bedroom."

"I couldn't hang it at the studio, and he didn't want it

after his last girlfriend broke up with him. What should I have done with it? Stored it in the garage?"

Laney rolled her eyes in manifest disbelief.

"Elena Degardovera Kinsellen. There is nothing in the least romantic between Fran and me." Well, maybe a few kisses. But they'd been to console Fran, nothing more.

"I didn't mean to imply there was." Unwrapping the ham, Laney picked off a bite and tasted it.

Its brown sugar scent drifted over the table to remind Autumn she hadn't eaten since breakfast. Sarita and shopping hadn't left time for lunch. "Did Reseda cook that? I'm starved."

"Uh huh. Before she left. Here, take this bite." She frowned. "I bake them like she tells me, but they never taste like hers. Okay. So you and Fran are buddies. Well, buddy, he has to be at the High in the morning, but he'll get here in time for dinner tomorrow. And he'll spend the night with us before going back Sunday for the reception. So stop worrying. Buddy."

It was no use. Laney would believe whatever she wanted. Autumn popped the ham into her mouth. "Ummm. Your mother makes the best hams."

"Yeah, Francisco loves them, too."

When they were younger, Fran had been a nuisance, constantly taunting Autumn about her skinny legs and flat chest. But at thirty-three, he had grown up.

While no one could measure up to Rennie, Fran was personable enough.

Her first and only male photographed in an intimate setting, Fran's pictures had been exceptional. He'd framed the best, the poster hanging in her bedroom, before his last affair soured. She'd gotten stuck with it.

A shame the Degardoveras took her concern for Fran as romantic interest, but there was nothing she could do about it.

Laney rummaged in a drawer for a knife. "Did you remember to make reservations for the pizza place tomorrow night?"

"Iris did, bless her. I don't know what I'd do without

that woman. She booked for ten people like you said. Who else is coming? Norma and Paul will make eight so…?"

Laney smirked. "You'll see."

Autumn didn't bite. Laney reveled in acting mysterious, but she never could keep a secret long.

"Great," Autumn said. "The more the merrier. I can't wait to see Norma. I can't believe she's still with Paul."

Norma Degardovera, notorious for dating a man for a few weeks and then dropping him, had been with Paul for over a month. Not yet a record, but close.

Laney, fully aware that it was time for Norma to break off her latest romance, shot Autumn a mischievous glance. "You like Paul? Okay, if you won't take Fran, wait until Norma dumps Paul and go after him. He's attractive, he's nice, he's got a good job, and he's one of the banking Talliafierros."

"Maybe she won't dump him."

"Hah. It's been five weeks. What's her record, that lousy sister of mine? Six weeks? Seven? She's like Fran. She'll make him fall for her and then dump him. You'll see." She huffed. "Paul's too hardheaded. He ignores us when Mom or I try to tell him how to handle her. I like Paul, too. If he'd listen to us, he could have Norma eating out of his hand."

"Uh huh." Autumn raised a brow. "If I recall, your advice didn't help Tyler or Abe. Not to mention Jamie and Will and—"

Laney flapped a hand. "They were different. No, I mean it, Autumn, hang around till she breaks up with him and then move in. Paul's a nice catch for someone and our Rosalina's too young. You might as well have him."

Autumn put her hands over her ears. Even Laney wanted to see her marry an outsider. "Norma's still with him, Laney. Maybe it'll work out. And stop matchmaking for me."

And for Rennie, darn Laney's too-generous, overly-busy heart. "None of the others are coming up?"

"No, Candela and Blanca couldn't get off work and Rosalina has to study for finals next week, poor baby. And

Eddie and Cristina," she added, summing up the whereabouts of her younger siblings, "went to Florida with Mom."

"Since when does Reseda go to Florida in December?"

Laney, through nibbling the ham, used a knife in efficient strokes. "One of her older cousins from Mexico City is visiting her daughter in Tampa, and Mom left today with the kids. She nagged me to go, too, but we've had this cabin rented for months and John needs the break. Let's put the turkey and ham on a plate and let everyone make their own sandwiches, okay?"

"I'll wash the lettuce."

"Chips, canned drinks, onions, cheese, what else? Oh, bread. And lettuce and tomatoes."

"And pickles. Gotta have a pickle with a sandwich."

"I'm right here." Rennie had come in quietly. "Sour face and all."

It was hard not to light up around him.

"Edible pickles," Autumn said. "Not curmudgeon pickles."

"Need some help in here?" Victoria was on Rennie's heels.

Autumn dived into the refrigerator to search for lettuce.

"Yes." In the kitchen, Laney became a drill sergeant. "Victoria, get out the plastic plates and cups on the shelf there. Rennie, silverware's in that drawer. And open that pack of napkins over there. Mayonnaise and mustard are in the fridge. So's the potato salad."

"I knew there'd be drudgery involved," Rennie muttered, but, accustomed to indulging the women in his family, he obeyed with his usual good humor.

Autumn arranged the lettuce, pickles, and cheese before adding sliced tomatoes and onions to the platter. "Should I mayonnaise the bread?"

"Let us do our own." Rennie didn't look up from putting ice in plastic cups. "We're capable adults."

"Oh? Do you know something I don't?" She was rewarded by the slow lift to one corner of his mouth.

After supper, Autumn joined the others in a raucous

game of Chicken Foot dominoes under the tall ceiling of the cabin's great room. Red and gold flames played and flung their iridescent glow through the glass doors of a wood-burning stove. Scents of hot chocolate and cider and roasted marshmallows floated overhead.

When the game was done, and people were yawning and stretching and making drowsy noises, Autumn moved to stand by herself in front of the fire. The lovely scent of burning cedar filled her nostrils.

She shouldn't have come. Not with Rennie here.

Her mood made her the first to retire as he and Victoria engaged in low conversation interspersed with chuckles. She brought her toiletry kit downstairs and brushed her teeth in the one bathroom before going back up to the room she would share with Victoria. Even after she lay down on one of the full beds, she couldn't sleep. Victoria's clear tones blended with Rennie's low murmur to drift up the stairwell.

What was he saying to make Victoria laugh like that? And what was Victoria saying to keep him talking?

Autumn put her pillow over her head.

Not until midnight did Victoria creep into the bedroom and climb into the bed beside Autumn's. Soon, Rennie's soft footsteps came up the stairs to the room across from theirs.

Autumn, trying her best to block out his movements, wished the walls weren't so thin. Light from his room filtered beneath her door, momentarily glazing the coverlet and wall but vanishing before bedsprings across the hall creaked.

She would give anything to have been born a different person. Gregarious, vivacious, personable. Unafraid.

As Jane had been.

Like Victoria was.

****

AROUND MIDNIGHT, AS Autumn pretended to be asleep in Helen, an Atlanta police car slowly cruised through the strip mall housing the studio. When it disappeared, Sam Bogatti, parked across the street, wrapped his gum and stuck it in his litter bag. Then he cranked his van.

At the back of the strip mall shops, a shiny new deadbolt protected the studio door, but the alarm system hadn't been rewired. Twenty seconds found Sam inside with his five-gallon jug of gasoline.

He shone a penlight on the counter. There it was, the message pad the receptionist had looked at when she talked about Autumn Merriwell going to Helen. He ripped off the top page with its name and phone number, then pocketed it.

A few heavy filing cabinets in a back room screamed "fireproof" but weren't locked. He emptied thousands of CD-ROMs into a pile in the middle of the floor before pulling out the drawers of regular office file cabinets filled with negatives.

Old negatives, but no sense taking chances. He dumped them, too, then added the cameras in case one had Sarita's images.

After soaking the stack with gasoline, he threw a lighted match. That would take care of stuff here. Bernie's computer guy would deal with the backup at AllSet if he hadn't already.

"Sayonara, Sarita," he muttered as the flames jumped up with an ominous hiss. "Too bad they won't have those pictures to remember you by. You sure did have something."

This job sucked.

He was going to have to get out of the business soon. Maybe in a few more years he could.

As alarms trilled, he quit the building and parked back at the crowded restaurant across the street where he could watch.

Six minutes brought out the sirens. Eight minutes later, flashing red lights and trucks squealed into the strip mall. Men jumped out to start unwinding hoses.

By then, the fire had caught hold and a crowd had gathered.

Flames broke through the studio roof and licked at the night sky before streams of water began to feed into their midst. Smoke swirled and eddied. Flickering orange tongues spewed out tiny particles of ash caught and driven by the wind to taint clothes and skin and lungs.

The smell infiltrated his van. Sam reached for his pack of gum.

Okay, that worked out great. The photography studio was gone, but looked like the blaze was contained, in no danger of spreading to the lounge or drug store at the far end.

Good. He'd hate to be responsible for destroying somebody's livelihood or getting innocent bystanders killed.

Sam was pretty softhearted.

He put the new stick of gum in his mouth and grimaced. No substitute for tobacco. He'd been thinking about quitting for a while, but his wife's bitching was what did the trick. That and her cough every time they went to bed. He'd figured he better go cold turkey and get it over with.

Ten months now, but he still wanted a cigarette.

The same way he wanted to be at home, curled up in bed against his wife's butt and looking forward to his kid's hockey game tomorrow.

Tough. *Ain't gonna happen.* He pulled his jacket tighter.

You had to take life as it came.

He'd call in the morning and get directions to this Helen restaurant, but there was no rush. Nobody'd find Sarita till her mother and stepfather got back from their trip to the islands on Monday. Plenty of time to finish the job.

Things were coming together. He knew where the photographer would be at tomorrow night. He'd find her, take her out by Sunday at the latest, be long gone by Monday. If he headed straight home from Helen, he wouldn't have to go through grimy Hotlanta.

Enough of this shit. His whole head was clogged up from the ash. He cranked the van.

The next thing was to find a motel for what was left of the night. Preferably one that offered movies on demand. A nice comedy or relationship movie.

All those action films had way too much violence to suit him.

Chapter Seven

AFTER A RESTLESS night focused on Rennie in his room a few feet across from hers, Autumn was the first one up Saturday morning. The coffeemaker, once readied and turned on, began to deliver its inviting aroma. She filled a cup from the hot stream, and then took it to the living room.

The draperies were closed from the past night, but she pulled one back from the tall windows to enjoy the vista of trees, sunshine, and the lake sparkling in the distance.

Branches of low-lying laurels quivered. She stilled. Something or someone was out there, coming toward the cabin.

A wild animal?

Yes. In plain view on the lake trail below the cottage, a deer with spotted chest and white ears and horns, its coat burnished by a beam of white early morning light, trotted confidently through the underbrush.

Oh, pretty! She barely breathed, scared he'd look up and see her spying from the window and run, but the buck came on without haste, oblivious or uncaring. Three more, a doe and two half-grown fawns, followed in quick succession, strolling up the trail as though it were their private domain.

No time to get to her camera. If she moved, they'd spook.

Before the graceful creatures passed out of sight around the cottage, they stopped. She shrank back out of view but bumped into an unyielding bulk.

Rennie. She smelled his woodsy scent, recognized his presence before he spoke. "It's all right, they haven't seen us."

His hands, below her shoulders, held her against him and warmed her through her sweater.

His whisper grazed her ear. "There's something on that little knoll, see? Maybe a salt lick. Or a plant they like."

She did see it. She concentrated on seeing it, on forgetting his chest touching her back, his hands on her arms.

The doe reached out a supple neck to munch on some shrub or grass out of sight behind the rhododendrons.

The deer. Don't think about Rennie.

Even if his chest did rub her back with each breath. That and his heat and his Rennie odor made the desire inside her rise to a physical ache nearly impossible to contain.

Over the hammering of her heart, she heard footsteps, and Laney's hushed whisper: "What are you two up to?"

"Watching the animals at breakfast. Be quiet and scoot over here." Rennie stealthily shifted so that Laney could slip in.

He left one arm around Autumn and draped the other around his sister and the three of them stood in silence, watching as the marvelous wild creatures ate their fill and sauntered out of sight.

"Well." Autumn was the first to exhale and disengage herself from the marvelous civilized creature beside her. "What a beautiful way to start the day."

Laney was more prosaic. "We *are* in the mountains, remember. This stuff happens. How about a cup of coffee for us insiders?"

"Another of the benefits of being an early riser." Rennie squeezed his sister. "Fresh coffee and picturesque visitors, girls. Who could ask for more? Does it get any better than this?"

"It gets lots better," Laney said smugly. "It takes more than deer and coffee to make my day perfect."

Rennie winked at Autumn. "What a shrew you've become. And today your anniversary, too. For two years you've been saying marriage is bliss and now you say you're unhappy."

"I didn't say that. I merely said deer and coffee aren't everything."

"Two years." At the table, he sat down gingerly on a wooden chair as if making sure it would support his weight. "You're an old married woman, Laney. And you and Norma both said you weren't going to get married until you were at least forty."

"That was before I met John, smartass. I saw at once that I'd better grab him before somebody else did." Laney, who despite her tartness exuded a lazy well-being markedly unlike her usual frenetic energy, got two cups, filled them full of hot coffee, and put cream and sugar into one. "I made a wise decision."

"No cream or sugar for me," Rennie said.

"Fix your own. This is for John."

Rennie's jaw dropped. "Dios mio. Waiting on him hand and foot. And this is the same girl who thought feminists needed to be more aggressive?"

His sister stuck out her tongue. "We all grow up. Besides, John deserves a cup of coffee in bed. He's had a hard week."

She tried but couldn't maintain her straight face. "Not to mention night. He worked extra hard in bed."

Rennie put his hands over his ears. "I'm shocked. You've got two unmarried people here, sister. Please don't confide your and John's sexual activities to them."

Laney smirked as she started back to the bedroom. "You're jealous because you don't have anybody to bring you coffee in bed." She stuck out her tongue.

"I could have coffee in bed if I wanted it," Rennie called after her indignantly. "Every day, I could have it."

"I don't think dogs can be trained to fetch coffee without spilling it," Laney threw back over her shoulder as she sashayed toward the downstairs bedroom and John.

Rennie chuckled and shook his head. "Sisters." Taking his coffee to the front windows, he stood sipping and looking out, his lean figure a dark silhouette against the bright light. Dressed in jeans and flannel shirt, he fit the rough surroundings.

Autumn commented on it.

He stuck out a boot. "I figured if we were going to do that fifty-mile hike Laney's planned for us, I'd better be appropriately attired."

"Five miles. Not fifty. But still a pretty good walk. Can we make it that far?"

"Easy-peasy." He reconsidered. "According to Laney."

Autumn sat at the table and drank her coffee and tried not to watch him. If Jane was gone, she could be more aggressive.

No, she couldn't. The thought of ending up with his pity again kept her silent. She couldn't go through that again. Better to write him off, let him go.

After breakfast, Victoria begged off the hike. She had a weak ankle that walking irritated, but she'd be happy to drive the others over to Anna Ruby Falls where the trail began.

Autumn cheered up.

After Victoria dropped them off at the pavilion, they fed trout in the burbling creek before climbing up the concrete walk to the waterfall and the wooded trail circling back to the cabin.

Autumn, Nikon slung around her neck, took a break at the end of the steep ascent. Twin cascades, falling from several hundred feet above, parted before re-merging in the lively creek below. Mist from its waters rose, wrapping her in its icy clasp. The air smelled fresh, like water and moss and pines.

She ought to swap lenses, use the one that could stop motion, get the water as it fell.

Before she could dig in her case, a shadow fell over her shoulder. Over the falls' roar, she hadn't heard Rennie come up.

He spoke first. "I didn't realize how much I missed this, how much I needed it. There's a trout, there under that rock. See it?" He pointed past her shoulder at the stream below.

She followed his finger. The fish lurked beneath one of several large boulders protecting a tranquil pool from the rough waters. "Big, isn't he?"

"He'd feed our whole group." The fine lines in Rennie's face had smoothed out. He seemed different. Happy.

"So what didn't you realized you'd missed?" she asked.

He flicked that smiling glance at her. "You know."

Understanding flooded. "Home. That's what you mean, isn't it?"

"I think so. Georgia's home to me, and I love it. Jane would never have been happy here."

The casual mention emboldened Autumn. "Do you miss her?"

He didn't answer right away. When he did, he looked at her, his grin widening as if he was pleasantly surprised at seeing her still there. "No. Yesterday, I would have said yes, a little. But today... This is the first time I've thought of her, and it's like I'm thinking of someone I barely knew instead of someone I planned to share my life with. Isn't that strange?"

His eyes were melting chocolate. Their noses were bare inches apart.

She thought for one wild, hopeful moment he meant to kiss her and leaned in. His breath brushed her, warm and benedictory as, instead of kissing her, he put out a hand and used careful fingertips to trace her face, from forehead to cheekbone to chin.

"Autumn, Autumn, how you've changed. I came back expecting you to be the same, but you've grown up and I'm a little lost. Maybe it's true. Maybe you can't go home again."

"No, it isn't true," she said fiercely. "You can. Home may not be what you remembered, but it's still here, Rennie, and the people who love you are still here. All of us."

His hand outlining her lips hesitated. Her vehemence had caught him by surprise. Why hadn't she kept her mouth shut?

"I suppose you're right," he said. "For sure, the people I love most are here."

"You folks ready?" John's jovial call summoned them. "We've got a long way to go before we get back."

Autumn jumped. How embarrassing, to be caught leaning forward, begging to be kissed like a stupid kid.

Rennie's hand withdrew, but his eyes didn't change, didn't move from her face. "No, home isn't what I remembered. But you're right, it's still home. And I'm happy to be back."

"Good," she said softly.

As they climbed the steps toward the trail, he began whistling beneath his breath, a tuneless sound that accompanied them as they entered the worn forest path.

Why hadn't she told him she was glad he was home? Why hadn't she told him how much she'd missed him?

Because she had no courage. Because she was afraid of another compassionate rebuff she couldn't handle. Not again.

But he'd been the one to touch her face.

Trunks of tall naked oaks and silver birches and red maples shot upward with myriad deciduous trees to erect a living wall that closed the hikers off from civilization. They made their way through the woods like Cherokees of old, skirting copious stands of evergreen laurel and rhododendron threatening to reach out and cover the trail, and clambering over rocks and logs that occasionally barred the path.

The terrain wasn't rough but by noon, when they reached the end of the trail inside Unicoi State Park, they all felt the effects. Plodding toward their cabin single file, conversation and jokes long since abandoned, Laney took the lead, with Autumn second. Rennie and John lagged in the rear.

When Autumn looked back, she caught them exchanging furtive words. She stopped beside a pine and waited.

"—don't want it spoiled," she heard John say. "So you've got to promise not to tell her. If you slip up—"

"Don't worry." Rennie was reassuring. "I'll see to it."

What were they planning? "See to what?"

Two guilty faces swung toward her.

"The breakfast dishes," John said blandly. "We left them soaking, remember?"

She didn't bother to hide her incredulity. "I wonder what you two are up to."

Their grins were smug and uninformative.

Okay, she wouldn't intrude on whatever it was they were planning, but she hoped it didn't have to do with pairing Victoria off with Rennie. Analyzing that almost-kiss at the falls had set her imagination whirling.

If she hadn't been so surprised, she could have said something, done something. If she hadn't worried about what he would have thought, she could have moved against him, brushed his lips with hers, tested his reactions and gone from there.

Maybe there would be another opportunity. If she was cautious and very determined and very persistent, maybe there might yet be a chance.

I'm not ugly. Men do look at me. Fran's been flirting with me for weeks. Why shouldn't Rennie? If I can show a little spirit, he might. What will it hurt if he turns me down?

Duh. Her pride. And any hope of getting him, too.

****

SAM BOGATTI, ABOUT to check out of his motel, made one last phone call, got the information he needed, and ended the conversation. "Thanks for the directions. When I get to Helen, I'm sure I can find your restaurant."

After he hung up, he stuffed a stick of gum into his mouth and looked at the note taken from the studio.

What did that seven beside the restaurant name and telephone number mean? Seven people? Or did she have a reservation there for seven o'clock?

He yawned, stretched, got up off the unmade bed, and picked up his bag. One last sweep of the room and bath ensured he'd got everything.

Seven people or seven o'clock. What the shit did it matter? He'd be there early and hang out till he found her. With luck, he could do a clean job and get away with no one the wiser.

But first he had to get to Helen. The woman at the restaurant said three hours from Atlanta, but the GPS said two hours and twenty minutes from here.

Time to get it over with and start home.

****

RENNIE'S SENSE OF well-being from the hike dissolved as soon as they returned to the cabin. Three other people, including Francisco and Norma Degardovera, waited.

Norma had brought her boyfriend, too, though he wasn't the cause of Rennie's discontent. Paul Talliafierro, he decided after a discreet examination of the banker who was his sister's latest conquest, might have more staying power than her other men. His freckled face and square shoulders held a no-nonsense air far removed from her usual flings.

While Rennie liked Paul's self-deprecating humor, he couldn't tell whether Norma liked it, too. She was as noncommittal as ever.

But Norma and her affairs weren't his problem.

His brother was the one who got under Rennie's skin. Ignoring Rennie's jaundiced eye, Francisco jumped up from his seat near Victoria and grabbed Autumn, hugging and kissing her in a most unbrotherly fashion.

The Degardoveras were a demonstrative family, accustomed to open displays of affection. But Francisco was lavishing way too much on Autumn. And in spite of her protestation that she and Fran were friends, Autumn didn't seem to mind.

She ought to. She'd had enough front row experience with Francisco and women.

Keeping one eye on his younger brother, Rennie made small talk with Paul. "So Georgia's about to get a Hispanic governor. What does the banking industry think about it?"

Paul, ignoring Norma's squeals from across the room where she was bombarding her sister and Victoria with some tale about the trip up to Helen, shrugged. "We're like all the other voters. Though it looks like Huertole's got a good platform."

"Business oriented, is he?"

Like Rennie and Francisco, Paul was a tall man, but his

body, unlike the lanky frames of the Degardoveras, was solid. A fighter's body. Rennie's question evoked a shrug. "Looks that way on the surface. One thing's sure, he's got the backers."

"Money's what it takes," Rennie agreed as a burst of merriment came from where his sisters and Victoria had clustered around Francisco and Autumn. He wondered what his brother was saying to make them giggle.

"Speaking of which, I heard a rumor yesterday." Paul addressed John, who was offering him a cup of steaming cider. "An ugly rumor. Connecting Huertole with South American drug cartels."

John's round face puckered. "So they're starting to sling the dirt already. That's what it is, Paul. A rumor. His parents came here from Colombia, so sure, he has relatives there. But Gus is squeaky clean, believe me."

"Oh, I do, I do." Paul blew on the hot cider. "But when something like that gets started, you know how it goes."

"We'll deal with it when we have to. Fran and I have our strategy all worked out. We plan to go public with Gus's personal finances as well the campaign accounts. That should squelch any rumors about illegal campaign funding. Right, Fran?" John looked toward Francisco for confirmation, but Fran was too engrossed in his feminine audience to notice.

John rolled his eyes at Rennie.

Worse, Norma, not content with Francisco's monopolizing Autumn, had joined with Elena in a subtle offensive designed to throw the two together.

His sisters needed to go soak their heads.

As Laney drew Victoria up from the loveseat and brought her toward John and Rennie and Paul, Norma pushed Francisco down on it. He, the turkey, took full advantage of his sisters' ploy to pull Autumn beside him and fasten a possessive arm around her shoulders, chatting all the while like it was the most natural thing in the world.

The devil take his whole family.

Rennie seldom allowed them to get on his nerves, but they were particularly obnoxious today. Did they have to be so obvious about pushing Autumn at Francisco? Not that his brother needed encouragement.

Come to think of it, considering the type women Francisco preferred, why the devil was he was hanging around Autumn? There was nothing about Autumn to make a womanizer like Francisco fall for her.

Nothing except those interminable legs and that miniscule waist and that long smooth neck and those clear blue eyes that narrowed when she got tickled about something.

She deserved better than Francisco.

Not that Rennie would let his annoyance show. He wasn't even sure it was annoyance that he felt.

But it sure was something. After Autumn's suggestive picture teeming with Francisco's sexual innuendo, he had expected them to be paired up.

Which made his reaction on seeing them together more incomprehensible.

"Move," Laney said, hitting her knee against his. "We're tired of Fran's monologue."

Rennie obediently shifted his legs so that Victoria and Elena could sink down on the floor beside his chair.

If Autumn was having an affair with Francisco, it wouldn't last long. Fran tired easily. It would be awful to see Autumn's heart broken. She was an old friend, almost one of the family. On the other hand, maybe Francisco was in love with her. Maybe he would marry her.

Whoa. *That* threw him in the dumps.

Later, having had the foresight to shower immediately after getting back from their hike, Rennie didn't need to fight for a turn in the lone bathroom. Instead, he went for a walk in the park. He needed to get away for a bit.

Something was going on inside himself that he didn't understand and wasn't sure he liked. He'd come home hoping to find peace but had found other, deeper desires emerging. Longings he hadn't known he possessed.

He wasn't sure he knew how to handle them.

Chapter Eight

AUTUMN, WAITING HER turn to shower, saw Rennie disappear out the cabin door and immediately looked for Victoria.

The reporter was on the deck with Norma and Paul, not outside waiting for Rennie.

Good. Did she dare follow after him? No, if he'd wanted anyone along, he would have asked. He'd probably gone out to his car for something. She'd wait.

He didn't come back.

Looked like it was going to take everyone a while to get ready to go out, so no use trying to get into the bathroom. Might as well do something productive. And if she ran into Rennie…

Gathering up her Nikon, she went outside and used the remainder of the afternoon to snap pictures of the scenery around the cabin. But she couldn't find Rennie, and the light wasn't right, and instead of her mind being on composition, it kept wandering to that moment by the waterfall.

After a while, her camera sagged. She was wasting her time. These shots would be trash.

Why hadn't she simply kissed him at the waterfall?

Because she was too scared, that's why. Scared of sticking her neck out. Scared of being rebuffed.

Coward.

Maybe it was as well she hadn't. He'd made it clear long ago she wasn't for him.

Drooping, she went back to the cabin where she was last in line to wash up. Then, before she could take her turn in the one bathroom, she learned that a simultaneous and extended shower by Laney and John—remarked on at length by Fran and Norma, to John's mortification and Paul's amusement—had left no hot water.

Laney, never embarrassed, shrugged her pretty shoulders and grinned like a Cheshire cat. "You'll have to take a cold shower," she told Autumn.

"I think *not*, thank you very much! It'll heat up."

Before the water warmed, the others began to mill beneath the beamed ceiling of the living area, clutching sweaters and jackets and gloves, impatient to leave for dinner in Helen.

Rennie wasn't among them.

Nor was Victoria.

Victoria could be upstairs getting her coat or outside taking a walk. She didn't necessarily have to be with Rennie. *Ragweed doesn't cause hay fever, either.*

"Y'all go on, Laney." How could her voice sound so placid? So normal? "I'll come along soon as I've showered."

Fran, deep in conversation with Norma and Paul Talliafierro across the room, overheard. "I'll stay and drive you in."

"Nope. I want to do my nails and some other stuff. I might even shave my legs for the occasion. If somebody'll leave me a car, I'll be along in a half hour or so."

"I won't go without you," Fran said.

Autumn said, "Don't be silly, Fran." The back door opened on Victoria, talking to someone outside.

Rennie, no doubt.

Autumn wanted to run away. "For pity's sake, go on, Fran. I'll be worrying the whole time I'm dressing. You know how antsy you get marking time. I'll work myself up into a tizzy thinking I'm making you late."

The Degardoveras screamed with laughter. "You've never been in a tizzy in your entire life," Norma said. "Do you remember that time Laney was driving us across town to take our PSATs and our horrid car—"

"Amy," Laney put in. "Rennie named her Amy Jean."

"Amy Jean," Norma acknowledged, "quit in the middle of Jimmy Carter Boulevard? Cars were honking, people gave us the finger, Laney started crying, and I was mad as a hornet."

"Hah. You were cursing like a sailor," Laney said. "Mom would have washed your mouth out with soap if she'd been there. But Autumn laid her seat back and closed her eyes and I swear, I think she slept till a tow truck came."

"What else was there to do?" Autumn tried not to listen as Victoria giggled over her shoulder at the back door. "Amy Jean had quit and that traffic cop called for a wrecker. No, I mean it, Laney, Norma. Leave me a car and y'all go on to the restaurant. I'll be along when I get bathed and changed."

Fran would have argued further but Victoria glided in and linked an arm through his. "Come on, Fran. You promised we'd share a pitcher of beer and an anchovy pizza."

"We can't leave Autumn." His protest, with Victoria clinging to him, weakened.

Victoria kept hold of him, but addressed Autumn. "You do have a driver's license, don't you?"

Competent, assertive, assured. Everything Rennie liked in a woman.

Autumn nodded. She even smiled. "Sure do."

Victoria turned back to Fran. "See? I'll bet the helpless little woman can find her way into town on her own, too. Come on, Fran, you promised." She pouted. On her, it looked good. "Nobody else likes anchovies. I've asked."

"Do go on, Fran," Autumn urged.

Why wouldn't they all leave and let her brood in peace?

"I'll be on as quick as I can."

After another few minutes of resisting, Fran gave in. "Here." He dragged out his car keys and gave them to Autumn, grasping her wrist with mock severity as she took them. "But if you're not at the pizza place in an hour, I'm coming back to look for you."

Autumn, freeing her wrist, dredged up another smile and

agreed that if she wasn't at the restaurant in an hour, he should come back for her.

Oh, go to the devil, Fran, and take Victoria with you.

How mean-spirited.

Although Fran and Victoria did make a nice couple. A power couple, that's what they'd be if they got together. And Rennie would be free for…

Hmmm. Food for thought.

With a little practice, she could become as conniving as Laney.

"We won't order anything till you get there," Laney promised as she looked for her coat.

"Make that we won't order anything with the exception of a pitcher of beer." John came up behind his wife with her pea jacket readied for her arms.

"Or two," Fran amended from the door.

"Uh oh, Autumn. You know what a pitcher or two means to Francisco. We'll be soused by the time you get there if he has his way," Norma warned as the group crowded through the kitchen. "Better hurry if you don't want to miss the fun."

"Rennie was right out here a minute ago," Autumn heard Victoria say as she and Fran went out arm in arm. "Let's see if he's already at the car."

Great. Victoria wasn't going to be happy with one man at her beck and call. She had to have two.

The cottage seemed stark and lonely without the merriment, when everyone had gone and she could take off her happy face and wish again she'd begged off the weekend once Rennie showed up at her condo. She could have pleaded the pressure of work, said she had to get Sarita's photos together by Monday.

The small interlude at the falls that had prompted her to gather up her courage might never have been.

Just as well. Humiliation at seventeen was one thing, but humiliation at thirty was something else. She was old enough to know better. What was that old saying? Once burned, twice shy? No need to stick her hand in the fire again.

After dragging herself upstairs to get her makeup case, she came back down and took a shower. At least the water had heated back up. Maybe it would leach out her sour mood.

Fran or one of the others could give her a ride home tomorrow so she wouldn't have to endure a trip back with Rennie.

She groaned, turned her face up to the spray.

The thought of not going back with Rennie was worse than the agony of being alone with him. And if she went with him, he'd probably want to talk to her about Victoria.

Why couldn't she be like Norma, forceful and unafraid? Norma had no problems laying out her requirements for men. She knew what she wanted and went after it. So did Laney.

She washed her hair and shaved her legs in the shower, but when she pushed back the glass door, she didn't feel any better. She hadn't expected to.

A gentle thump came.

Like the back door closing.

But everyone had left.

Spooked, hand frozen in the process of reaching out for a towel, she let the steam curl up around her and listened.

The noise did not repeat itself.

The woodstove. That's where it came from.

Sure. Logs popped and crackled and fell. A wood fire could make enough noises to unnerve the faint of heart like her.

That's what she got for making Fran go on. Of course, if Rennie instead of Fran had offered to stay with her...

"Darn you, Rennie Degardovera," she muttered. "What are you? Some kind of sorcerer? I refuse to live my entire life eating my heart out for you."

That made her feel better, braver. "Either I'm going to get you or forget you. So there."

Sure. As if she had any say-so over her recalcitrant, foolish, sentimental heart. Still, her decision revived her.

Wrapping one towel round her hair and another around herself, she stepped out into the steamy room, looked into the foggy mirror, and cracked the bathroom door to help dissipate the mist. Though she listened hard, she didn't hear another thump or any other unexpected noises.

"Old house noises," she muttered. "Ghosts."

She propped a foot on the john lid and slid her towel down to swipe at her leg.

Was that blood? Oh, great. She'd nicked her ankle shaving. That's what she got for letting Rennie Degardovera upset her. She bent over to see how bad it was.

A door closed.

Footsteps padded down the hall.

She stiffened. Before she could move, the bathroom door flew wide open, and she was caught with one leg up in a pose that could have been used for a male magazine.

She gasped and pulled at the towel to no avail. It stayed stuck beneath her foot.

Rennie, shock rounding his eyes and mouth, stood framed in the doorway.

The towel wouldn't come free, no matter how she yanked.

"I'm in here," she said unnecessarily.

"Madre de Dios," he said as unnecessarily.

The door didn't close.

She gave up trying to conceal herself, and made a tiny hopeless gesture with her head and shoulders toward him.

He stood suspended in consternation and astonishment…and something else.

His mouth softened while his body tightened, swelled, and smoothed the wrinkles of the faded jeans to accommodate his bulk. His thighs flexed beneath the taut fabric, as if every muscle, every cell, and every tissue of his body were preparing to run.

But his feet didn't move.

Nor could hers. Despite her deficient charms exposed to his critical eye.

Under his stare, a tingling began deep inside her belly, despite its imperfections naked to his view. Her upraised leg revealed everything, but she still couldn't move.

The interminable moment ended.

"Sorry, Autumn." The syllables came out hoarse and choppy. He was as disconcerted as she. His hand fumbled, found the doorknob and pulled it toward him. "I'm sorry."

She bit back a scream as the door closed and separated them.

Damn, damn, damn. Why had he sneaked in like that?

She dried her body off with hard scouring motions, detesting the hateful, straight, insufficiently female body that he had now beheld in all its inadequacies.

"I'm sorry, Autumn," he called again through the door. His voice had regained its normalcy. "I thought everyone had left for the restaurant."

"It's okay. I'll be right out."

How could she sound so composed when her heart pounded like a jackhammer and her stomach felt like upchucking? Of all people, why did it have to be Rennie who came barging in to see her naked, without makeup and her hair in a towel and...?

Any hopes of stimulating romantic interest were doomed after he'd seen what little she had to offer.

Damn, damn, double damn.

She yanked on a robe and zipped it before compelling her jumpy hands to apply foundation and blush and lipstick and mascara and liner.

Better. That was her professional face looking back from the mirror. Her heart had slowed. She wasn't gulping for breath.

She was back in control.

What was the big deal? He'd seen nude women before. A lot better-looking women than me, she told herself as she went out. Jane had been small but curvy, and there must have been others Autumn didn't know about.

Rennie would be okay with the whole thing. He probably hadn't noticed her flat breasts and skinny legs. And if he had, he probably didn't think a thing about them.

Maybe he hadn't noticed.

In the great room, she found him by the front windows where they'd glimpsed the deer that morning. A trace of cinnamon sweetened the air. Coals rustled in the stove. He whistled some unintelligible tune between his teeth, and one broad shoulder leaned against the frame as he contemplated the dusky forest.

Gray twilight outlined pine trees and bushes, changed them into large sinister splotches trying to smother the night lights that marked the trail around the black waters of the lake.

An interesting scene, but not one deserving of such absorption.

It was her. He couldn't face her.

She cleared her throat. "The hot water was used up by the time everyone showered," she said to his back. "I had to let it heat back up. That's why I was late. I thought you'd gone on with the others and I was here by myself."

He turned his head enough for her to see his profile. He still wouldn't look directly at her. "Hey, don't apologize. My fault. I saw the cars leave and assumed you were with the rest. I shouldn't have burst in on you."

"It's okay. I'm through in the bathroom if you want to get in."

"Thanks." He went down the hall, carefully keeping his eyes to the front, but his consideration didn't matter. She was already scooting toward the stairs. He sounded strange, as if he was still embarrassed by his intrusion.

Of course he was. Any nice guy would have been embarrassed, and Rennie was definitely a nice guy. She was being silly about the whole thing. If Laney or Norma had been in her place, they would have shrugged it off. Why couldn't she?

After drying her hair, she looked for her hairbrush and realized it was still in the bathroom. She finished dressing, donning slacks and her new holiday sweater before pushing the jingle bell earrings through her lobes. Then she fastened her fanny pack around her waist, pushed it to the rear out of the way, and taking a big breath, went back downstairs.

Rennie wasn't in the great room. Glancing down the hall, she saw his tall form inside the bedroom door.

What was he doing in John and Laney's room?

To let him know she had seen his trespass, she called,

"Are you through in the bath?"

"Yeah." He sounded absentminded, but not upset at being caught among his sister's things.

Not that it was her business what he was doing. Autumn retrieved her hairbrush and worked on her hair.

"Autumn."

She stepped into the hall. "Yes?"

"Would you mind helping me out?" He was going through Laney's bag. "It's good you're here. Laney doesn't know it, but John's taken a room for them tonight at that hotel by the river."

"Tonight? Oh, for their anniversary." Delight for Laney erased mortification. "How great. I wondered why they wanted to spend their anniversary with us."

"John never intended to. He packed his things for me to take over there, but he wants me to get Laney's stuff. Can you pick out what she'll need? Like, here's her pajamas and toothbrush, but what about underwear and all that for tomorrow?"

"Not those." She took away the flannel pajamas he held and pushed him aside.

So that's why he and John had had their heads together on the walk today. Nothing to do with Victoria. How stupid she was. "Here, let me do it. Laney bought a gown just for tonight. I was with her when she picked it out. It's here somewhere."

She found the new nightgown hidden away in a side pocket. When she pulled it out, the black silk swirled sensuously over her arm.

"That would suit you." Rennie gave her his sleepy grin that made her heart scrunch up in a tight aching ball.

Heat rose to her face. "You think so?"

"With your hair and coloring, it'd look great. Some blondes can't wear black, but you can."

Unaccountably pleased at the casual compliment, she said lightly, "Thank you, kind sir. I'll take you shopping with me next time I go."

"Just whistle. I'm good at sitting outside dressing rooms. Mom and my sisters trained me well."

She hadn't thought her heart could lighten, but it did.

In fifteen minutes, they had the bag packed.

"We'll drive over to town and drop it off at the hotel after dinner." Rennie hesitated. "Listen, I'm sorry about barging in on you, Autumn. The house was quiet and locked up. I honestly thought everyone had gone."

"Hey, you've seen naked women before. Forget it. I have."

Her words fell between them, calm and disinterested, sounding for all the world as if she meant them.

****

RENNIE COULDN'T FORGET.

The sight of her, one slender leg bent as she pulled ineffectively at the towel caught under her foot, kept running through his mind. He kept seeing the way the tiny waist flared into the smooth butt and how the nipple on one small cone-shaped breast jutted straight out as if shocked at his intrusion.

She had been all big eyes and long legs and alabaster flesh.

He'd wanted to run over and throw her down and spread her out and lose himself in that sweet area between her thighs. And that was a hell of a way to be thinking of Autumn.

Autumn!

He put Laney and John's bag in the trunk of the Lexus.

She was like his kid sister. Not to mention a part of Atlanta's top circles, a past debutante, the kind of girl meant for the boy most likely to succeed. A clean-cut old money Ivy Leaguer who'd give her towheaded, blue-eyed children and a columned two-story white house for living happily ever after. A man who'd take her to the opera and the ballet, who'd buy her porcelain and caviar and diamonds.

Not a Degardovera. She would never have a Degardovera. She would never eat sandwiches off paper towels or visit relatives who lived in Mexican shacks with dirt floors.

He swallowed, mouth dry from remembering the soft shoulders, the inviting thighs.

This wouldn't do. He couldn't think about Autumn naked.

Had Fran seen her that way?

Hell.

****

SAM BOGATTI HAD hung around Helen all afternoon.

A nice little tourist trap. After locating the pizza place, he'd wandered along the streets and browsed in the shops where he bought his wife a candle and enjoyed a cappuccino. Then he'd wandered some more. When he figured it was time for the photographer to put in an appearance, he'd found a cold bench near the rest rooms and the pizza place.

There he waited.

And waited some more.

It was after seven before his target walked by. A tall dark man trailed her, caught her elbow when she stumbled on a rough sidewalk. She looked up at him and said something with a smile.

Pretty woman. Prettier than the brochure picture.

Sam took his time getting up, and then followed them into the building and down a corridor to the door of the restaurant. When he entered, a gust of warm air blasted past him, air redolent with marinara, sausage, beer, pine boughs, and wood ashes uncomfortably reminiscent of the fire the night before. Country music moaned over the babble of excited and inebriated hilarity.

He shouldered his way inside, but couldn't get anybody to seat him for fifteen minutes. What was up with that? He hadn't noticed a crowd coming this way. The line in front of him wasn't that long. He was a customer; they ought to be jumping to seat him.

Forget it. You don't need the stress.

These things happened, and he was patient. He'd learned at the start you couldn't be in this business and not be patient.

As he waited, he chewed his gum and looked over the restaurant. No, there weren't that many customers but the place was small. A male cashier did nothing but sit at the door and answer the phone while a lone waitress in blue jeans and red-checkered shirt rushed back and forth to the kitchen.

The harried woman did seating as well as serving.

When at last she motioned him toward a table between a fireplace large enough to burn a small tree and the noisy party including Autumn Merriwell, he didn't hesitate.

What the shit.

He hadn't expected the place to be full, and he certainly hadn't expected to have to wait this long to get inside, but here he was and he'd make do.

Even if it did mean sitting at a table where his back was against that of his target.

What frigging luck. A single man at a table for four. His leather jacket and jeans might not stand out, but someone could remember him.

His heart rate rose. Time for a few mental stress exercises. Breathe, breathe. In, out.

Didn't matter. Nobody'd connect him to the people at the next table. He hadn't spoken to them. They hadn't spoken to him.

Still, maybe he should change the plan.

He chewed on his gum.

Nah, no need. He'd watch his step, make sure he gave none of her group a reason to notice him.

He was good at fading into the woodwork. Average height, average looks.

His grasp of anonymity was one of the skills that made him invaluable for these kinds of jobs. And when all was said and done, this was one more routine assignment to wrap up before heading home.

Sarita, now. That wasn't routine. That woman hadn't been anything close to ordinary.

He should've turned down the contract.

But Bernie had given him plenty of plum jobs in the past. He owed his old pal.

Thanks to Bernie, he had enough money stashed away for a comfortable retirement, and that day wasn't so far away. Another eight years—maybe ten; that would see his youngest kid out of high school and through college—and he could swing it.

Sam took off his overcoat and spat out his gum in the inevitable wrapper. This one went in his pocket.

No need to leave any of his DNA floating around.

He kept his head averted as he ordered but picked up scraps of their conversations.

"—revved up by what the polls said—"

"—so glad Mom decided to get away—"

"—happy you're home. Athens isn't that far—"

"—can't believe it's been two years since—"

"—know television is a hard field to break into—"

"—notice Rennie's car? Big brother's in the money—"

"—idea for a news story. I know this man who—"

Huh.

Sam almost snorted. These people were too wrapped up in themselves to pick up on a stranger at the next table.

Coffee came in a foam cup. Pizza was served on its pan with a deli sheet slapped down in lieu of a plate.

Jeez. He wasn't fussy, but not even a paper plate?

The pizza was okay, but it wasn't like Leo's at home.

He ate methodically and rapidly.

This might turn out pretty good.

The Ruger wouldn't do in a crowd, but he'd expected as much and left it in the van. The knife would work. He bent his knee, touched the smooth handle in its usual place on his ankle.

Yeah, okay, he'd use the blade.

If things worked out, if she gave him the slightest opening, he would slip in and take her from the rear.

One quick thrust into the little place beside the small of the back, and the last loose end would be tied up.

Any luck at all, he could be miles away before anyone realized she'd been stabbed.

And man, he thought as sudden nostalgia for his wife yelling in the stands and his oldest kid racing toward the puck hit him, was he ready to go home. A week was too frigging long to be away.

He risked a glance toward his target.

She looked like a nice dame. Too bad she was an incriminating one.

You shouldn't have taken up photography, lady. You shoulda been a stewardess or something.

Chapter Nine

THE NOISE AND bustle and pizza smell that smacked them in the face didn't help Rennie's frame of mind. Too bad he and Autumn couldn't have stayed at the cottage, read the paper or played a game of cards, had a quiet evening to themselves.

Sure. Right.

After that stunt he'd pulled, barging in and gawking like a horny teenager, it was a wonder Autumn was speaking to him.

Come on, you're making too much of it. These things happen.

He nudged her into an empty seat across from Francisco. Then, before his brother, caught between Victoria and an older woman, could rearrange the table, he slid in beside her.

Francisco, flirting with both women, didn't catch the strategic maneuvering till it was too late. His face darkened, but he didn't say anything before turning back to Victoria.

Looked like Francisco had toned down his personality. But not a lot.

"Rennie, Autumn, this is Dani and Gus Huertole," Laney said gleefully. "Did you see what they gave John and me for our anniversary?"

The Huertoles. Georgia's would-be first couple. It seemed they had taken time from their busy schedules to attend the party, and had brought John and Elena an elaborate Christmas tree ornament as a gift.

Autumn exclaimed when Laney passed the ornament to

her. "It's the state capitol, with gilt on the dome for the gold plate. It's beautiful, Laney."

"Are you spending the night?" Rennie asked Danielle Huertole on the other side of Francisco.

"I wish. It's so lovely up here." Her languid wave revealed a plain wedding band. Stylish in a red and green scarf draped over a black sweater, she sported small wreath earrings to match the brooch pinning the scarf. Her smooth pageboy glistened in the light. "Sadly, we have to go back tonight. I have last-minute things to do for the jewelry exhibit opening Sunday."

Victoria leaned across toward Francisco, elbow on table, chin resting in her hand, fascinated by whatever he was saying. At her shriek of laughter, Danielle turned that way indulgently.

Women usually were indulgent when it came to Fran.

"The gilt's from Dahlonega gold," Laney said. "It says so in the brochure. There were only a few made."

"Look at the details." Autumn passed the ornament to Rennie carefully. "Such craftsmanship."

"Beautiful." He took it gingerly. Looked like a regular ornament to him. "The state capitol. A symbol of what's to come, eh?"

Gus Huertole heard and let out a booming laugh. "We can hope. But yes, things are promising. Dani and I are optimistic." He didn't look at his wife, which was fine because Dani's attention was on Fran.

Only it wasn't. When Rennie passed the ornament back to Laney, he realized Dani had tuned out his brother along with her husband.

Her eyes looked weak, remote, as she slumped on the other bench.

Maybe she was fighting off a cold or migraine. She sure didn't look like the persuasive businesswoman Victoria had proclaimed her.

But that might be her style.

After giving orders for beer and pizza, Gus Huertole turned to Autumn and waggled his brows. "So you're the woman I've heard so much about. The one who takes such, um, interesting photographs. I've been told your pictures are works of art."

He was a personable man in his fifties, handsome with a dark mustache and graying sideburns. His distinguished appearance didn't quite agree with a robust figure that looked more like that of a prizefighter.

Autumn's blush in the bathroom flashed through Rennie's mind, but she showed no discomfiture at Huertole's irreverence. "Hmm. I wonder who told you that? Fran, I bet."

"I'm sure I never used the word 'interesting,'" Rennie's brother protested from across the bare wooden table. "I distinctly recall using the words 'sensual genius'."

Huertole agreed with mock humility that further recall did bring the word genius to mind. "Perhaps I got it wrong, Fran. I beg your pardon, Autumn."

"Don't say things like that." Francisco clapped his hands over Victoria's ears. "We have a news reporter in our midst, Gus. Never admit you're in the wrong, at least not in front of Vicky."

"Fran," his sisters shrieked. "Leave Victoria alone."

"Vicky knows I was joking." Francisco made a face. "Don't you, Vicky?"

Giggling, Victoria used her hands to remove his. "Hmmm. Sounds like you've got something to hide."

"Oh, grow up, Fran," Laney said. "And stop manhandling Victoria."

Rennie, fully aware that Laney and Norma had marked Victoria for him and not his brother, and completely indifferent—he'd long been inured to their machinations—shut out the controversy and concentrated on his pizza.

While Huertole and Autumn fell into a conversation about photography, Dani was talking across the table, discussing some kind of ad layout with John Kinsellen.

"—sure you're right. The sports shirt will doubtless go over better." A slight accent betrayed her South American origins. While Agustin Huertole had been born in Texas, his Argentine wife had come in on a student visa to attend Vassar. They had met and married in New York, moving to

Atlanta when Huertole's company had transferred him south. After twenty-odd years in the state, most people considered them Georgians.

Rennie knew from his mother and sisters that Huertole had begun his political career as state representative and gone on to become state senator. Now Huertole and Georgia's entire Hispanic community hoped he would be governor-elect.

Dani Huertole, as chic and sophisticated with her Spanish grandee bone structure and svelte figure as Autumn was with her cool blonde elegance, belonged to the wave of political wives who balanced their careers with their family life.

Francisco had said she would soon take a leave of absence from her job as assistant director of Atlanta's High Museum of Arts to help with the campaign. But whether her husband was elected or not, Dani Huertole planned to keep working.

That might be what was wrong. The stress of her job and the campaign might have put the pallor in the thin face.

As Victoria had said the day before, Danielle Huertole was a savvy woman despite her lackluster appearance. She showed a quick comprehension of John's explanations as to why they would have to postpone a fund raising drive planned for January, and at Victoria's casually worded insinuation about drug money in the Huertole campaign, dismissed the rumors with a waggle of her manicured fingers.

"I assure you, the one drug my poor husband is familiar with is the one made from the coffee bean. That, I must admit, he is completely hooked on."

Huertole was fortunate in his wife. The candidate himself might be too imperious to handle the business end of an election campaign but maybe under Dani Huertole's supervision, he would come across in his ads better than he did in person.

When Dani overheard Huertole talking to Autumn about the studio, she transferred her attention to them. Her eyes, Rennie noticed, were not brown as he had assumed, but were rather a series of dark spots on a gray-green background, striking despite their weariness.

"My husband is fascinated with photography." The brunette hair in its modish bob swung back as she gave Autumn a smile that would have seemed natural had it not been for those glassy eyes. "I admit, I've heard so much about you, Autumn, that I'm fascinated, too. However did you hit upon such an unusual vocation?"

"My grandfather started the studio, and then brought my uncle in." Autumn summarized the studio's past history and her own involvement, ending, "I didn't set out to do erotica, but it seemed women were excited to find someone they could trust to take their pictures in professional poses like the centerfolds in magazines. The ones their husbands and boyfriends buy for the informative articles."

The people around her laughed, but Dani didn't. "You aren't what I expected, but I suppose you hear that all the time."

"Occasionally."

"I would love to see some of your work."

Autumn shook her head, smiling slightly. "I don't have many examples, I'm afraid. Most of the women I photograph prefer to keep their prints private."

"Naturally," Gus Huertole put in. "I can't imagine any respectable woman having such pictures taken and permitting them to be displayed for purely salacious interest. You shouldn't expect it, my darling."

The way Dani held up her chin at her husband was the tiniest bit challenging. The curl of her upper lip was the tiniest bit caustic.

Here was a surprise.

Rennie glanced around. There were some deep undercurrents between husband and wife, but no one else seemed to notice. Perhaps he was imagining them.

Gus Huertole moved a millimeter away from his wife. Like he didn't want to hear what she was about to say.

Interesting.

"I'm sure, my dear," Dani Huertole, despite her low voice, held her husband's attention with a steely gaze, "that

Autumn is most circumspect and trustworthy, and that her clients have every reason to feel their photographs are secure with her."

Autumn shifted on the bench uneasily so her shoulder pushed against Rennie's. "I hope so. I try to give my clients what they pay for."

Danielle stared at her husband but spoke to Autumn. "Perhaps after the campaign, I can come by and talk with you about some photography for myself. I'm sure Gus would love a sensual photo of me. He complains my pictures make me look too cold."

Her husband could not control his start. "I hardly think it wise to—"

"You'll be governor, my dear." His wife turned away from him. "Not me. Your reputation will be quite safe since no one can blame you for my peccadilloes."

"That isn't what I meant."

Danielle shrugged.

Huertole flushed and pressed his lips together. A tiny muscle moved in his jaw, his lips drooped. Despair? Fatigue?

The conversation moved to the chances for snow.

What was that all about?

Autumn had noticed Gus's reaction, too, and cast a worried glance at Rennie. He winked at her. She went back to her pizza.

Francisco was busy captivating Victoria while occasionally throwing a word to Autumn to ensure she wasn't neglected. Except for his brief abortive affair with Sarita, Fran had a knack for handling women.

Rennie had never once begrudged that knack. Until now. When Autumn was one of the women being handled by his brother, he didn't like it one bit.

As soon as the group finished eating, the Huertoles pled the long trip back to Atlanta and their opportunity to get a full night's sleep for the first time in three weeks. They made quick farewells and swept out.

Once they'd gone, the atmosphere lightened. The others lingered over coffee, chitchatting until the impatient Laney urged them up. "Come on, people, there are lots of things to do. Why sit around on a hard bench when we can go outside and hear caroling, maybe take a trolley ride?"

"Or a carriage ride," Norma said.

"A carriage ride! That's even better." Laney agreed with her sister too quickly.

Rennie hid a groan.

They'd obviously planned the stratagem beforehand, but Laney looked at Autumn as if the idea had just occurred. "It'll be so romantic, clopping along at night with the holiday lights twinkling everywhere. Let's take one."

"Yeah." Norma looked at Autumn, too, as ingenuous as her sister. "You and Fran in one, Rennie and Victoria in another, then Laney and John, and Paul and me."

Paul was a soft-spoken, likable man. He'd never be able to stand up to Norma's bullying, more was the pity. Norma soon tired of men she could manipulate.

Rennie was as surprised as the others when Paul refused. "I imagine the others can make their own arrangements, Norma. As for me, I'm going over to the Festhalle at nine for the dance like we planned. Then I have to head back to Atlanta. You can come with me if you like. Or not."

There was an indrawn sigh from Norma's siblings at Paul's flagrant disregard of her stated behest. Norma was accustomed to getting her way, but Paul hadn't yet learned what was expected.

Everyone's eyes went from Paul to Norma.

She chose to be conciliatory. "Darling, we can do both. First we go for a ride, and then we can go to the Festhalle."

Paul checked his cell. "We won't have time. It's already twenty to nine. I've heard a lot about the Festhalle so I don't want to miss it. I may never get back up here again."

Norma's good humor began to unravel. "You don't have to miss it. If we take—"

Paul got up. "Anyone want to walk to the Festhalle with me? We can view the lights on the way."

Silence, then Autumn was the first to hop up. "I'll go, Paul."

Rennie smothered his grin. She couldn't stand conflict.

How she'd become so attached to the Degardoveras who were constantly in a state of flux was a mystery.

"Even if I don't dance, I like to watch." Autumn stepped out over the bench, leaning back to keep from crowding a man behind her.

Rennie had better support her. "Me, too. And I need to walk after all that pizza and beer."

Everyone else followed, his sisters smoothing over their miscalculation by dropping the subject.

If Norma wasn't careful, Rennie thought as he noted the way Paul, seemingly without effort, began coaxing his sister back into good humor, she might end up with a broken heart. Paul wasn't like her past flames, but Norma might not have enough sense to realize that until it was too late.

Serve her right, the little hellion. She and Laney were both scheming, manipulative females who did their best to control the men in their lives. Husbands, lovers, and brothers. A man had to be quick to keep ahead of them.

He caught up to Autumn.

****

SAM BECKONED FOR his check as soon the people at the table next to him stood up. Holding his coffee in front of his face, he dawdled as they filed past chattering.

Though he kept his gaze to the side, he soaked up every detail of the photographer, especially the bright blue cape she wore over a colorful sweater. Its lapels swung wide open, revealing a belt as the hem fell to her hips.

The belt wouldn't be an obstacle nor would the hip-length cape. He'd come up underneath and strike below the waist.

He glanced at the check. Jeez, that much money for mediocre pizza served on a frigging piece of paper? These damned tourist towns were nothing but rip-offs.

He left a nice tip for the waitress anyway—she was good but overworked—and he didn't ask the cashier for a receipt. He didn't need one. Bernie's client would spring for this meal without substantiation, like he'd also spring for the other expenses on Sam's say-so.

One of the perks of the job.

Aw, it wasn't too bad except for the time away from home. He was getting older. Traveling had gotten to be a hassle. He missed his wife and boys.

The good thing was, once he was through here, he'd be one step closer to quitting. Another couple hundred thou or so should do it. The hard part was accounting for the money, but Bernie had that handled, with the IRAs and investment swaps and all.

He trailed Autumn Merriwell and her blithe group as they moved across the street into an area of small glittering shop windows and brightly painted cafes that comprised an older section of town. There, on the knoll above the river, they spent a few minutes arguing before splitting up.

"Let's take the street car to the Festhalle," one of the jazzy brunettes said stridently. "Come on, people. Don't you have any spirit of adventure?"

"Go ahead," one of the tall men said. "I'm adventured out and you would be, too, if you'd been dragged fifty miles through the wilderness."

The other jazzy brunette shrieked. "Rennie, you know you loved that hike. And it was five miles. Nothing!"

They had to be family, the four Hispanics. They looked too much alike to be anything but brothers and sisters.

After a spirited debate, part of the group walked up the street, recrossing it to assemble where musicians trumpeted Christmas carols from a bandshell.

The two remaining couples, including the photographer and the brothers, strolled down the sidewalk toward the river. The fourth in their group, a stylish chick with a self-assurance that bordered on arrogance, met someone she knew.

The two couples stopped. The woman made noises of delight. "Ryan, I don't believe it! What are you doing way down here in Georgia?"

Sam chewed his gum and shifted from foot to foot in front of a glassblower's window where he pretended the wares were immensely fascinating and totally unlike anything he could buy in the mall at home.

The redhead was carrying on like she'd found a long-lost

relative. "Ryan's a producer at a station up in Michigan where I worked for a while. Let me introduce my—"

Station, eh? Radio? TV?

TV. Her white teeth and glossy looks shouted boob tube.

Maybe a broadcast personality. She sure didn't let anyone else talk.

"Autumn here is a photographer—you'll never guess what her specialty is—and Fran. He's campaign manager for a gubernatorial candidate. And this is Rennie," she gushed, entwining her arm through that of the tall man who had accompanied Autumn Merriwell into the restaurant.

Putting her hooks in the dude.

"Dr. Lorenzo Degardovera, a computer professor at UGA. We're all having the most, the most—oh, how shall I put it?—the most invigorating weekend."

"Laney's out of earshot so go on, tell the truth," the other man beside the photographer urged. "We're trapped in a cabin that we're lucky has running water."

"Fran." She flirted her eyes at him but clung to his brother. "It's rustic but nice. We're having a wonderful time."

Sheesh. Sam tuned her out and shifted his feet.

A shadow caught his eye.

The Merriwell dame had heard enough, too. Either the polite smiling and nodding and exchange of pleasantries weren't to her taste or else, and far more likely—Sam grinned—she'd had enough of Miss Personality moving in on her boyfriend.

Whatever. Either reason worked. She was edging away to wander down the street toward the river. Alone.

Things usually worked out for the best, didn't they?

Blam!

"What the—!"

His heart hit his throat as he sprang for the protection of the building. A couple of older women between him and the photographer jumped, then squealed and pointed.

Fireworks.

He relaxed. No sign of popping lights. The photographer

must have seen some down the river though because she stood motionless on the dark bridge, staring downstream into the night.

His heart rate slowed.

Jeez, that had surprised the f-bomb out of him. And when he was doing so well with the four-letter words, too.

Not a good example for the boys, his wife had decreed.

Sam meandered down the dim sidewalk, but he didn't get a good view of the brilliant colors in the sky until he reached the wooden slats where the bridge began.

His target had leaned against the railing to watch them burst overhead.

Two older couples chatted quietly as they crossed the bridge. A few seconds later, a boisterous group of college kids romped past. The guys stopped to make some oblique overtures to the photographer. When she turned a cold shoulder, they muttered something and resumed their tipsy progress over the bridge.

That's right, dipwads, move on along. Get out of my way.

Her coat hem billowed as she pulled the lapels together. Beneath the gentle darkness, her profiled figure made a forlorn silhouette.

He could take her where she stood. Pause like he was watching the fireworks and then slide the blade beneath the bottom of her jacket, stick it in, and twist it.

In his head, he worked it out. How the blade would catch, then pierce her flesh and slide upward to the lungs.

Yeah, it felt right. If he was careful, there wouldn't be much blood. A little cry wouldn't be out of place in the town noise surrounding them.

Go with the gut.

Sam put his foot on the railing as if to tie his shoe and slipped the blade from its ankle sheath.

The steel haft was cool, but not heavy. At home in his hand. Concealing it up his sleeve, he sauntered toward where she leaned over the rail.

A couple stepped on the bridge so he stopped by the rail, too.

Nice little river. Its frothy current rippled over and

around large boulders. Some of the rocks were jagged and sharp. The roiling water looked cold.

He'd never been to the Alps, but this might be how the villages over there looked. Maybe he and the wife could go on vacation to Switzerland one day. After the boys got out on their own. After he retired.

He didn't concentrate on the photographer or the knife or what he was about to do. Better to clear his mind.

The couple moved past, arm in arm, intent on each other.

Now. Sam took a few steps until he was directly behind her, then glanced over his shoulder. No one nearby.

The few people on the end of the bridge, like the photographer, were intent on the sky. A particularly dazzling eruption brought out exclamations, but Sam focused on the unsuspecting woman, whose blue jacket fell to her hips and swung in a wide inviting arc.

The blade dropped out. He grasped the handle.

This is it, baby.

One step and he slipped the point up and under the hem of her cape, thrust the blade home.

The tip met the expected first resistance before punching through.

And stopped cold.

Huh?

No yielding of soft flesh. The blade met something too solid to penetrate and jarred his arm to the shoulder.

The photographer stumbled and with a soft cry, tipped over the railing. Her hands shot out, clutching for a handhold.

What—?

No blood. No time to wonder why. He sleeved the blade before anyone could see.

Someone screamed. The photographer.

Get out. He'd lasted in the business this long because he kept his cool. No losing it now.

The people on the bridge started his way. Others saw and followed. The group she'd left earlier rushed past, their attention on the woman dangling from the bridge rail.

In moments, Sam had melted into the confusion.

Chapter Ten

SOMEBODY PUSHED ME. Why? What happened?

Autumn tried to keep her balance. Failed. She hit the protective railing of the bridge but couldn't keep from falling.

Her head turned down. Heels turned up.

Someone whimpered. Her.

Everything unfolded like slowed movie frames.

This isn't happening.

The rail stayed within inches of her eyes at a strange and different angle from where it should have been. Her body kept turning.

Of their own accord, her hands reached out, found a purchase on one of the supports and scrabbled for a grip. Her feet finished their revolution over the side of the wall. The rail vanished from view, but she had hold of something.

Her body twisted. She stopped plummeting.

Somehow, miraculously, her hands had closed around a pipe beside a bridge support.

Hanging by the flimsy junction of hands and metal, she swung over the rushing water.

She couldn't climb up. She couldn't get a better grip.

Her hands were already losing strength. Her fingers, no matter how frantically she squeezed, continued to slide a fraction of an inch at a time.

She was going to fall into the rocks.

Someone screamed.

Was that me?

Her hands slipped to the bottom.

Useless. She couldn't hold on.

Someone caught her arm before she could fall, someone who held her wrist in an iron grip that cut into her flesh and made her eyes tear up.

The pain moved from her wrist outward. Her arm felt like it was being jerked from its socket. Her face banged against the bridge.

But she no longer fell.

Above her head, Rennie struggled to keep her from the rocks gouging the waters below. His lips, drawn back in a snarl, made him look more like an attacker than a rescuer.

"Put up your hand." His teeth gritted. Sweat beaded on his upper lip.

His face was not that of her unruffled Rennie. It was feral, urgent, determined. Another time she would have been terrified.

Not now.

Her weight threatened to drag him over the side. His body strained to support hers.

"Give me your other hand," he yelled over the moaning wind.

She tried to do as he instructed, but there was no handhold.

Gales of air, frigid and harsh, blasted from under the bridge. Her legs and body swayed in midair, shoving her against the stone and preventing her from catching onto the rail.

"I can't." He could never hold her. She'd fall onto the rocks.

Fran's face materialized beside Rennie's, and his hand snaked out, caught her other, flailing arm.

In a second, the two men had snatched her up, out of the inimical wind and away from the hazardous waters, over the rail to safety.

Fran tried to draw her toward him, but Rennie was the one she wanted. She rushed into his chest, blind and unheeding of what she revealed.

The wool of his sweater rubbed against her face. His arms circled her and his scent enveloped her.

His voice was urgent. "Are you all right?"

"How in hell did you fall?" Fran put his hand on her shoulder as if he would detach her from her shelter. "My God, it's lucky we started down this way when we did. Another minute and... Autumn, what happened?"

She couldn't answer. She clung to Rennie. Blood pounded at her ears.

Trembling began in her knees and spread to her hips and arms and shoulders.

"She's all right," Rennie said over the top of her head.

She kept her face buried in his sweater.

"Autumn," Fran started. "Let me—"

"She's all right, Francisco," Rennie repeated. "Just scared. Let her catch her breath."

"What happened to her?" somebody, a woman, asked.

Alien hands tugged at her, trying to separate her from Rennie. Fran. She tightened her grip.

"Give me a moment," she managed to say, her voice muffled. "I can't—let me stand here a moment." She sounded shrill and hysterical and quite unlike herself.

She wasn't all right, but Rennie wanted her to be and she had to pull herself together so as not to disgrace herself in front of him. She *would* pull herself together.

I won't cry, she chanted to herself. *I won't cry, I won't cry, I won't cry.*

"Is she all right?"

"How did she fall?"

"What happened?"

Voices. From all sides. Murmuring, clamoring, excited. She peeked out from her haven.

Laney and Norma and Victoria and others. All bunching around. All concerned. All jabbering.

She burrowed back into Rennie's sweater.

"Are you all right?" Fran's words resounded in her ear. His hand clamped on her shoulder and tried to pull her away. "Autumn, are you hurt?"

"Leave her alone." Rennie's forceful tone subdued

Fran's insistence. "Let her get her head straight before we go asking questions."

She shuddered. Rennie understood.

Grateful, she huddled deeper into his chest, the soft lining of his down jacket cradling one cheek and his thick sweater rough against the other. She wanted to stay here like this, with his scent in her nostrils and his heartbeat in her ears, safe and secure.

He let her stand in the welcome protection of his arms, patting her back, holding her, rocking her back and forth until she calmed and her wobbly legs could support her.

Then he gently weaned her from his steady embrace. "Okay now, Autumn? Think you can stand up now?"

She let her arms drop from where they were clutching him. His face was still grim, scary. Not like the man she loved. "Yes. Clumsy." It was hard to step away, but she did. She even managed a shrug. "It was clumsy of me."

A small circle had formed. Everyone stared at her. The Degardoveras. Victoria. Victoria's friend. Strangers who hadn't the vaguest idea of what had happened had gathered to see the cause of the commotion.

She hated their curiosity, the way they pointed and talked about her among themselves.

Rennie would hate it, too. No wonder he looked so forbidding. He was upset with her for making such a spectacle of herself. And him.

She'd turned that voracious spotlight on him. No wonder he was annoyed.

"I'm fine."

There. That was her own voice, cool and impassive like nothing had happened. She'd trained herself long ago to put on a serene front when her aunt scolded her for crying. Aunt Laura had told her crying wouldn't bring her parents back, that it would make her ugly so no one would want her.

Aunt Laura had been stern, but her training had never failed Autumn. It didn't now.

"I'm fine," she repeated.

"Are you sure?" Fran laid an arm over her shoulder.

"What happened? How did you slip over the rail?" Victoria's concern was overshadowed by eagerness.

Hoping for the worst, but then Victoria was a reporter.

People, seeing she was all right, resumed their activities.

Not Victoria. "You weren't standing up on the rail trying to take pictures or anything, were you?"

Autumn didn't mind Fran and Rennie's questions, but darned if she was going to let Victoria interrogate her like she was stupid enough to climb up on the bridge rail and fall off.

She shook her head and stepped back toward Rennie.

Rennie put a bracing arm around her, joining his bulk with Fran's to form a protective shield against inquisitive eyes. "Autumn's got more sense than that, Victoria. Besides, she didn't bring a camera tonight."

"Then how did she happen to fall?" Victoria persisted.

Safe between Rennie and Fran, Autumn could answer without terror. "I don't know what happened. I was standing here looking at the fireworks and then I—I fell." She remembered the hard blow to her back, put a hand round to feel her fanny pack twisted to one side but still there. "It felt like someone bumped into me."

There hadn't been a tug, like someone trying to wrench the pack away.

Maybe they'd reached for it but misjudged, shoved her off instead. "I remember somebody hitting against my back. Hard. I guess they pushed me off balance."

That had to be the answer.

She added with more assurance, "Someone ran into me, and I staggered and went over the rail before I could catch myself."

Nothing else would fit. The jab to her back had been too fierce for an ordinary brush of bodies. Someone had been running and had slammed into her accidentally.

It wasn't likely someone had been after her fanny pack. And if they were, guess they'd think better of tackling someone on a bridge next time.

Victoria opened her mouth, but Autumn circumvented more questions. "I'm all right now." She managed a credible semblance of a smile. "Thanks to Rennie and Fran. We're blocking traffic. Maybe we'd better move out of the way."

Rennie didn't remove his arm from her shoulder. "You must be shook up. Sure you can walk?"

"Yeah." Her legs still quivered, but she'd walk under her own steam if it killed her.

"Okay. Good." To the others he said, "Autumn and I are going back to the cabin. She's had a shock and I'm tired. We're going to skip the rest of the festivities."

Autumn stopped short. "No, I'm fine, really I am. Don't leave on my account, Rennie."

"You may be fine but I'm not." In the gray light beneath the strands of twinkling lights, his harshness gave way. "You scared the stew out of me. Look." He held out his hand. "I'm still shaking. If you're as calm as you seem, you're damned well a robot. We're going back to the cottage, Autumn. We can come back later if we feel like it."

"But I'm—"

His arm tightened on her shoulder, and he whispered at her ear, "Besides, we have some business to take care of. The hotel. Remember?"

"Oh." Laney's things. Conscious of Fran's curious eyes, she said, loud enough for the others to hear, "Okay. Maybe you're right. Maybe I am a little unsteady."

Fran's eyes narrowed. He looked at his brother instead of Autumn. "I'll take Autumn back."

"You can't. We brought my car instead of yours. Besides, I'm going back to the cabin anyway."

"Then I'll come with you." Fran took a belligerent stance.

Rennie shrugged. "Suit yourself."

"Oh, good grief. Stay and enjoy yourself, Fran," Autumn cut in.

How ridiculous that he might think Rennie wanted her. She would have laughed. Except that she felt too rocky and too annoyed at Fran's possessiveness. She wasn't a prize he could snatch away from his older brother. "There's no need to break up the party because I'm going."

Fran didn't like Rennie taking her off, but Victoria, bless

her, added her entreaties. "Come on, Fran, Autumn will be fine. Don't leave me by myself."

Fran hesitated, but in the end couldn't hold out against Victoria's pretty coaxing. "All right, go on with Rennie." He glowered at his brother. "But you'd better take care of her."

Autumn didn't need anyone to take care of her, and opened her mouth to say so, but Rennie took her arm. "I kept her from falling over the wall, didn't I? Don't worry about Autumn."

As they started toward the car, her last glimpse of Fran revealed him sulking.

Rennie noticed, too. "Francisco's annoyed. He thinks I'm after his girlfriend."

"I'm not his girlfriend." She stole a sidelong glance at him, but he'd reverted back to his usual self, uncaring as to whether or not she was anyone's girlfriend.

Her tiny sigh was inaudible.

They fell in with a crowd walking toward the nearby hotel where they'd parked the car. Once Rennie got John and Laney's bag out of the trunk, they went into the lobby.

At the elevator, they joined others waiting to go up. A man, vaguely familiar, stepped on at the last minute. Kind of skinny. Average looks. Not handsome but not ugly. So ordinary it would be hard to do a decent portrait of him. That bland face would be impossible to shoot.

Now she placed him.

He'd been in the pizza place. Another tourist visiting Helen for the Alpenlights except without a wife or kids or anyone else to eat with.

"Push two," Rennie said in the hushed tone reserved for elevators full of strangers.

She was in front of the controls.

He held up the key's tag where a big 216 jumped out.

She hit two. No one else said anything. Looked like they were getting off on the second floor, too.

Except for the ordinary man from the pizza place. He stayed on the elevator and chewed his gum.

****

HEADING BACK TO where he'd parked, Sam Bogatti soon

had the van moved over to the hotel. Traffic was congested, but that was okay. Things were looking up.

After the screw-up at the bridge, he'd almost gone back for the van so if the photographer and her man drove off, he could follow them. But he'd trailed along on foot a little way. Lucky he had, else he wouldn't have seen them get their luggage.

They were staying at this hotel, and he'd seen exactly which room she'd be in tonight.

Yeah, his luck was changing.

With that nasty surprise at Sarita's when he'd looked at those photos and seen Bernie's house of cards come tumbling down, plus the failure tonight to close the books, he could use a change.

Whatever his knife had hit, it had stopped him cold.

Sam couldn't understand it, and that bothered him. He was a craftsman who did things according to certain rules and expected things to turn out accordingly.

Worry about it later.

So when after thirty minutes he turned into the hotel lot, he parked far away from their Lexus.

No sense in tempting fate.

Okay, decision time. Gun or blade.

A lot of people were here in town, maybe moving up and down the hotel halls.

But not in the room. There'd just be the photographer and her man. He'd wait till the hall was empty.

Knock, shoot, and get out.

Yeah. He'd tried it quiet with the blade, but that had crapped out. And with two of them, he'd have to be quick. Fat chance he could get by with doing the woman without taking out the man.

Had to be the gun.

Figure out scenarios.

Like what would happen if Autumn Merriwell came to the door alone. If her boyfriend came to the door alone. If both of them came together.

If she opened the door and the man was in the bathroom, he might get by with one hit.

Get real. More than likely, her man would open the door, or he'd be in bed where he could see Sam when the woman did the honors.

Plan on taking out two, and then he wouldn't be caught off guard, like what happened tonight on the bridge.

What the shit could have blocked his knife?

Let it go. Concentrate on getting the job done.

He looked at his watch. Say an hour. That would give him a chance to get acclimated and incidentally, give them an opportunity to fall into bed and have their jollies.

This would be their last chance.

He wasn't an unkind man. This was simply business. He needed to get the job over with so he could head home.

Jeez, he wanted to be home.

Don't think about it. His wife would still be there tomorrow, and his kid would have another hockey match next Friday night. He'd be back for that one.

His gum was hard and tasteless. He discarded its gray wad, using the wrapper before storing it in his litter bag, and put a fresh stick in his mouth. Too bad it wasn't a cigarette; he sure could use one after that frigging washout on the bridge

Then he reached back behind his seat for the case containing his Ruger and its silencer.

****

AFTER DEPOSITING JOHN and Laney's bag in their delightful and, compared to the rustic cabin, luxurious suite, Autumn and Rennie left.

When they were settled in the Lexus, she said, "You don't have to take me back to the cabin. I'm okay now. We can go back to town if you want to."

The sound of distant merriment made the silence pronounced. His eyes flicked at her and away. The weak outside lights carved hollows, changed his face to a mask. "It's been a long day. A cup of hot chocolate in front of a cozy fire sounds a helluva lot better than being forced to dance the Chicken Dance in front of a bazillion people. Doesn't it to you?"

Hot chocolate in front of the fire with him? Heaven.

Autumn could almost forget the lingering shoulder ache. Even her helplessness at dangling over the Chattahoochee's waters cutting through the boulders. Her terror.

Almost.

She shivered.

"It's okay." He took his free hand, squeezed her arm at its fleshy top beneath her shoulder. "It's over and you're safe."

"You always did know what I was thinking."

"Not always. You're good at hiding your feelings."

She should be. She had learned early to hide them during those first long weeks after her parents' deaths.

That was why she'd adored the Degardoveras on sight. They vented their emotions unabashedly, laughing and shrieking and crying whenever the impulse seized them, and they didn't mind her occasionally venting hers either. If she could be more like them, warm and boisterous and outgoing, perhaps Rennie would feel differently about her.

Who was she kidding? She was a timid cold fish pretending to be a woman. Her accident tonight had proved what a clumsy coward she was.

By now, she ought to know better than to let one moment beside a waterfall raise her hopes. Particularly after that debacle in the bathroom when he'd viewed everything she had to offer and politely turned his back. He hadn't even felt comfortable enough to joke about it.

As Rennie brought in chunks of wood for the stove, Autumn went upstairs to take off her coat. She laid her fanny pack down on her bed and stopped short.

The heavy fabric was slit.

She fingered the hole, then opened the zipper to take out her wallet. It was gashed, the leather pierced. When she opened it, a big gouge in the flap stood out. Even a credit card was dented.

Like someone had stuck a knife in it.

No. Couldn't be. But what else would have caused it?

She took the pack and her billfold down to show Rennie.

Bent over at the stove, he whistled his tuneless song and prodded a piece of wood with the poker.

"The weirdest thing, Rennie. Look at this."

The pleasant whistle stopped. "Lose your money?" He shut the door and propped the poker in its place. "Was it a pickpocket after all?"

Then he saw the slit in her fanny pack. When he took the wallet, any good humor had disappeared. He inspected it, touched the slit leather.

She bit her lip. "Something hit me in the back when I fell. I figured someone had run into me. But now, this seems kind of like, whatever it was that hit my fanny pack, must have cut it."

He opened her wallet.

Oh, no.

She kept her photos on her cell phone except one. Rennie's senior high school picture hid her driving license in its front window. She could see him first thing when she opened her wallet.

Why had she kept that photo, old and out of date as it was? But it should have been safe. No one ever looked inside her wallet. Certainly not Rennie, who'd been gone for years.

He saw his own face but made no comment.

"What do you think?" she asked hurriedly, to draw his attention away.

He fanned out her charge cards and took his time answering. "I think credit cards are good for something besides credit. And I think you're lucky you had your butt pack on. Whatever sliced this went right through. It could have sliced you as easily."

Nausea swelled. She put a hand to her mouth.

"Hey." As on the bridge, he put a brotherly arm around her. "It's okay. Nothing happened. It's over."

"I was scared." She hugged him, holding him tighter than necessary.

"I know. I was scared, too." He laid the wallet on a nearby table and shifted her around so that he could enfold her in both arms and pat the back of her shoulder at the same time. "And I wasn't the one hanging off the bridge by my fingernails."

Emboldened, she buried her face in his shirt and let her hands slide down to rest on his hips. As his hand drifted up and began kneading her neck, she tightened her hold on him.

His heat penetrated through her scarf to her throat, through his sweater to her breasts, through their two pairs of slacks.

The faint cedar cologne mingled with his body oils, and the soft rise and fall of his breathing accompanied hers.

Her heartbeat heightened, pulsed in her ears as she became conscious of something else. Something dark and wanton within her. Something solid and tense and excited between them.

She couldn't move, could hardly breathe.

Not again. She couldn't make a fool of herself by mistaking his reactions.

This happened all the time, didn't it? A pretty girl, cleavage, the curve of a leg.

Anything like that turned men on. Some men got hard brushing against silken fabrics. And his hand was wrapped in her scarf, cupping her neck, massaging her shoulder.

Rennie's chin lifted to rest on the top of her head. Her breasts lay against him, their weight pulling at her, draining her will.

Why didn't he do something? Push her away, pull her closer, raise her face and kiss her?

Lord, she wanted to kiss him.

But she couldn't move, and he didn't.

The two of them stayed perfectly still, arms tight about each other, bodies melting against each other, his chin resting on her hair so that her forehead nestled in the hollow of his neck. His skin felt fiery hot.

Not as hot as her breasts where they pushed into his chest. Not as hot as his sex through the corduroys where he pressed against the top of her thighs.

"Are you all right?" The words above her ear were distant. Taut. Strange. Rennie's voice, yet not his voice.

"No," she whispered, and her whisper cracked from the longing that rose up and filled her throat and vocal cords.

He moved his chin then, and she could tell from the direction it moved that he was looking down at the top of her head. "What's wrong? You aren't hurt?"

"No." Again the croak.

She lifted her face, intending to tell him she was fine, but his eyes met hers and she was drowning in their dark liquid and with an incoherent mutter, he bent down and she stretched up until their mouths met and merged.

Soft, damp, warm. Everything she wanted.

She belonged here in his arms. She belonged.

From the time she was eleven years old, she had dreamed of kissing Rennie. Under his mouth, she floated in a white haze of surprised pleasure and aching desire that erupted into full-fledged need. Her lips opened to take his tongue, and it pushed into her mouth as if it had every right, hot and eager to explore each area, yet restrained, slow, prolonging its investigation and the urgent promise.

Sex with him would be like that.

Some faraway corner of her mind knew it. The blood rose and threatened to drown her mind.

Sex would be slow and sweet and exquisite, building up to a blinding, crashing climax.

Barely realizing what she was doing, she cupped her thighs around him, pushing against him, molding her breasts and stomach into him until she was ready to do anything, promise anything in order to make him a part of her.

Rennie pulled his mouth away. He exhaled with a suddenness that reminded her of the pricking of a large balloon.

She deflated as quickly as one.

When he removed his lips, he didn't let her go. He took her head in one hand and turned it and laid her cheek against his chest and held her there.

His heart beat furiously in her ear pressed to his shirt, the ebb and flow of his blood joining hers as he clung to her, compressed her to him. His free hand massaged her back and hips. She heard him swallow, felt his throat's constriction on the top of her head through her hair.

"This—I—this won't do, Autumn." His voice rasped. Not Rennie's voice. Not casual or calm. Then he gently nudged her back, away from him, removing the heat he generated.

They generated.

"We can't."

She came back to earth.

Chapter Eleven

SHE WANTED TO scream. But that wasn't her way.

Reluctantly, silently protesting, Autumn let Rennie push her away until they stood face to face, two feet apart.

She gasped for breath, swallowed.

Her mouth, her breasts, her body. All hot and trembling and aching for him. Rennie.

Who had wanted her for a moment before he caught himself.

"We can't, Autumn," he repeated.

"No. I know." And she did. Whatever emotional needs Rennie harbored could never be satisfied physically. Rennie wouldn't make love to a woman unless he committed himself, wanted to live with her. Marry her.

And he didn't love Autumn.

He started to take a step toward her, but stopped. His mouth twisted as if he tried to speak but no words came out.

"It doesn't matter." She'd caused his conflict between desire and integrity. She'd end it, make it easy for him. "Don't worry about it, Rennie."

"I shouldn't have let it go so far. Autumn, anything else wouldn't, it wouldn't be right. Francisco—"

"I told you Fran and I are friends! That's all we are!" He thought she was in love with Fran. She clenched her fingers so tight the nails hurt her palms.

"I hope so." As if released, words tumbled out. "Don't you see, Autumn? You deserve someone better than

Francisco, better than me. Better than anyone like either of us. You need a man who can give you a good life, someone who understands where you come from and who can live up to… You deserve more than either of us could ever offer you."

This outpouring was foreign, unlike Rennie. She tried to laugh, but the sound was strained, clearly showing her misery. "What if I think you're wrong?"

"You might think it now, but later you'd change your mind. No, Autumn, I can't… If we kept kissing, it would lead to something else, and then you'd despise me."

"I wouldn't."

He paid no attention. "You're too—you're so different than us, Autumn. You'd never be happy with someone like us."

How many times did he have to say that? How long did he have to stumble around trying to find reasons for rebuffing her that wouldn't hurt her feelings?

The truth was he didn't want her. Period. Not for himself. Not for Fran.

She wasn't good enough to be a Degardovera.

He wasn't finished. "You need someone like Paul, someone who's more—"

Despite the hot surge that swelled her veins and lifted her breasts and filled her groin, despite the shame of her throwing herself at him, his excuses broke through. "Paul?"

Great. Not only did he not want her. He thought she deserved nothing better than a staid, dull banker.

Talk about humiliation. She might have personality problems, but this was the ultimate slap in the face.

Well, she had some pride left. "I guess I know what I need, thank you very much. And it isn't anybody vaguely resembling Paul Talliafierro. Why don't you say what you mean, Rennie? That you don't want me, that I should leave you the hell alone?"

She meant to rush upstairs and hide until she could compose herself, but when she turned, he caught her elbow and whipped her around so fast that the long side of her hair flew straight out.

He had recovered his fluency. "No, no, Autumn, I meant you need somebody who shares your kind of background, someone who knows the right kind of people, someone who's not, who's a member of the Piedmont Driving Club. Someone who knows the ropes in your set and who won't disappoint or shame you."

"My set? The Driving Club?" Her jaw dropped. "One of the so-called movers and shakers who spends days planning how much money he can bring to Atlanta or make from the poor souls who live here? Or one of those dilettantes who golf rather than work like mere mortals? Is that what you think of me, Rennie?"

Scalding fury, egged on by hurt, gushed up and replaced the earlier drowning sweetness. She wrenched her arm away, forgetting her arm socket was sore till the pain hit.

She winced, wrapped an arm around the sore shoulder to ease it. "Thanks so much. Thanks so much, Dr. Degardovera. I'll have you know I've never set foot in the hallowed Piedmont Driving Club except for the stupid debutante parties Aunt Laura made me go to. Or whenever Uncle Parnell took me with him. And they wouldn't have belonged to it except Aunt Laura's father joined when it was the thing to do for business. Believe me, I'm perfectly capable of choosing the kind of man I need. I don't need anyone to do it for me. You—you're a real shit."

He caught her wrists again, held her in spite of her struggles. A low gurgling sound rose from his throat.

Laughter.

She had bared her soul and faced his ridicule, and he had turned her down. Again. Now he was laughing at her. "Let me go!"

Twisting away, she yanked her arm away.

His grip tightened. His chuckle deepened, turned into a breathy moan of annoyance. "You irrational woman, can't you see what I'm trying to say? I wouldn't do for you, Autumn. Neither will Francisco. If you and I—or if he were to make love to you—you'd hate either of us within six months. We don't know the people you know, Autumn, we haven't grown up the way you have. We aren't the kind of people you're accustomed to being around. Can't you see that?"

"What!" She couldn't believe her ears, that Rennie of all people would be a secret bigot. "Oh, I see all right. Thanks so much for your learned opinion on my friends and my character, *Dr. Degardovera*." She was as near to losing control of herself as she had been in her entire life. "For a doctor, you're the most ignorant man I've ever met and I've met quite a few, believe me."

With a final heave, she jerked loose and escaped before she completely gave way to a temper she never lost.

So he thought she was a socialite, did he? One of the ex-debutantes whose days were filled with clothes and skiing trips and island jaunts and charitable balls. Or worse, one of the fast group Fran ran around with. Men and women who hooked up without bothering to learn each others' last names.

I thought I loved him but I don't even know him.

Upstairs, she slammed the door and stood in the middle of the dim room, putting her hands to her flaming face and shaking all over.

She'd never been so mad.

She should never have allowed him to hold her, kiss her. But she had. And she was foolhardy enough to kiss him back when she knew in her heart he didn't think of her that way.

A banging on the door made her drop her hands.

"Autumn, let me in."

"Go away!"

Anger died.

How humiliating. She had betrayed herself. Not only had she clung to him—wrapped herself around him like a lust-struck cat—but she'd all but begged him to make love to her.

Never again. I'm over you, Rennie Degardovera. For good this time.

He kept banging on the door. "Autumn, open the door."

"Go away."

"Damn it, let me in so I can explain."

"Go away, go away, go away!" She couldn't think of anything else to say except, "Leave me alone."

She wouldn't cry.

The door ripped open and he burst into the room.

Her eyes popped, her mouth fell open.

He had forced the flimsy lock.

This was not Rennie. Rennie would never break into her room like a madman.

But he had. His eyes flashed and a curly lock of hair fell over his forehead while his face had more color beneath its normal brown tint than she had ever seen. It was a stranger who filled the small bedroom and menaced her.

She stepped back, away from this disturbing intruder. She couldn't come up with words strong enough to express her outrage. "You, you—Don't you touch me!"

He stopped and lowered hands that had reached out. The volcanic eruption died so that he was again the Rennie she loved. "I never meant to hurt your feelings. All I meant to say was… Ah, Autumn. I couldn't make you happy and you of all people deserve to be happy."

Any remaining anger evaporated.

He believed that he was wrong for her, that she would be better suited to a plodding banker like Paul Talliafierro.

Maybe he was right. She would never be warm, outgoing, or assertive like the Degardoveras. Maybe she *should* find a nice staid man like Paul to share her life with.

She sighed, saw the broken lock. "We'll have to pay to get that door fixed."

"What? What door?" He was disconcerted. "No," he said, waving a hand impatiently as she opened her mouth to pinpoint exactly which door she meant, "don't explain, it doesn't matter. We've got to talk. We can't leave it like this between us. I don't want you to be upset. I don't want you to think I don't care about you."

"It's all right, Rennie. I was mad with myself and taking it out on you. I wanted you." What the heck, why not turn herself inside out? Why not make her degradation complete while she had the nerve? Then maybe she could find a convenient black hole to climb into. Or a lake. Uh huh, there was a nice big lake right outside the cabin she could use to drown herself in.

"I wanted to go to bed with you, Rennie." She studied her nails. They were their normal short and unpolished ovals, but concentrating on them meant she didn't have to see his disgust. "I wanted to make love with you, and I thought you wanted to make love to me. I thought we could share something together. Sorry. I misread the signals."

"You…" It was his turn to pause. His voice twisted, unwilling to say the words. "You didn't misread the signals."

The room about her stilled. She dared a glance. The bare bulb overhead shone down with barely enough light to put a sheen on his curls and expose his face.

It looked as drawn and miserable as hers must.

Hope, disintegrated and thrown to the winds, rematerialized. She waited, afraid to question him, afraid to breathe for fear he'd say something to contradict what she thought she'd heard.

His eyes beneath thick eyebrows were unfathomable in the gloom of the bedroom, his mouth screwed up and vulnerable, almost pleading. His tongue slid over the bottom of white teeth as if trying to keep words from emerging.

They came out anyway, low and ragged. "There's nothing I'd like better than to go to bed with you, Autumn, to make love to you. You don't know… I'd give anything to be able to do it. But it would change everything between us. We couldn't be friends any more if we went to bed together."

"We couldn't?" She blinked away the pricking in her eyes.

"No."

He was using the 'friend' excuse. What he meant, no matter what he said, was that he wasn't interested. She'd broken off relationships herself saying she'd rather be friends, broken them off even though she'd liked the man. When she'd known deep down she would never love him as she loved Rennie.

Pulling back was the honorable thing to do when someone attracted you, but you knew it wouldn't work.

And Rennie was honorable. Unfortunately.

She never shed tears in front of anyone, and this was no place to start. Not here in front of Rennie. She wouldn't break down, but she couldn't stop loving him either. Both habits were too ingrained. "I understand, Rennie. It's quite all right."

"Autumn." The words sounded as if they were being dragged from his throat. "You're not like us."

"No, I'm not. And you can never care for me because I'm too different. I'm not your type. I'm a boring, pitiful woman you feel sorry for but will never love except as a friend. Thank you very much, Rennie. You've made your feelings crystal clear. I understand you perfectly. I won't bother you again."

So there. She sounded brittle but composed.

He reached out a hand, caught her chin when she would have turned away, forced her to look at him. "I do care for you, Autumn. You don't know how much. I could so easily give in."

His head swayed toward her, stopped. His eyes, their deep brown almost black, bored into hers.

Hurt filled her, compressed her lungs. "Then what more do you want from me?"

"I could make love to you, right here and now," he whispered. His grip on her chin tightened, pressed against the bones underneath until it seemed his hand would become a part of her jaw. "You felt me, you know I want you. I could easily throw you down on that bed and forget everything I believe to make love to you. But afterwards, what then?"

Hope wasn't dead after all. He wasn't sending her away as he had when she was seventeen. He was about to kiss her again and if he did, what he'd said earlier didn't matter, couldn't matter.

She swallowed. "Afterwards we'd still be the same people, Rennie. We'll still be friends."

"No." He bent closer. "We wouldn't be the same. Habits

and faults and differences that are tolerated in friends are fatal for lovers."

"So you're saying you could make love to me and enjoy it, but you don't think sex would make up for my faults," she said slowly, feeling her way.

He leaned forward. "Don't put words in my mouth. You don't have any faults, Autumn. And I have too many. That's the problem."

His breath stroked her cheek. He was going to kiss her and when he did, they would make love. This time there would be no pulling back.

Downstairs, a door opened.

Whatever might have happened was lost.

The murmur of voices drifted upstairs, and then Norma called, "Autumn, Rennie. Where are you? Paul and I've come to say goodbye before we head back to Atlanta."

"And to give Paul time to recover from that polka before he has to drive back." Fran's teasing words floated up the stairwell followed by Victoria's uninhibited, hearty guffaw.

Rennie's lips, about to touch Autumn's, pulled away.

He dropped his hand from her chin and stepped back, pale as she'd ever seen him. "I guess the Festhalle wasn't so much fun after all."

She would die, she would surely die.

So close to holding him, kissing him, loving him, having him. And still as far away as before.

One more minute, that's all it would have taken. One more minute.

They looked at one another.

His quick breathing slowed. She forced her own lungs to take long deep gulps of air.

"I'll go down, tell them you aren't feeling well." He turned away too quickly.

Stunned, she watched him leave.

He did care for her, no matter what he said. And he did want her. She had felt the desire coursing through his skin.

He had admitted he wanted her.

Her heart lightened. *He does care about me. He does.*

"I'll come down in a few minutes," she called to his

back, wondering how she was going to explain the broken door lock to Victoria. She'd have to say she'd locked herself out and Rennie had had to break it in. That sounded pretty lame.

Maybe Victoria wouldn't notice.

Hah, a nosy reporter not notice a busted door?

After her heated face cooled, she had to go downstairs and sit in the great room as if she wanted to be there, smile and make conversation and discuss her unfortunate fall off the bridge as if nothing of consequence had happened between her and Rennie.

This isn't finished. I may not be the person he needs, but I won't give up until he says there's positively, absolutely no chance for me.

He had wanted her. He had admitted he wanted her.

Not that he showed it now. He sat on the loveseat with Victoria on one side of him and Norma on the other.

Norma kept sneaking perplexed glances at Paul. Norma didn't understand why he was so casual toward her, why he didn't behave like the rest of her boyfriends.

Autumn sympathized, but she had her own problems.

And her biggest problem smiled across the room and bedeviled Norma about being spoiled and too used to having her own way, before later explaining the responsibilities of his new job at the University to an attentive Victoria.

The old feelings of being on the outside tried to return.

Not that she was left out. Fran, his earlier suspicions at her going off with Rennie waning, was overly solicitous. He insisted she take the comfortable stuffed chair and brought her a hot lemon, bourbon and honey concoction he swore would fix her aches and pains by bedtime.

Paul was considerate, too. He covered her feet with a blanket so she wouldn't be cold before Rennie got the woodstove blazing, and then pulled out his phone to entertain her with pictures of his cat and toddler nieces.

Norma fumed quietly. She liked to be the center of attention.

Too bad. Autumn would gladly have given her the spotlight. People fussing over her wasn't her style.

Especially since Rennie carefully stayed far away from her for the rest of the night.

After Paul and Norma left for Atlanta about ten, the others took turns in the bathroom. When Victoria exclaimed about the broken lock on their bedroom door, Autumn shrugged, saying she'd stupidly locked it from the inside when she started out. "So Rennie had to break in for me."

Her taking the blame made him, she noted with satisfaction, flick that dark glance her way for a second.

Too bad she couldn't read anything from his eyes. Only when she was lying in bed did she remember the gash in her fanny pack.

She was glad Rennie hadn't brought it up to the others. That would have made them hover over her even more.

****

SAM BOGATTI DIDN'T allow himself to get annoyed.

Ever.

But this morning his stress exercises hadn't helped, and he was close to forgetting that anger was a no-win proposition.

They were a nice-looking couple, the poised Hitchcockian blonde and the tall olive-skinned Hispanic. And Sam, having a tender heart and a compassionate soul and knowing it would be their last chance, had given them ample time last night to have their fun. He had patiently waited over an hour before slicking back his hair, snagging a waiter's jacket, and knocking on their door.

He'd waited, knocked again.

No answer. They weren't in. They'd evidently made whoopee and gone out on the town again. From what he could see, Helen was one big party scene so he shoulda expected it.

But he hadn't, and instead of doing the job and heading out as planned, he'd been forced to check into a motel down the way and spend another frigging night away from home and man, was he pissed at them for giving him the slip.

Never mind. He smoothed his hair and straightened the

jacket that was a little bit big. At seven o'clock in the morning now, the lovebirds should be sound asleep in their room.

His natural optimism returned.

This might work out better. From what he'd seen the past night, everyone in town ought to be hung over and groggy, including the lovebirds. He might not have to take out the man, too.

Sam detested unnecessary slaughter.

When he knocked, a woman's voice answered.

Excellent.

He readied the gun beneath the towel. "Room service, ma'am." An old ploy, but effective.

A few minutes passed. The inner chain rattled, and the bolt clicked back to let the door open. A sleepy face peered out.

A woman's face beneath a frizzy cloud of dark hair.

"Did you order room service, baby?" she called over her shoulder, stifling a yawn.

The gun, half-hidden by the towel draped over his arm, was whisked out of sight. "Smith? Allen Smith?" he had the presence of mind to ask. Quick on his feet, Sam prided himself in being.

"No, I'm Mrs. Kinsellen." She frowned at his towel.

He made a pretense of looking at the door number. "Oh, terribly sorry, I must have the wrong room."

A man's voice, raspy from sleep, called out a second before the door closed, "Who is it, hon?"

Sam didn't hear what she answered. He was striding down the hall, stripping off his borrowed waiter's jacket and fuming.

Shit, what a close one. Who the shit is she?

Someone familiar.

His mind was already churning, sorting new facts, filing them into old.

Ah. He had her.

One of the jazzy brunettes in the photographer's group last night, the one clinging to a placid man happy to be clung to. Yeah, the man back in the bed who had spoken as

Sam escaped. Somehow this couple and the other had switched rooms on him.

Shit.

Now, now, take it easy, don't get your bowels in an uproar.

Stress was the cause of most heart attacks in middle-aged men. And excess weight. He'd never had a weight problem, and hitting the gym three times a week helped his stress levels. But for moments like this, he had a set of mental exercises.

Breathe in, breathe out. Imagine floating in a clear pool of water in warm sunshine. Imagine petting the dog's silky ears. Imagine lying on the beach listening to the ocean.

Okay, heart was back to normal, temper under control.

He looked around the hotel for the Lexus, but it was gone. The blonde and her man must have borrowed the room for a while last night.

Never mind. This little setback could be handled. All he had to do was watch and wait. The two lovebirds upstairs should lead him to the Merriwell chick if he waited and watched long enough.

And patience was part of the job.

He moved his van to a place where he could monitor both hotel doors.

****

THE KITCHEN OF the cabin was crowded, too crowded for Autumn. There was no chance of being alone with Rennie this morning, with everyone fixing their own breakfast and chattering.

Elena and John came in, with Elena bubbling over about their night at the hotel.

"—wonderful, lying in that Jacuzzi in front of the fire. I still can't believe John thought of surprising me all by himself." Laney planted an enthusiastic kiss on her husband's beaming forehead but spoiled her accolade by adding, "He's usually so unimaginative."

John helped himself to coffee. "I saw it was either find a hotel or spend another night listening to people going in and out of that one bathroom beside our bedroom."

"Oh, John, don't spoil your romantic gesture." Laney did

a happy pirouette before turning to Autumn and Victoria and confiding, "The thing was, the bed creaked so much—"

"Elena." John spilled his coffee. "Do you have to share everything?"

"—that someone next door kept bumping on the wall and screaming at us every time we tried to do anything innovative," she continued, sending a mischievous look toward her husband that quickly dissolved into perplexity. "Then some dimwit bellman woke us up at the crack of dawn this morning, can you believe it? And you know what?" Her brown eyes, slanted like Rennie's, widened. "He was carrying a gun under a little towel draped over his arm."

"A gun?" Autumn and Victoria echoed.

Fran groaned and rolled his eyes.

"Laney," her annoyed husband injected with a long-suffering expression that said he was far too familiar with her vivid imagination. "You didn't see a gun, hon."

"It was a gun."

"We've gone over this. It couldn't have been a gun."

Her eyes flashed. "You weren't awake, John, you were practically comatose after spending half the night in the Jacuzzi and the other half getting a whole-body massage. You were in bed and never saw the man. He had a gun."

"It was a coffeepot or a serving spoon or something you mistook for a gun."

She flushed bright red. "Serving spoon?" She jabbed a finger into her husband's chest. "You're crazy, John." She jabbed him again. "I tell you he had a gun." Another jab. "You think I don't know a gun when I see one? You think I'm a dummy?" One last jab.

"Stop that. You're as dingy as that weirdo next door."

She screamed and hit him with the side of a fist. "Kiki isn't a weirdo and neither am I. Take that back."

He dodged when she would have hit him again. "Cool it, hon. Remember your work with battered spouses."

While the others observed, Rennie braved the storm. "Yeah, cut it out, Laney. You're getting to be as bad as Norma. We'll all testify for John if he decides to divorce you."

"You butt out, Rennie. This is between John and me."

Rennie held up his hands. "John, call on us as witnesses if you decide to take legal action."

Autumn tactfully nursed her coffee as Laney sat down, sulking. Anger looked good on Laney. For that matter, any emotion looked good on Laney. Like her siblings, her dramatic Spanish face was eye-catching, no matter whether she was happy or sad.

Frowning seemed to be the order of the day. Even Fran, in his khakis and button-down shirt, seemed preoccupied. At least till Victoria elbowed him and earned a grin.

As Autumn and the others nibbled at toast and cereal, Laney tried her best to pick a quarrel with John. "The next time someone shows me a gun, I'll shoot you with it. Maybe then you'll admit I was right."

John, accustomed to his temperamental wife after two years of marriage, stopped arguing. He refused to do anything but shake his head in an amiable manner supposed to deescalate Laney's anger but in fact doing the exact opposite.

Autumn fingered the rim of her cup. A gun.

Had Laney actually seen a gun? Surely not. The Degardoveras, with the exceptions of Rennie and his youngest sister Cristina, tended to drag every ounce of drama out of ordinary situations. Laney, while not quite as theatrical as Norma, was still pretty good at performing.

A slanting glance toward the one never-ruffled Degardovera showed him disinterested in his sister's antics. The corduroys and bulky sweater didn't mask his slim hips and wide shoulders as he stood, mug in hand, looking out a tall window and brooding.

Neither Autumn nor he had said anything to each other except for the inevitable morning greetings. He must have been rethinking his admissions to her advances because he'd avoided her all morning.

Heat warmed her cheeks.

All right. If that was how it was to be.

She got up to put her cup and bowl in the sink and turned her back to him. They had a three hour drive back to

Atlanta this afternoon.

Alone.

Try and get away from me then, Dr. Degardovera. She would make him accept her as a desirable woman or alienate him forever.

This friend stuff was getting old.

Fran, as Laney's diatribe increased in volume, made a spurious leap up from the breakfast table in a patent attempt to stop his sister from further browbeating his brother-in-law.

"Anybody want to go for a short walk to the lake before we have to leave? It isn't far to the trail from the deck. If we start now, we can be back in an hour, plenty of time before checkout at noon. Victoria?"

"I don't know, Fran," Victoria demurred. "I'm not much for hiking. My ankle tends to swell if I walk far."

He bent over her, stretching both hands out to the back of her chair as if to trap her between his arms, and gazed into her eyes. "Vicky, even a couch potato like you can do this walk. Come on, sweet thing. I'll carry you if you can't make it. I promise."

"I don't know." She threw a flirtatious glance toward Rennie. "Are you going, Rennie?"

"Sure," he said in his easy manner. "I'm game."

Autumn was the lone holdout.

"Come on, Autumn, it'll be fun." Fran left Rennie to keep Victoria from backing out while he came over and tugged at Autumn's hand. He entwined his fingers in hers, flashing the intimate smile that seldom failed to bring the feminine object of his attentions to her knees.

Autumn, immune to Fran's charms, unwound her hand. "I think I'll laze around here." Her shoulder still hurt from the fiasco on the bridge.

Besides, Victoria had resumed her proprietary air toward Rennie this morning. There was no reason to tag along while the chic newscaster hung onto his every word.

And Autumn didn't want to chance ending up alone with Rennie until she could be sure they would have time to finish what she intended to start.

Sooner or later he would offer considerate apologies and reasoned arguments for not making love to her. Unless she had time to break down his resistance, his apologies would be one more block in the barrier between them.

When she thought about throwing herself at him, she got sick to her stomach.

But what else can I do?

How often had she tried to become a part of her uncle and aunt's closeness, and how often had she been disappointed? How often had she joined in the Degardoveras' adventures only to find herself eventually sent back to her aunt and uncle?

All her life, she'd been left on the outside, looking in at happiness.

If she lost her chance to be a part of Rennie's future because she was afraid of rejection...

Well, she wouldn't. That's all there was to it.

In the end, everyone except Autumn went down to the trail.

Chapter Twelve

As HIS BEIGE van crawled down the deserted street, Sam Bogatti checked out the positions of the isolated cabins.

Cars took up most of the parking spaces in front of the lower cottage where the couple from the hotel had disappeared, but that didn't matter. He wasn't about to park there.

Smoke rose from the chimney pipe. The photographer would be inside with her friends, curled up beside a warm fire. Laughing and enjoying herself. Unsuspecting. Must not have heard about the fire or she'd have rushed home. Maybe his luck would hold and he could take her before she got word.

As Sam chewed his gum, he brooded.

Seemed a shame, wasting a pretty woman like that when she had a good-looking boyfriend and no small talent for taking sexy pictures.

Everything to look forward to, future looking all rosy.

Except it wasn't.

Life was a bitch.

"The wife's right. I'm too soft-hearted. I've got to toughen up. Can't worry about everybody."

Parking down the street across from another set of cabins, he lay back against the headrest. In his rearview mirror he could see the front of the cabin hiding his mark.

From the number of cars, several people were inside. He didn't want to take her out in front of witnesses, but he couldn't stay here either. Not for long. Park officials were the worst of bureaucrats, the kind who routed out unauthorized vehicles and ticketed them. He for frigging sure couldn't afford to be questioned or recalled after what was going down today.

Ten fifteen.

They'd check out and leave for Atlanta soon. No way was he trailing them back down there. It'd take him another half day to get started home.

Either he could knock on the door and risk being seen, or stay here and wait, hoping she would come outside where he could get to her. And he didn't have long to decide.

Below him, on a path circling the lake behind the cabins, a group of exuberant hikers swarmed into sight. Despite the distance, he recognized the couple from the hotel. With them were the two brothers and the perky TV broad from last night.

Nobody else. He sat up for a closer look. Yep, no blonde photographer among them.

The group disappeared behind trees.

Leaning back, he considered. Autumn Merriwell might not be inside the cottage.

No, odds were good that she was. The rest of the walkers had been with her last night in the pizza place, along with that older couple and the other sister and her admirer. The older couple had left early—he'd heard them say they had a long drive back to Atlanta—but the second brunette and her stocky man had been with the group milling around afterward.

They weren't with the walkers. That meant maybe three people in the cabin. He could cope with three.

Okay, he'd wait here and watch the entrance a little longer. If everything seemed okay, he'd try the door. Wouldn't take two minutes to get in, do her and whoever was with her, then get out.

He stroked the Ruger. Its cold smoothness cleared his mind.

Yeah, he was right to use it. No time for niceties out here in the boonies. He'd played around long enough, been frustrated once too often. Give her five minutes and if she didn't come out, he'd go to the door and finish it.

As he put the silenced Ruger in his lap and took a ski mask from the console compartment, his rearview mirror showed a Ferrari pull up and park in front of the cabins. He stiffened at a splash of blue emerging.

The blue-coated driver leaned back in before straightening with some plastic grocery sacks. Her jacket hem flared like a cape while the morning sun reflected blonde highlights.

Bingo. Patience was rewarded. *Thank you, lady luck.*

Cranking the van, he swung it around. Behind the parked cars, he rolled down the window just as she reached the steps leading down to the two cabins and stopped.

With her back toward him, not six feet away, she dug into her purse like she was looking for a door key. The blue jacket stretched out nice and inviting across her shoulders.

An easy mark.

One smooth movement and the Ruger lay steady on the window frame.

He popped her three times. Once through the head and twice in the back.

She crumpled to her knees.

Plastic sacks hit the ground. A roll of paper towels and a six-pack spilled out into the dirt alongside a carton of light bulbs.

She fell on her face beside them, bright blood spreading over the blue coat.

Nausea struck.

Jeez, his stomach. This part always got him.

Think about something else.

Stash the gun. He inhaled and exhaled as he stuck the Ruger under the seat. The queasiness subsided. He drove off.

If she wasn't dead when she hit the ground, she would be in minutes, bleeding like water from a faucet.

No one had seen him. The few people he'd spotted since entering the park were the hikers lost on the trail below and the drivers of occasional cars on the main road.

His license plates were obscured by mud. He was safe.

The weekend was shot to hell, but for consolation, he'd be home in time for the kid's hockey practice Tuesday afternoon.

A weight lifted.

As he wheeled the van down the hill toward the park exit, a man emerged from the woods and started down the road toward the cabins.

Sam drove past him, putting his hand up to his face. But the walker never looked his way.

Dark face, dark hair, athletic build.

The photographer's boyfriend. Too bad he had to come back to that. And too bad a woman with Autumn Merriwell's talent for taking pictures had to die.

Sometimes his conscience bothered him.

You're getting soft, Sammy.

Time to think of leaving this business. He could look into buying that motel in Florida his brother-in-law kept yammering about going halves on.

Nah, he was tired.

The past few days had been hell, what with Sarita—Sarita Sartowe!—turning out to be his target, and then the screw-up with the photos and the trouble finding the photographer.

All over now. He'd put in a few more years, then retire like he planned.

He found a decent music station on the radio, stuck a fresh piece of gum in his mouth, and kept driving.

Going home. Yeah, man.

****

AUTUMN JUMPED. HER eyes flew open. Her heart raced.

What was that?

Dazzling white light highlighted cedar paneling, black stovepipe, and brown carpet under dark high-beamed ceilings.

Where was she?

The park cabin. Helen. Rennie.

The bright light came from sunshine streaming through tall windows. The woodstove window glowed red in front of the loveseat where she sat with feet up on an ottoman and head on a cushion.

She'd been thumbing through a magazine while the others went for a walk.

Ah. Now she remembered.

Her heartbeat slowed to normal.

I must have dozed off.

She rubbed her eyes. Something seemed wrong. Out of place. The cabin lay silent except for the crackle of burning wood,

What had cut through her sleep so abruptly?

And she *had* been asleep. Fast asleep.

A strange turbulence charged the air. Sitting up, she stretched, then mentally shook herself. She was being foolish. Worrying about what she would say to Rennie and what he would say to her had worn her down.

A noise—physical and not supernatural—had awakened her.

Backfire. There hadn't been much traffic on the road by the cabin, but loud cars abounded wherever you went nowadays.

Or firecrackers. It could have been a firecracker. There'd been lots of them in Helen last night.

She yawned and listened, but heard nothing more.

What time was it?

Rennie had agreed that checking out at eleven would give them plenty of time to eat lunch and catch the live glockenspiel at two.

Ten thirty-five. He and the others hadn't been gone long enough to circle around the lake.

Restless, she picked up the magazine dropped on the floor. It was the latest issue of a popular Atlanta magazine, and the cover showed a smiling Danielle Huertole in businesslike navy suit and white ruffled blouse. She stood with her arms crossed, posed so that the High Museum of Arts loomed in the background to her side.

HIGH MUSEUM's COUP, read the headline. *ASSISTANT DIRECTOR BRINGS PRICELESS TREASURES TO THE ATL.* Further down in smaller captions, another article started: *Will Dani's Gus Become Georgia's Gus? Supporters Say Sí, Pollsters Say Probably.*

Fran must have brought the magazine up to show John so they could gloat over the free publicity for their candidate.

A sudden thought made her frown. Could Fran's warmth toward Victoria have an ulterior motive? She hoped not. It would be wonderful if Fran and Victoria hit it off.

Come on, be honest. Fran's happiness was the last thing on her mind. She was thinking that with an attractive, sexy television personality out of the way, she'd have no competition for Rennie.

For shame. Whatever character she had was rapidly going down the tubes.

Discarding the magazine, she lay back and stared into space.

She had to figure out what to say to Rennie on the drive home. This morning he had ignored her like he was embarrassed. After the way she'd thrown herself at him last night, conversation was bound to be strained going home.

That could be why he was avoiding her today. Because of her outright assault on his virtue.

Heat rose up her neck. Had she been that aggressive? Had she really ground against him until he'd had enough?

One thing was clear. No matter what happened, their old easy friendship was ended. Either she would make him see her as an available sexual partner rather than a little sister, or else they'd retreat to being mere acquaintances.

Far too late to go back to where they'd been before.

Nor did she want to.

****

WHEN RENNIE STARTED to hike toward Smith Lake with the others, he kept remembering Autumn. She had watched them leave with the set face and false brightness that reminded him of the frightened child who'd first entered the Degardoveras' lives.

She didn't deserve to be so miserable. Him being the cause made it worse.

A quarter of a mile down the trail, where it crossed the

road leading back to the cottages, he stopped. What was he doing, tramping through the woods while she was so desperately unhappy? He needed to talk to her, to explain that yes, he was attracted to her but that he couldn't take advantage of his friends.

Especially her.

Autumn was the last person in the world who deserved to be stuck with someone like him. No matter what she thought now, sooner or later she'd find out the truth about him and Sarita. If they became lovers, he'd have to tell her himself.

But no matter how she found out, he'd lose her respect and disgust her so much she'd never want to see him again. He needed to be straight with her, and the sooner, the better.

"I forgot something," he told the other hikers. "Meet you back at the cabin."

As he headed for the road as the quickest route back to the cabin, a crackle broke the woods silence.

Then a van passed, heading toward the main road.

Not unusual but...

A growing uneasiness drove him until, rounding a bend, he saw the dark rooflines of the cabins.

Lining the parking places off the road between the cabins and him, stood the row of cars. His Lexus along with John's Ford and Fran's Mazda.

The ditzy neighbor's Ferrari took up the last space.

Everything was fine here. Nothing was out of place. He wa1s imagining stuff.

No. Something was off.

Was it the dead silence? After the previous crackling, not a sound, not even a squirrel's chatter, enlivened the air.

Maybe it was the morning sun diffused through the concealing overhead mist that painted everything—trees, shrubbery, and cottages—with an eerie gray translucence.

Whatever it was, it made him mindful of his surroundings.

Then he saw her, a twisted heap lying face down between the cars and the steps leading down to the cabins.

One arm pinned down an empty plastic bag, and her jacket was stained red.

No!

The blood in his veins changed to ice. The pit of his stomach threatened to spew its contents.

Later, he didn't remember covering the yards separating them. Only the anguish. "Autumn, Autumn!"

Rolls of paper towels lay to one side, a six-pack of beer to the other.

Blonde hair was discolored by a deep brown-red. One small hand rested on a box of light bulbs as if she had tried to rescue them when she fell.

Rings covered the fingers, rings that didn't sparkle in the overcast light.

The ice melted in a flash of thankful heat.

Rings.

Not Autumn thank you God not Autumn. Not Autumn thank you God not Autumn.

His heart, crammed into his throat, fell back into place. His stomach settled. Sanity returned.

Her face, pressed as she was against the pine needles layering the packed earth, was hidden. But he knew.

Kiki Ballencer, the woman who had exclaimed over Autumn's jacket and his own likeness to Elena.

Blood clotted the blonde hair and stained the blue wool.

Rennie didn't want to touch the unmoving form, but he knelt down and felt for a pulse.

The dead woman. Autumn.

The blue coat. The blonde hair. Both like Autumn's.

But Autumn was safe; Kiki was the one hurt. What was going on?

Was Autumn all right?

He jumped up and rushed toward the steps and the cabin.

Please, please, don't let Autumn be like Kiki.

He didn't know what he was terrified of finding or why this disjointed urgency, but he flew past the azaleas and down the railroad tie steps, fumbled for the doorknob and rocketed inside.

"Autumn," he called, and again, panicked when she didn't answer. "Autumn!"

"Rennie?" Autumn, partially hidden where she lay on the loveseat, sat up. Her mouth and eyes rounded. Blood drained from her face at sight of his. "What is it?"

She was safe. "Autumn!" His legs went limp.

"Rennie? What's wrong?" She half-rose so that one foot rested on the floor, the other knee on the cushion.

He'd scared her.

No wonder. He was so scared himself he'd snarled at her. "Nothing. Nothing's wrong." He caught a breath, bounded to her.

Autumn was here and she was all right.

Conscience made him stop short, kept him from taking her into his arms and hugging her hard. He panted from wrestling with it while his hands clenched and unclenched.

"Rennie?" She stood up.

"Autumn. Thank God."

"Rennie, tell me what's wrong!" There was a groggy, tousled aura about her. She trembled.

To hell with his conscience.

In two steps, he'd caught her, kissing her face and hair and any other place he could reach. He clutched her to him, afraid she might be taken away at any moment. He touched her eyes, her ears, her nose, her throat, murmuring, "Autumn, Autumn, Autumn."

She didn't fight him or object. "Rennie, what's wrong? Rennie?"

He lifted his mouth from her soft skin. "Kiki's...I thought she was you." He buried his face in her hair, breathing in her rose scent, rejoicing in the fine strands stroking his cheek. "I thought she was you, Autumn. I've never been so terrified in my life. Madre de Dios, I thought she was you."

"Kiki? Is she hurt?" Unlike the night before, Autumn was the first to draw back, the one recalling responsibilities. "What's wrong? Does she need help?"

One more moment to hold her. Just one more moment, he told himself. Then he steadied as her hands rested on his chest and her eyes looked at him with a trust that made him want to damn responsibility and carry her off to a place where she would be safe and they could be together.

He was confused, out of his head. He needed to pull himself together, get back to normal.

Except nothing was normal any more.

"Kiki's—I think she's dead." He pulled his cell out. "Damn, I forgot there's no signal here. Autumn, I need to run up to the lodge, have them call an ambulance." He pushed back her hair, mussed and tangled from his frantic caresses. "Someone needs to stay with her. She… It, it's too late for her but I have to go get help."

She understood immediately. "Let me put on my shoes."

"No!" He couldn't ask her to stay with that ruined husk. "Maybe you'd better go up to the lodge and I'll stay."

She stood. "I'll do it, Rennie."

Back to the old Autumn. No hysteria, no tears.

The panic belonged to him when, at the door, she grabbed the blue jacket off a duffel bag packed and ready for the trip back to Atlanta.

That coat was dangerous on her. It looked too much like the blood-soaked jacket that hadn't protected Kiki.

No time to worry why, but she couldn't wear it.

"Don't put that on." He jerked the coat from her and threw it down, stripped off his own down jacket and held it out. "Humor me, Autumn. Please."

One mystified look, but she put on his jacket without question.

Bless her. Either of his sisters would have argued if he told her to get out of a sinking boat.

At Kiki's body, she gave a quick intake of breath before lifting her hand to her mouth.

In his too-big jacket, she looked fragile and defenseless. He couldn't leave her alone with Kiki's pathetic corpse.

She read his mind. "I'm all right. Go on."

He caught her shoulders in both hands, squeezed them bracingly. "I'll be back as soon as I get help."

"I know." She sounded like Autumn. Unruffled. Capable. "I'll be fine, Rennie. Go on now."

If she had been Norma or Laney, he would have had to waste time dealing with the inevitable hysterics. But Autumn never dissolved into tears. Still, he lingered. "I'll hurry."

"I know. Go on so you can get back. I'll be fine."

He started to run, hating to leave her, hating she'd have to stay alone with the thing on the ground, hating every step that took him away from her.

A family at the next cluster of cabins were loading suitcases in their SUV as he ran by. They greeted his tale with suitable shock and volunteered to send help from the lodge.

Autumn, sitting on the steps near Kiki's remains, looked askance when he ran back.

"I found some people up the street," he said between gasps. "They're going to the lodge to get help." He bent over, rested his hands on his knees and inhaled oxygen to his starved lungs.

"Good."

In the midst of the unexpected tragedy, her calm was remarkable. How he did love her for that.

She looked at where Kiki sprawled. "She was so animated. So alive. It doesn't seem possible that she's dead. What happened, Rennie? Did she fall?"

"I don't think so."

"You don't?" Silence. "Her husband?"

Had it not been for the blood coagulating into dark red splotches, the small form would have seemed that of a large rag doll, dropped and abandoned by an uncaring owner.

He didn't like looking at Kiki's body, didn't want Autumn to look at it either. "I don't know." He dropped down on the railroad tie beside her, put his arm around her and turned her face toward him, away from Kiki. "I don't know, Autumn."

"Who else would have done it?"

He shook his head.

She must be shocked, but she covered it up well. "How horrible to think a marriage could end up like this. What could make a man want to do this to his wife?"

"I don't know. Jealousy, maybe. Money. We don't know the whole story. Probably never will."

Somewhere in the back of his mind was a germ of truth, something he needed to remember. But he couldn't think of it. Whatever it was eluded him.

Beneath his arm, she shuddered. "I can't imagine anyone hating another person enough to do something like this."

"Of course you can't." He squeezed her. She had no idea of the evil in people, his Autumn. For that matter, she had no idea of the depravity to which a normal person could sink.

Even ones who tried their best to be upright and moral.

He didn't want to be the one to break her rosy glasses. His teeth clenched. *I won't be.*

She laid her head on his shoulder. He shouldn't have let her, but he did. Together they waited.

They didn't speak again until after the emergency team came.

Chapter Thirteen

A PROTECTIVE NUMBNESS had descended over Autumn the moment she saw Kiki's pitiable body. Murmurings of bullet wounds from White County EMTs and deputies caused the sense of unreality to linger.

Kiki was murdered, but Autumn couldn't take it in.

Investigators asked her and the others question after question, many of them unanswerable.

"I don't know," came most of the replies.

But sometimes it varied. "I didn't meet her at all," said Fran.

"I spoke to her for a minute," said Victoria.

"We talked long enough to find out she was terrified of her husband," said Laney.

"We were walking and didn't see anything," said John.

Autumn was as vague as the rest. "I was sleeping. Something woke me up, but I don't know what. I didn't hear anything."

Rennie remembered seeing a beige van when he came back to the cabin, but he hadn't noticed the driver or the tag plates.

As they waited, Autumn kept thinking that if they'd talked more to Kiki, accepted her invitation to go over for dinner, maybe Kiki wouldn't be dead.

I should have been nicer to her.

No matter how pushy Kiki was, no one deserved to end up on the ground covered in her own blood.

Afterward, the only thing Autumn recalled clearly from

that afternoon was the pearly gray light cast from the cloud-distorted sun and the chill that would not leave no matter how many layers she put on.

Her numbness was beginning to wear off by the time the sheriff dismissed them.

Fran and Victoria immediately left for Atlanta. He was due back in Atlanta early to prepare for the High Museum reception that night, and Victoria saw an opportunity for a news story; Kiki's estranged husband, the ex-football player, was a possible suspect and she was personally acquainted with him. Fran had been happy to oblige when she begged for a ride.

Part of Autumn's reviving brain noticed how well the two were getting along.

Fran's interest in Victoria might be due to his trying to wangle favorable coverage on CNN for Gus Huertole. Or it could be due to Victoria's glamor. Or there was the chance Fran thought Rennie was interested in Victoria, which meant Victoria was simply another way to score off his big brother.

Well, she wouldn't worry about Fran. Or Victoria, who might also have an ulterior motive. The reporter been pumping Fran about Gus Huertole and his wife, asking about their finances and influence in obtaining this new exhibit for the High Museum.

Not that it mattered.

Whatever the reason the two had hit it off, Autumn was glad, particularly since Rennie's uninhibited display that morning.

He no longer avoided her, but neither did he treat her any differently than before. If anything, he had withdrawn into himself like he'd done when she first asked about Jane.

How was she ever going to make him admit his interest in her?

Assuming he *had* an interest in her.

No, he must. After the way he had rushed into the cabin, grabbed her up, held her, kissed her. He wouldn't have been so panicky if he didn't care for her.

Those weren't brotherly kisses, either.

Uh uh.

So why had he urged Laney and John to join him and Autumn for a belated lunch in Helen? "We can view the last live gluckenfeel of the weekend," he added enticingly.

If Autumn were a gambler, she would have bet he was putting off being alone with her for as long as possible.

That was okay. They had a long drive back to Atlanta. With nothing to do but talk.

Both couples were subdued as they window-shopped and waited for the glockenspiel to begin. Kiki Ballencer's murder, despite none of them having met the woman before this weekend, had laid a pall over the festive getaway.

"Do you think Autumn's fall last night was connected to what happened today?" John asked Rennie in a low voice as Laney hovered over a display of music boxes.

Autumn didn't miss Rennie's flicked glance and tiny hesitation. "I don't know. I did think the coincidence ought to be mentioned and that's why I told the investigator. With the jackets looking so much alike, it just seemed…strange."

Laney tore her eyes from a particularly enchanting box shaped like Cinderella's coach. "It was Kiki's husband who did it, I'm sure it was. I know you think she was laying it on kind of thick, John, but she was running scared. And he's had brushes with the law before. I've heard rumors of their domestic problems for months through the battered women's shelter."

"You may be right, but it won't hurt Autumn to stay with someone for a few days," Rennie said. "At least until they find the guy."

"She'll stay with us," Laney said.

"Good."

Autumn raised her brows. Was he seeing her as a friend or sister to be protected? Or as a woman he cared about sexually? "I don't need a babysitter."

"I didn't say you needed a babysitter."

"The same thing."

"Rennie's right, Autumn," Laney said. The cold air had pinked her cheeks and made her dark eyes sparkle. Wavy black hair fell from beneath a crimson beret onto a bright green turtleneck and maroon pea coat. A few snowflakes and she could go on the front of a Christmas card. "It won't hurt to be careful. In case something's going on we don't know about. You'll stay with John and me."

"No, thank you, Laney. I've slept on the sofa bed in John's office before. I'll pass."

"You could come to Mom's." Rennie refused to look at Autumn. "She has plenty of room."

So Rennie thought she was a helpless female, did he? She wasn't.

Okay, maybe she was a little concerned, especially after Kiki's death. But her fall off the bridge and Kiki's murder had to be coincidences. That was all they could be.

She wouldn't play his game. "Let's have one last funnel cake before we leave."

"I've got to pick up my candle, too." Laney glanced at her watch. "He was supposed to have it ready by now."

The funnel cake tasted flat, and everyone except Autumn ended up with powdered sugar all over their clothes. Laney brushed off John and smeared it all over his jacket front.

Rennie declined his sister's help.

Autumn didn't offer hers.

Afterward, they walked over near the tower where they could get a good view of the glockenspiel. After waiting twenty minutes in the cold, the show wasn't nearly as entertaining as Autumn had imagined.

She wasn't the only one disappointed.

"You mean that's it?" Laney exclaimed once the people disappeared from their balcony. She huffed and put her hands on her hips in disbelief. "We stood around all afternoon in the cold to watch a bunch of people come out on the porch and wave their trombones or whatever around? And fake trombones, at that. This is disgusting."

"Now, Elena," Rennie chided. "What did you expect? Didn't you know what a glockenspiel was? What did you think it would be like? I thought it was lovely. The musicians played—or maybe mimed is a better word—their part to perfection. And the dancing was very, very alpine-like. Well worth the trip to Helen and our sojourn in a primitive cabin with few conveniences and not enough hot water for six adults."

Autumn tucked her Nikon away in its case. "They were supposed to be French horns. If you didn't want to stay, Rennie, you should have told me."

"And miss the show? Heavens to Murgatroyd! I wouldn't have dreamed of it." Rennie exuded a positively saintly air.

"I think that was a broom the man on the right next to the end was carrying," John offered. "I mention it because I know Laney would never recognize one otherwise."

"You pig." Taking off her glove, Laney ran her cold hand up beneath her husband's sweater.

He yipped and tried to get away.

"Children, children." Rennie's grin glimmered. "Can't you behave? Here's a cafe, Autumn. You said you wanted a cup of cappuccino before we start home. Come on, let's sit down while Laney picks up her candle."

Autumn had hoped, after the undeniable evidence he had given of his feelings for her, he would talk to her about his reaction the past night.

Instead, he had retreated into his role of big brother and friend.

What was she going to do? He'd already seen her with all her clothes off, so stripping naked and prancing around in front of him wouldn't accomplish anything.

At last they started back to Atlanta, alone, but when they passed the old mill leading out of town and before she could broach the subject uppermost on her mind, Rennie said, "You can't go back home. Not till we find out what happened to Kiki."

Nausea swelled. She refused to think about Kiki in her blood-soaked jacket amid strewn groceries. "You're being paranoid."

"Listen, Autumn, someone tried to stab you last night on the bridge."

"No, no, it—"

"Yes, they did. Anyone looking at your butt pack can see what happened. Those detectives realized it, too. And today a woman wearing a coat like yours was shot to death. Something's wrong."

She didn't want to believe it, tried not to believe it. But could his taking those things so seriously mean that he cared for her in more than a friendly way?

If only he would take his eyes off the road.

No clue from his profile.

She swallowed. "I'm not a fool. I realize the two things may be connected, but don't you think the most likely thing is someone mistook me for Kiki last night on the bridge? After all, it was dark and I had on my coat like hers. Kiki told us herself her husband was threatening her. Doesn't it make sense to think he mistook me for her, before he got a chance today to—"

Images from that morning flooded, blotting out those of the vivacious woman they'd met Friday. Her stomach flip-flopped.

Digging into her purse, she found a tissue and blew her nose, then cracked the window to let cold air revive her.

"Autumn, come to Mom's, stay there for a few days."

"There's no need. Don't be silly."

"A woman's dead." Dark eyes flicked at her and back to the road. "I don't think I'm being silly."

She lay back against the seat and closed her eyes. The fresh air quelled her nausea. "I'm going home."

Unless he could give her a far better reason to stay away from her condo than he had given so far. Like he loved her and was afraid something might happen to her. Like he wanted her at Reseda's because he wanted her close by.

What might have been a sigh in another man signaled Rennie's impatience, but he didn't argue.

For several miles, they rode along in a chilly silence, until Autumn whipped up her nerve. "Did you mean what you said last night?"

His hands tightened on the wheel. "What I said last night."

"Yes. About… You know."

He gave her that Rennie glance again, where his head didn't move but his eyes darted over to her face and back to the road. The tires made a humming noise. "I said a lot of things."

"*Rennie*." Had the kiss made so little an impression on him? "You said you wanted me."

His profile turned harsh. His hands gripped the steering wheel. "Of course I meant it. You're a sexy, desirable woman. A man would be a fool not to want you. That doesn't give him the right to act on his wants."

"I see." If she didn't speak up, her courage would sift away. She swallowed. "So I'm good enough to have for a friend, but not good enough to have for a lover."

"Why are you doing this?"

"Doing what?"

"Putting words in my mouth." His voice was clipped.

"Rennie, you said you cared for me. Do you?"

"Of course I do."

"As a friend? Or something else?"

"Leave it, Autumn. Please." He sounded tired.

She left it.

You coward. But how much further could she humiliate herself and him?

Conversation in the Lexus was nonexistent as they sped down Highway 400. The two of them shared the tiny space but each remained insulated. Both leaned back against the leather seats and let the air become a barrier between them. The tinkle of Scott Joplin's ragtime broke the silence. The afternoon light touched trees with rusty leaves on bare limbs and gloomy pines and other evergreens. A perfect setting for her mood.

But when he pulled up to her condominium soon after dusk, after the car was stopped and before they got out, he turned to her. "I've been sitting across from you the whole time I've been driving, trying to pretend nothing's changed between us, that you're the same and I'm the same. But it isn't going to work. We can't be friends any more. We've gone past that."

"I know. I was wondering when you'd catch on."

Don't sound so snippy. He's giving you an opening.

Either the shock of falling over the bridge or seeing

Kiki's body made her reckless. "It's as well we don't try to be friends, Rennie. Maybe we need to let it go." *Jump in before you lose your courage.* "Or maybe there's something else we can be." *Say it, just say it.* "I love you. I always have."

The slim hand resting on the wheel tightened into a fist. He stared down at it and away from her.

She'd gone too far.

His voice seemed remote. "You told me that once before, after I graduated from UGA. When I left home."

She started. "You remember? I thought you'd forgotten, put my emotional collapse down to adolescent hormones."

"Of course I remember. You told me you loved me, begged to go with me to California." The one corner of his mouth she could see, lifted as if he found the memories amusing.

Heat seared her cheeks as she recalled the scene she had made, the hysterical blubbering of the teenager she had been. "You laughed."

Please don't laugh now.

The smile vanished. He looked at her. "What else could I do? You were seventeen, and I had an assistantship waiting. I knew by the time I saw you again, you'd have forgotten me and fallen for someone else. Kids change their minds a hundred times before they settle down." He slapped the wheel. "What kind of scumbag would I have been if I'd encouraged you in thinking you loved me, if I'd taken advantage of you? Give me some credit, Autumn."

She covered her eyes. She couldn't let him see how he'd hurt her. "I thought I'd die when you said I was too young to know what I was saying. But I meant it."

"I was right. You were too young, and I was... I shouldn't have laughed. I'm sorry, Autumn. I should have been more sensitive, more understanding. I wasn't laughing inside, believe me. Inside I felt pretty awful."

So like Rennie. Shouldering the blame for her poor judgment. "No. You were wonderful, so patient and sweet while you explained why I couldn't go away with you, that I was confused because I was so young, and had lost my mom and dad, and was so unhappy at Uncle Parnell's. You said that one day I'd find someone I loved. You said we'd always be friends. But you were wrong. I did love you then. I've loved you for a long time now, and I can't seem to stop."

"Autumn."

"No matter how I try. I don't want to be friends anymore." She leaned over. "So if you can't feel that way about me, too, maybe it's better if we make a clean break. I don't think I can take seeing you and being with you as a friend when I want you all the while for a lover."

There, she'd said it all. She'd revealed every secret of her soul for him to ridicule.

Which, being Rennie, he would never do.

He put an arm over the console and hugged her in a chaste, affectionate fashion. "It wouldn't work. You and me together. We're too different. Our families, our backgrounds, everything about us. I'm not what you think I am. In the end you'd be sorry, maybe even despise me. And I couldn't stand for you to be unhappy."

Her heart dropped. She felt cold, like a stone statue that would never come to life. "Don't you know I could never despise you? Why can't we at least try it?"

His arms dropped away. "Come to Mom's, Autumn. Don't stay here alone."

Hopeless. It was hopeless.

She opened the car door. "Open the trunk so I can get my bag out, will you?"

The entire weekend had turned out as terrible as she'd feared.

****

INSIDE THE FOYER, welcomed by waxed hardwood floors and the small flower photos her uncle had loved, Autumn took off her jacket and automatically glanced toward the answering machine.

Squeaky strolled out to its beep.

Beeping and blinking. Lots of blinks. It didn't stop.

Surely she hadn't received that many calls at home over the weekend. Something must be wrong with the machine.

"Hey, Squeaky."

A quick pet before she punched the button.

An excited voice of an acquaintance who waited tables near her studio said, "Autumn, if you're home, pick up, there's the most awful fire going on near where your studio is. It's right there in those shops by your studio. I've tried your cell but you don't answer. Pick up if you're there."

"A fire."

Autumn stared at the machine. Near her studio. Her possessions. She pictured them engulfed in flame. "My cameras, my equipment. No. No!"

Her heart drummed.

Rennie came up behind her as a voice she didn't recognize, awkward and halting, came on. "Um, Ms. Merriwell, this is the manager of Grenokes Walk Plaza where your studio is, um, located. Please get in touch with me. Um, as soon as possible. There's been a, um, a fire at the Plaza."

Rennie touched her back. "Your studio may be all right. Don't panic yet."

But the studio wasn't all right.

A third message from the fire department played and then another from a fire investigator. The manager of the shopping center had called several more times, as had people who worked near her studio and others who had heard the news.

The machine gave out of room in the middle of the last message.

"The studio. Everything's in it. Cameras, lights, meters, backgrounds." Autumn's heart had settled but she was numb. "Surely everything can't be gone. The negatives of pictures my aunt and uncle took. My negatives. My CDs." She put a hand to her suddenly aching head, trying to gather her thoughts. "No, wait. They may be all right. Aunt Laura made Uncle Parnell invest in fireproof filing cabinets to store them in years ago. But everything else… The heat alone would destroy it all. I'll have to go over right away."

She looked around, searching for the minivan keys, finding them on the key rack hanging by the door.

Rennie's lean fingers, bronzed with clipped nails, closed

over her shaking hand. He quietly removed the keys and returned them to the rack. "I'll drive you."

Squeaky meowed loudly.

"Let me feed her." Going into the kitchen, she set out fresh water and food, then scooped the litter box. Squeaky hated a dirty litter box.

She couldn't stop talking. "All my aunt and uncle's cameras were in there. An antique Rolleiflex and an old Graflex. The ones I use every day, my Nikon and the Hasselblad. And last month I invested in a new camera for taking passport pictures."

After she washed her hands, she found him holding her jacket, waiting for her to slip into it.

She couldn't stop going on about the studio. "My first camera my father got me when I was four is there. Oh, and the Kodak Brownies collection. There's one my mother got from her father when she was a child, and several cameras Dad and Grandfather and Uncle Parnell had. And some others I've bought. I had a display using them and some of Mom and Dad's old snapshots of their dogs and Mom's dolls and playmates." She sniffled.

"Let's wait and see what's happened before you give up on it, shall we?" Rennie adjusted her jacket. "There may be some smoke damage and nothing more. Your cameras may be fine."

The bleakness that had overwhelmed her in the cabin returned, stronger than ever, pressing so hard she couldn't breathe. "No. They aren't fine."

****

As RENNIE DROVE, Autumn turned her cell back on and listened to more messages about the fire. Her unusual talking jag was over.

The silence troubled Rennie, but he let it ride until he pulled up to the strip where the studio had been. Then he cursed at seeing the devastated shops.

Before the car fully stopped, Autumn was getting out. By the time he joined her, she stood dully in front of the ruins.

"I knew it."

He put his arm around her shoulders.

She was stiff and unmoving. "When I heard that first message, I knew."

He squeezed her.

No use trying to tell her it would be all right. The fire had destroyed the entire section of the strip shops with the studio. All that remained was a blackened mass of blackened, crooked beams and crumbling walls.

Her work, her entire career was gone along with the photographs inherited from her aunt and uncle and grandfather.

She handled the destruction well. No conspicuous tears, not for his Autumn, but her anguish was palpable.

After a few moments, she pulled out her cell and called the manager of the shopping center.

He listened to her side of the conversation, mostly questions, until she frowned. "They do? But why? The fire department? Yes." Without searching or fumbling, she took a small pad and pen from an organized purse. "Give me the number."

When she hung up, her face, drawn from the shock of the damage, had set in stark lines. "They think this was arson."

"Arson?" A notion, seeded from the incident on the bridge and Kiki's murder, sprouted.

Everything had to be connected. This fire, too.

Her hands trembled as she put her cell back in her purse. "The manager wasn't very polite to me. Not like he usually is. I think he believes I set it."

"What?" Anger inundated him. He hugged her, not hard; her frame felt fragile against him. "It would have been kind of hard for you to set a fire since you were in Helen all weekend, wouldn't it?"

"I guess I could have hired someone." Her voice was lifeless.

"That's ridiculous. It won't take long for them to see it."

Less ridiculous was his conviction that the fire had something to do with Helen. The bridge. Kiki Ballencer.

And Autumn didn't even realize there might be a link.

"Autumn, there may—"

She drew back. "Will you take me to the firehouse, Rennie? I need to talk to them."

Better not say anything yet. "Sure."

Despite it being a Sunday evening, they found someone at the fire station willing to talk to them.

"My negatives and CDs were in there. Are they all right?" was her first question after introducing herself.

Rennie was proud of her composure. None of his family, with the possible exception of his deceased father, would have been so reasonable.

She went on, "They were in fireproof cabinets, so they should have been safe."

"We did find the cabinets." The fireman opened and closed a desk drawer. "But the drawers were open."

"Open?"

Autumn and Rennie stared at him.

"The fire started in front of the cabinets. We suspect the contents were emptied out and the blaze started there."

Rennie swore.

"My negatives? My CDs? Gone?"

Her lips quivered, turned into those of a child who watched a dog being run over. "Some of them went back years, decades. Most of the negatives were portraits my grandfather took."

She closed her eyes and rolled her head from side to side. "The stuff on the computer is backed up off-site, but the other… We kept meaning to get them all scanned in but never… I don't think I can bear this."

Rennie took her hand, but she didn't notice. He rubbed her cold fingers.

The fireman clucked. "Fires are bad. We don't know for sure what caused this one, but we'll have people sifting the ashes soon, Ms. Merriwell. We can tell more then. If you'll go into our main office tomorrow morning…" He wrote a name on a card, pushed it toward her. "Talk to our investigator there. They should know more by then."

Autumn took the card and looked at it unseeingly.

Too dazed to function. He was the one who had to ask, "Was it arson?"

"We can't say for sure at this point." The man fingered his collar.

"But you can guess."

The man tugged at his collar hard, like it was way too tight. "Well, from what I understand, the way the cabinets were open, the way fire burned from the middle area outward, then yes, I'd guess it was set deliberately." He turned to Autumn. "I suppose you'll be notifying your insurance company, Ms. Merriwell. They'll want to work with us, I'm sure. To see that you can collect the insurance as quickly as possible, I mean."

Her lips pressed together. Rennie could almost see her don the regal calm that was her disguise for dismay and anger. And fear.

"I'm sure they'll be interested in working out the insurance payouts. But I'm more interested in catching the arsonist than I am in collecting the insurance. Besides negatives spanning sixty years, I had several irreplaceable cameras in there. My Graflex, my Rolleiflex, my Brownie collection. Some have been—" The crisp tone faltered. "Some had been in my family for decades. Whoever did this ought to have to pay."

"Yes, ma'am. He'll pay all right," the fireman assured them.

"If you catch him," Rennie murmured.

The man twisted a ballpoint pen in his hands. "If we can catch him. Or her. Yes."

On the way back to her condo, Rennie stopped at a deli. It was nearly deserted at the late hour, but they got sandwiches and decaf coffee. He wasn't hungry, but he ate so she would.

It didn't work. She toyed with stale chips but mostly held the steaming coffee in both hands. He did get her to take a few bites of the tuna sandwich, but when she pushed her basket away, he leaned back in the booth. "Okay. You can either go to Mom's or I'll stay with you. Which would you prefer?"

"Don't be ridiculous. I'm fine. It was a fire. Other people have gone through them and survived, and I will, too."

He didn't like her pallor or the taut way the skin stretched across her cheekbones. "Look, Autumn. A knife or something like it stuck you in the back and pitched you over that bridge last night. If it hadn't been for your butt pack, you could be dead. This morning, a woman wearing a coat like yours was killed. Now we find your studio's burned to the ground. That's a little too much coincidence. I don't think any ex-husband shot Kiki. I think someone's after you."

Her expression didn't change. "I've thought of that."

So she'd reached the same conclusion.

She ran a finger around the rim of the foam cup. "But why? I don't know anyone who would want to hurt me. And to burn my studio, destroy my cameras, my photos—" She took a tiny sip.

He followed the pulse in her throat as she swallowed. "Do you think someone could have taken exception to the kind of photography you've been doing lately?"

"My photography?"

"Erotic stuff. Nudes. You know." He ran a hand through his curls. "Maybe some kind of nutty fundamentalist got his dander up. You know how intolerant they're getting. Down here in the South we have our loonies when it comes to Bible-thumpers."

"In this day and age? Come on, Rennie. That might be true in rural areas, but we're on the outskirts of Atlanta. People are a lot more broad-minded here. Besides, I don't take photographs for magazines or newspapers. They're for individuals. They're personal, private. I think you're on the wrong track."

"Never got any letters or threatening phone calls?"

"No. Except from some man who thought he'd dialed Merriwell Used Cars. Look, Rennie, I don't do pornographic stuff. And not that many people know what I do." She took a sip of decaf.

"How did you get started?"

"I did a portrait for a customer shortly after I joined Aunt Laura." Her hand twisted on the coffee cup. "She wanted to do something special for her husband's fortieth birthday and had thought of posing in a hot tub. When I went out to her house, we had a great time thinking of different outfits for there and also her bedroom. She loved the pictures and showed some of them to her friends and they wanted some done. Then they told their friends, and it kind of snowballed."

"Do you advertise?"

"No. I've done several hundred people since then, and the women have all come from word-of-mouth recommendations. Even Sarita Sartowe heard about me through Reseda. Your mom told Kaneka about me, and she told Sarita."

The words brought him back to reality. His mother cleaned the mansion where Sarita's mother and stepfather lived. Reseda Degardovera washed fine china and polished real silver for her clients.

While her own family ate sandwiches off paper towels and drank soft drinks and beer straight from the can.

And Degardovera relatives in Mexico lived in dirt-floor shacks like the one Reseda had left thirty-eight years before.

No matter how successful he was, Rennie could never get away from his heritage.

I'm too tired to think about what this means. He yawned in spite of himself.

Autumn, sensitive to others, immediately pushed her cup aside. "You're exhausted, Rennie. Let's leave so you can take me home. You need to go on and get to bed."

As if she wasn't exhausted herself.

"Didn't you hear a word I said? You could be dead or hurt. You aren't going to stay at your place alone where anyone can find you. It's too dangerous until we know more about what's going on."

"Rennie." Reserve forgotten, she reached across the booth and touched his hand. Fire leaped through his skin. "You look worried."

He set his teeth. "Mom's place or me on the sofa. Take your pick."

She drew back. "You're serious."

"Listen, I was going to Athens tomorrow, to look for a

place to live. You don't have anywhere to go, not with the studio gone. Come with me."

He wanted to touch her hand, but didn't. She might be upset and in need of comforting right now, but their embrace the past night and its aftermath told him what his comfort would lead to.

No matter how he felt, and he was beginning to think he'd been fooling himself about Autumn for the past thirteen years, he wouldn't take advantage of her and do something she would most certainly regret later.

"We'll ramble around Athens and visit all the sights," he coaxed. "We can spend the night at Mom's house and leave straight from there, what do you say?"

"Sorry." The imperturbable princess was back. "Any other time, Rennie. But now I've got too much to do. A lot of calls to return and a lot of work finding a place for a new studio. I'm not going to be run out of my home or my business."

"Then I'll stay with you."

"Fine. You won't even have to sleep on the sofa. I've got a spare room." One delicate brow arched. "I need some milk and bread. Can we stop at the Kroger store?"

"Sure."

Spending the night with Autumn. All he needed.

He ought to go home, make sure his body was safely removed from temptation. But he couldn't. Not and make sure she stayed safe. "We'll stop wherever you like."

As he waited in the car while she ran into the store, he wished the idea of sleeping in Autumn's spare room didn't sound so appealing. She'd be in bed across the hall, all soft and inviting and wearing a seductive black nightgown like that one of Laney's while he…

He was going to have to take a cold shower.

Chapter Fourteen

REFUSING RENNIE'S OFFER of help once they reached her condo, Autumn took charge of the plastic grocery bags and their interesting contents herself. "You can carry the milk."

Since she'd agreed to let him babysit her, one priority had sent thoughts of death and fire to the back of her mind.

Maybe Rennie did believe she was in danger. Or maybe he subconsciously wanted to stay with her for other reasons.

Didn't matter. She was going for broke tonight.

"There, everything's like I left it," she said when he had made a circuit of the upstairs and downstairs with Squeaky trailing behind. "If you want to go along home, I'm sure there's nothing to worry about."

"You're stuck with me, lady."

She lowered her lashes so he couldn't read the plans taking shape. No sense in scaring him off. "Fine."

The spare room was directly across from her bedroom. She was on her home court. And she intended to seize the advantage to sweep aside Rennie's scruples.

Besides, his presence reassured her. Despite her protests, this strange weekend had spooked her.

No, she wouldn't think about that. Easier to look at Rennie's long, rangy form and luxuriate in his presence.

There was no Victoria around to lighten his mood, but he didn't seem to mind. In fact, he looked pretty satisfied at having to spend the night with Autumn.

Not that he planned to spend the night *with* her, exactly.

He intended to keep her company, drive away the ghosts

of Kiki and the fire-ravaged studio while they puzzled over whether or how they were connected.

The important thing was that he was here in her condo.

When she got out fresh sheets, he came to the spare room to help. Squeaky, vying for attention, got on the bed when they stated to make it up. Autumn kissed the little head, put her out into the hall and closed the door.

Without Squeaky's help, the yards of cotton billowed smoothly across the bed, forming a tangible connection between her and Rennie as they worked in companionable silence. Once their fingers met while smoothing the linen, and the touch set her burning. She was convinced his eyes whispered of desire and perhaps something deeper before they were averted.

He did care for her. And not like a sister, or else he wouldn't have kissed her that way last night. Neither would he have rushed to her and clung to her this morning when he found out she wasn't Kiki.

When they finished making up the spare bed, the affronted Squeaky sneaked in to claim a place on the clean sheets.

He didn't notice because he was chuckling at the guest basket with toothbrush, toothpaste, mouthwash and other sundries she set out. "How efficient. I should have expected as much from you. Do you treat all your guests this way?"

Was he making fun of her? "Yes, and I use disposable razors if you need to borrow one. I draw the line at loaning my clothes, though, no matter how much you beg to use my Wonderbra."

His eyebrows shot up. His gaze involuntarily went to her breasts.

She shrugged. "They may be real but they're maximized. So now you know all my secrets."

"Do I?" He sounded edgy.

Good. "Yes. I don't like sharing my toothbrush and I'm flat-chested. You must have noticed that yesterday."

Oh, and by the way, I love you.

The reminder of the scene in the bathroom brought a quick inhalation, but he didn't pick up her cue. "And no loaning me clothes, eh? Sure about that? I love that snowman sweater."

"Positive. Anything but clothes." All right, he wanted to keep things light. She could oblige. "Besides, I doubt my things would flatter you, Rennie. Pinks and lavenders are more suited to your complexion than blues and browns."

"If you won't loan me your clothes, how about your jingle bell earrings?" He flapped a wrist. "I've been green with envy ever since you jingled them my way last night, sweetie."

"You're as bad as Fran."

His good mood faded.

Oh, pooh. He and Fran were adults now. That troubled boyhood contention between them should be over.

Even if Fran did act like she was a pawn in the one-upmanship game, Rennie wouldn't retaliate.

He wasn't flirting with her because Fran liked her.

Fran was the one who wanted whatever Rennie had. Rennie had let his younger brother cut him out at dances and borrow his clothes without complaint. With his sunny nature, he never minded that Fran stole his girls and beat him in tennis. Or if he did, he never showed it.

"Okay." She backed away. "All set. Throw Squeaky out and close the door or her snoring will keep you awake." In the hall, she waved toward the bathroom. "Towels and washcloths on the shelves. Soap and shampoo in the shower. If you need anything else, let me know."

He stepped past her into her bedroom to stare at Fran's photograph that dominated the wall.

She recognized that look. Did he still think she and Fran were even slightly involved romantically? She'd put a stop to *that*. She strolled over to him, crossed her arms. "I'll give it back to him one of these days."

"Will you?"

"Uh huh. He'll have a new girlfriend before we know it, and he can have it for her."

"Can you give it up that easily?" His voice was flat, noncommittal.

"I don't want it."

"Don't you?"

"No. Never did. It just kind of landed here."

She wanted Rennie and almost said so.

No, she'd told him already. No sense in beating him over the head.

Avoiding his brother's photograph, Rennie wandered further into her room. He picked up a water sphere, one that played music and let snowflakes drift down over an ice skater with her back arched gracefully as she endlessly spun round with tiny foot and hand in the air.

Autumn watched him as he wound the music globe and shook it. His invasion of her space didn't bother her like anyone else's would.

The flakes drifted down, the skater turned. He held it up. "Everything's perfect in your house. Even this."

"Laney gave me that for Christmas when we were little."

"I remember. The funny thing is that it isn't out of place here. You know how to pull it all together. What curtains to hang with what upholstery, which paintings go on what wall, what bric-a-brac to set on your dresser." The swirling flakes seemed to enthrall him.

"I collect things that I like." What was going through his mind? What was he was leading up to? "As for putting them all together, if they look okay together, fine. If not, tough."

"I've always envied people with so much confidence in their tastes that they don't care what others think." He set the sphere down carefully.

He didn't have to be so distant. So brooding.

"What does taste have to do with it? Everyone's different." Somehow she'd lost the slender thread of their old childhood connection. He was moving beyond her and she couldn't catch up. "Everyone makes their nests as comfortable as they can. That's why a home is called a home."

"Sometimes it doesn't work out like that." He glanced toward Fran's picture and away. "I have a painting," he said slowly. "I wish you could see it. It isn't at all like the stuff you have hanging. I'm not sure it's the kind of thing even a geeky computer nerd like me ought to have in his apartment, but I like it. I wonder what you would think. It's wild and unwieldy. Flamboyant."

"Sounds like you."

He didn't grin. "Nobody important painted it. And it's on black velvet."

So that was it.

He was pointing out again how different she was from him, telling her that she would never fit in with him and his life, that they would never be suited. Why couldn't he understand she didn't care about superficialities?

"Funny, I've never thought of you as a nerd, computer or any other kind." She held her voice steady. "And I'd hate to think you were surrounding yourself with things you thought your scholarly image needed. If you like a painting on black velvet, I can't see that anything else matters."

"But what if it's in bad taste, Autumn?" His dark gaze swung round, fastened on her. "What if it's so atrocious you're embarrassed for me?"

This dancing around was getting ridiculous.

Come out and say it.

She uncrossed her arms. "I like you, Rennie. No. I love you. I've already told you I love you. And I love you too much to want you to do things or buy things or change your life to please me. Is that what this is about, your stupid preoccupation with who you think I am, or who you think you are?" Anger grew. "What do I have to do to convince you I love you for yourself, whoever you are? I've demeaned myself, laid myself out like a doormat for you, and you won't even step on me."

"Autumn—"

She moved toward him, holding out a hand. "What else do I have to do?" She caught his shoulders and looked him in the eyes, holding her mouth up next to his.

Kiss me, you idiot.

He gave an angry exclamation before bending down.

What started off as an impatient gesture turned into a fierce kiss totally unlike the ones showered on her when he found her inside the cabin after Kiki's death. This kiss hurt her mouth and left her helpless. His hand caught her breast and kneaded it with a discomfort that would have made her pull away had she been capable of movement.

She couldn't think. She was mindless, dazed. Delirious. He did care, did want her. He couldn't deny his need after this.

Don't think.

She opened her mouth and pressed herself against him.

In the midst of her response, he pushed her away and stepped back. "*Madre de Dios.* Don't you see, Autumn? Don't you understand why you can't love me, why we can't do this?"

"No."

Her voice stopped him. His chest rose and fell with harsh, ragged breaths.

Her own lips stung, her own lungs gasped for air. "I love you, Rennie, and you can't change that. No matter what you say, what you think. I've known you since I was five years old and I love you."

His shoulders slumped. "I didn't... Autumn."

She loved that face, with its deep-set brown eyes and the aquiline nose and the wide mouth pliant from her kisses.

He licked his lips, screwed up his eyes as if to make her disappear. "I'd drive you away. Sooner or later you'd be sorry you ever thought you were in love with me. But God help me, every time I get near you, it's all I can do to remember how you deserve so much better than me."

"Rennie." She moved into him. "Stop belittling yourself." Then she waited while his arms came up, inch by agonizing inch, proving his will wasn't strong enough to stop them. They locked around her until she stood in her own circle of warmth. "I do love you. I meant it when I was seventeen and I mean it now. I can't stop loving you."

His shoulders sagged, his head dropped. "I'm too tired to fight you anymore. Heaven help you, because I love you, too. I guess I always have."

Her heart sprang and flipped.

He still tried. "I didn't know, couldn't believe it when I started thinking of you like this. I didn't want this to happen."

"Shhh." She turned her face up and they kissed, a comfortable enterprise lacking the earlier fire and urgency.

There would be no interruptions, no second thoughts this time.

She knew it and so did he. His lips and fingers moved over her face as if memorizing each inch.

When her heart threatened to burst, she rested her head against his chest and he laid his face against her neck. For a long moment they held each other that way.

How strange. I can feel his breath leaving his nostrils and entering mine, feel the blood rushing through him like mine, feel his heart beating in time to mine, feel his flesh warming mine. If I listen real hard, I bet I can hear his thoughts. As if we were one person.

His hand eventually slid down, cupping her butt, drawing her to him. He didn't stop her when she opened her legs to take him against her, did not stop her when she ran her hand under his sweater.

He slid her own top up, found the fastening of her bra and undid it. Her too-small breasts spilled from the figure-enhancing binder, but he caressed one like it was perfect.

All without haste, all without frenzy.

Because this time we'll finish.

As his head bent, she sighed, arched her neck so his lips could reach its curve, pulled in her stomach so that his fingers could slip down inside her slacks. He splayed his hand on her stomach gingerly, afraid he'd hurt or frighten her.

As if he could. This was what she'd wanted for years.

She unsnapped her slacks herself so his fingertips could touch her, could slide down her belly to the curls.

"I can take them off." Giddy with anticipation, she tackled the zipper.

"No." He laid a hand over hers.

"I want to take them off. Please let me take them off." She wriggled her hand, trying to make him release it. Her intimate parts clamored for his attention.

"Not until we can make arrangements to do things right."

"Right? This is right."

"Autumn." His voice held back laughter. "I don't do this all the time. I don't carry rubbers around with me."

"Oh. That. What do you think took me so long at the store?"

She would have giggled at his shock except that she had a shrewd idea it was better not to make fun of a man when the joke had the least connection to his sexual prowess.

"You bought condoms at the grocery store?"

She could have sworn his body relaxed. Was he turned off? Had she done something wrong? Been too aggressive? Taken too much for granted?

She hurried on. "Yes. Just in case." She went and got them. Coming back, she closed the bedroom door in Squeaky's annoyed face. "I hope this is all right with you."

"You planned this? You knew we'd make love?"

Was he annoyed? "I hoped."

"Autumn, I… Once we do this, there's no turning back." His voice was hoarse.

"I'm sick and tired of hearing your dire predictions about what will happen if you make love to me. Let's do it and worry about what happens later."

Dark eyes flew open.

He swooped her up and laid her on the bed. As she drew off her sweater and unzipped her slacks, he ripped off his own clothes.

While she threw back the coverlet and climbed between the sheets, she heard fabric tear, heard a button bounce against the wall. She snuggled down and waited.

"What's taking you so long? Oh."

He had removed Fran's picture and set it on the floor facing the wall.

She smothered a smile.

****

RENNIE PROPPED FRANCISCO'S photo against the wall, the back turned out. He would be damned if he let Francisco's likeness leer down at them when he made love to Autumn. The first time ought to be special. He'd go slowly, do it right. Then she'd be safe from anyone like Fran.

That was all that mattered, that she be safe. He'd give

her everything she needed because he wasn't the same person he once was. She deserved better, and he'd be better.

For her.

When he climbed into the bed, he took his time adjusting the sheets before turning to her. Her hair, when he pushed it back, smelled faintly of roses. Her eyes were clear and blue.

Who was he kidding? He'd never been with a woman like Autumn. His two intimate relationships had both involved women who carried too damned much emotional baggage.

One had been anxious to forget an abusive father by making every man she met love her. She'd also tried to boost her self-esteem by bringing everyone close to her down to her level.

The other had been determined to put a deprived childhood far behind by climbing the rungs to monetary success as quickly as possible and dumping anyone she feared might hold her back.

But Autumn was whole, self-sufficient. He was unnecessary to her financially or emotionally because she was poised, lovely, intelligent, and stable. She could have anyone she chose.

But she said she loved him, and Autumn never lied.

Tension he hadn't felt within him uncoiled. Being here with her felt like finally finding himself.

He rolled into her waiting arms and lost himself and his insecurities in the heat that surged through his body and overwhelmed his senses.

She was so sweet. When she pulled him against her bare skin and cradled him to her breasts, he forgot his doubts and took his time, relearning each ridge, each bone in her face and shoulders, before moving his tongue from her ear and running it down her neck. Tasting the dainty breasts, the flat stomach and navel, the slick warmth that welcomed his intrusion.

All the time she lay willingly beneath him, spread out like a prize for his plundering. When he found her center, she began to tremble.

He held her hips and teased her with his tongue. Her hands in his hair tightened with each whimpering breath, until suddenly she rose beneath him, crying out and arching her body in utter abandonment.

He wanted to shout, to plough triumphantly into her. But he stilled his longing and stretched out beside her until her breathing steadied and her heartbeat calmed. When her hand found his length and would have caressed him to breaking point, he nudged it aside and began all over again on her. Her flesh was dewy from his success, slick from her satisfaction.

And when he recognized her soft whimpers from earlier, knew she was close to climax, he slipped inside her, reveling in her tightness, her heat, her need for him. As she gripped him and held him to her, she whimpered again, pushing up at him, trying to end what he had begun.

"Please, Rennie. I can't wait."

"Yes, you can," he whispered. He pulled back and drove into her. "Long enough."

She screamed and flailed like a wild creature, her contractions forcing his seed to spew out in a hot shower that brought on his own silent scream.

I am lost, he thought in the midst of his delirium. *I should have been strong enough to keep her from making this mistake.*

Eventually, her starry romanticism of what he was would curdle under the glare of reality. But whatever she decided in the future, whatever roads she took that might not include him, he would be hers forever.

That's why he was so afraid of Autumn, because he knew loving her would mean losing himself and whatever hard-earned self-respect he had achieved; because he could never live up to her standards. And that meant nursing a new hurt when she realized she had been mistaken in him.

Chapter Fifteen

AUTUMN LAY ENTWINED with Rennie. Her happiness turned the dim bedside lamp radiant and enhanced the muted colors of her bedroom. The musk of sex touched the air.

His shadowed body propped slightly over hers as he ran one hand up and down her naked hip, and talked about the future. "You'll have to go to Athens with me now," he was saying when her cell music played.

She ignored its ring. "Why?" Surfeited, she wanted nothing more than to lie still and listen to Rennie make plans. "Don't," she said when he reached over to pick up her cell.

"You'd better." He handed it to her.

She sighed.

Rennie never shirked responsibility. That was another thing about him she loved. But this one time, after his earth-shattering admission he loved her, he could have been irresponsible. Just this once.

She cradled the receiver between her neck and ear, wanting to pout. "Hello."

Rennie grinned before he bent over her chest. His tongue brushed one exposed nipple, delighting her, making her heart thud and her mouth quiver against the plastic cell. Making her stomach clench with remembered delight.

"Autumn," Laney's piqued voice came over the wire, "I've been calling Mom's house for hours. I thought we'd decided you were going back there for the night."

"No, Laney." How demure she sounded. "We didn't decide that. But it's okay. Rennie's here with me." She laid a hand on his bare chest. Muscles twitched at her touch. "And he's going to stay here tonight."

"Oh, good," Laney said, blithely oblivious to the true situation. "John and I've been talking. We think Rennie's right, that you shouldn't be by yourself. Kiki's death probably had nothing to do with you, but you can't ever tell. Him being there will keep you from worrying."

"Yes, it will. Rennie's right here to take care of me so I'm not worried a bit." She circled his nipple with her thumb, let her fingers trail down to his navel and then his erection. "He's taking excellent care of me. Believe me, I'm fine."

That was an understatement.

Laney didn't notice. She had no idea Autumn's world had turned on its end. "Oh, good. What I was calling about was your TV. Is it on?"

"My TV? No." She had better things to do than watch TV. And chatting with Laney wasn't one of them.

"Turn it on to WSB. They're showing some of the reception on the late news."

"Reception?" A total blank.

"For this opening at the High Museum, silly. Guess who they interviewed? Francisco!"

"Fran?" Autumn widened her eyes. "It figures. It was a woman reporter, right?"

"Of course. They showed a teaser just now, and he was so cute. I knew you'd want to see it. And Rennie, too. The report's coming up on the news at eleven."

Autumn yawned as she powered off and transmitted Laney's instructions to Rennie. "I guess we'd better go watch."

His grin, slow as molasses and twice as sweet, spread. His hand touched her stomach and started a new tingling. "We don't have to if you don't want to. Francisco won't know."

Tempting. So very tempting. "Of course he'll know. He'll grill us unmercifully as to how his tux looked, how he sounded, whether every hair was in place, if they showed the right profile. Then when he finds we didn't think enough of him to turn on the TV, he'll be crushed."

"Not for long. His ego's too big." Rennie spoke without the least hint of malice. There was no smugness behind his words because he was in bed with a woman Fran wanted.

Was there?

No. Rennie hadn't made love to her because he thought she was involved with Fran and wanted to pay off old scores.

He hadn't. She was sure of it.

Rennie would never do anything like that. Not to her and not to Fran.

He wasn't like Fran.

Well-being suffused her, warming her, making her feel as if her very toes were happy. Why hadn't she ditched her stupid pride and gone after Rennie years ago, before he'd ever met Jane? She could have followed him to California, and they could have been together all this time.

Except he'd have sent her back home.

No matter. The present more than made up for the past.

In the middle of his stroking her, when the gentle warmth inside her was on the verge of becoming full-blown heat, she wavered over going downstairs. "I could run down and set up to record. Then we wouldn't have to interrupt this for Fran's big interview."

"I'd forgotten about Fran." He lay back and groaned. "We'd still have to set it up and watch it later. So let's get it over with. He'll make us replay it in front of him if we miss the real thing. But look on the bright side. It won't take long and we can come back to bed."

"All right. But only because you say so."

He ran a finger down between her breasts and around her navel. "You know I'm right. Little brother'll give us a pop quiz tomorrow. We'll have to know the answers or we'll never hear the end of it."

"Uh huh." She wriggled as he tweaked a nipple. "But it might be worth it."

He abruptly rolled over and sat up on the side of the bed. "No, it wouldn't. He can get ugly. Remember that time

Norma stole his mirror and he lectured her for an hour on dishonesty, immorality, and making wrong decisions? And she had to listen because he threatened to tell Mom if she didn't. Do you need a robe? We'd better go now before it's too late. Anticipation will make it better, I promise."

Downstairs, TV turned to the right channel, they shooed Squeaky out and curled up in her easy chair. Not until toward the end of the newscast did the report on the High Museum come on.

By that time she had unzipped Rennie's jeans and they were engaged in another activity, one in which her bare fanny sat on his lap while she lay back against his chest and gently rocked back and forth.

They had to take time off in the middle of their exercise to watch the interview.

"We should have waited for the tape," Rennie muttered as she made him stop his lascivious exploration of her bottom.

"Shush."

As his hands reached around her waist to part her thighs, she took hold of them and held them still. "Anticipation makes it better. Remember?"

First the camera swept through some of the exhibits.

"At the High Museum tonight," the pretty reporter began, leading into her shtick about the Louvre's unprecedented decision to loan its renowned *Ornaments for the Human Body* exhibition for a three months' display in Atlanta.

Precious jewels and metals dotted the collection, the earnest young woman explained.

"Take, for instance, this set of Byzantine earrings and necklace. They're made of gold, emerald crystals, sapphires, and pearls. But some of the truly invaluable pieces are made of less costly materials, such as this pair of 16th century armlets from southern Nigeria, carved of ivory and inlaid with copper. Or this eleventh Dynasty Egyptian wesekh-collar of composition beads—"

That collar. Those brilliant colors.

Autumn sat bolt upright.

"Ouch. Careful how you bend." Rennie tightened his hold on her hips and immobilized them as she settled back. "What's wrong?"

"I don't know." But she did. Or thought she did. "Except... Rennie, that necklace, the one with the beads."

"What about it?"

"Sarita wore it in our photo shoots."

With her back against him, she couldn't see his face but she could feel him switching from pleasure to business.

"I doubt it," he said after a moment. "At least not that one. It would stay under lock and key. Sarita might have a necklace that looks like it. Maybe."

She wriggled, trying to twist so she could see him. Carefully so that she didn't injure anything. "Why would she? Nobody wears things like that today. I thought at the time it was an unusual choice because Egyptian jewelry isn't that fashionable." She saw his skepticism. "I think she wore that same necklace. And some of that other stuff looks awfully familiar, too. That ivory bracelet, for one."

He didn't scoff. Instead, as if her squirming on his lap had reminded him of other things, he turned her back around toward the TV, bringing his hands under her arms and catching her breasts and pulling her to his chest. Holding her tight against him, he somehow managed to roll her hips across him and back, provoking lovely extended billows of pleasure.

Still... "Rennie, it *is* the same necklace."

"Okay. And how, beautiful lady, would Sarita have got that particular necklace out of the museum's custody and back?" His breath warmed her ear.

"Um, I don't know, would you do that again, please, that thing with—Oh, there's Fran." She caught his thighs, stopped him, momentarily sidetracked from the agreeable tension he'd elicited.

"—all due to Danielle Huertole's hard work and personal contacts," Fran was telling the interviewer as he gave generous credit to his boss's wife for bringing the exhibit to Atlanta. He stood before the High Museum, his swarthy good looks spotlighted against its stark white tiles.

"She's the type of person who, when she makes up her mind something should be done, does it. Gus and I are glad she's on his side in this upcoming campaign."

The pretty blonde beamed at Fran. "So Gus Huertole is definitely going to run for governor next year then?"

"You heard what he said in his speech tonight." Fran looked striking in his tuxedo, credible with a frank gaze, and perfectly at ease despite the microphones stuck in his face. "People want Gus to run, and providing he has the resources, he intends to give them what they want. From the way our phone's been ringing off the hook the past few days, we should have plenty of volunteers and contributions. See me later," he added with a twinkle to the reporter questioning him, "about that donation you promised in return for me answering your questions. Fairly sizable, I believe you said?"

Something unconnected popped into Autumn's mind. "I wonder if Sarita knows someone at the museum. Like maybe Danielle Huertole."

Rennie shifted beneath her.

He could have been restless to finish what they'd begun.

Or had her oblique accusation of Sarita purloining valuable jewelry upset him? He'd gone through high school with Sarita and dated her long before she became famous. When he'd left for California, still before Sarita's early success, Kaneka had given him her address so he could find her and make sure she was okay.

Had he? Reseda had never talked about him hanging out with Sarita while he was out there, and she would have boasted now that Sarita was so big.

Or would she? Reseda never had approved of Sarita. Sarita had collected a lot of boyfriends and she loved to play them against each other. Reseda had disliked Rennie dating her.

From behind her, Rennie sounded remote. "In Sarita's line of work, she's acquainted with a lot of people. But even if she knows someone at the museum, I'm pretty sure she'd never get hold of that necklace. The Louvre takes pretty good care of security for their things, I feel sure."

She was mistaken. He'd shifted at the mention of Sarita because he was uncomfortable with her sitting on him like this.

And if he sounded cool, it was because Sarita didn't concern him any more. Any tenseness was the same tenseness she felt having him inside her. It had to be. She moved on his hips, tightening her thighs, manipulating him in a way that brought on his gratified, "Oh, yes. Do that again."

Leave it alone.

She couldn't. "You don't think that since Dani Huertole was responsible for the exhibit, she might have loaned the necklace to Sarita for the photo sessions?"

"We aren't even sure they know each other. I wouldn't worry about Sarita or the necklace. What difference does it make whether she's wearing an antique or a copy? You've got your photos safe in your van." His hands that had been stroking her back, glided around toward her breasts.

"I guess you're right. And I'm lucky the thumb drive's still there. If I'd taken it to the studio…"

She shuddered. He buried his face in her back. His tongue flicked at the bottom of her neck.

Sarita's photos were safe. Though everything else left from fifty-eight years of hard work had gone up in smoke. "I dread starting over. The thought of pulling a studio together from scratch makes me want to cry."

"You can do it." His hands went round her waist, drawing her back hard against his chest. "Don't think about it now." His hands crept lower. His voice thickened. "Think about this."

She lay back against him, happiness returning with his arms tight around her. "I hope you're right, that I can build the business back up."

His caresses heightened her desire.

He couldn't be holding anything back from her. The Degardoveras never withheld, but gave freely to anyone they loved. She was the one who kept herself under such tight control that she'd almost watched Rennie walk out of her life rather than risk his rejection.

She couldn't stifle a gasp as he found a certain spot. But the necklace troubled her. "I wish you could see Sarita's proofs. Then you'd believe me about her having that necklace."

"I do believe you. Maybe Sarita saw it, liked it, and had a copy made." His tone said he was tired of hearing about the necklace while his hands said he wanted to discuss far more pressing matters.

No sense in letting Sarita's jewelry spoil the moment.

Not with the wisps of excitement collecting and thickening in her belly as he lifted her and thrust her down hard against him, catching the sensitive place each time until her body involuntarily began to match his strokes and their rhythm quickened and their breathing quickened and his heat exploded within her and made her cry out in the midst of paroxysms.

They went to bed later, but they didn't get much sleep that night.

****

SAM BOGATTI DIDN'T get much sleep that night either.

He'd driven straight through from Helen to Illinois, arriving home late Sunday night to hear about the hockey game—their team had won four to three and his kid had scored one goal and had two assists—and to endure his wife's censure for missing church.

"It's my work, cupcake," he placated her. "What can I do?"

Later, after they climbed into bed, he curled up against her and patted her butt, laid his head on the pillow next to hers, and died.

When the phone rang, he was lost in a dream involving a big Nordic blonde and summertime streams and white fleecy clouds over alpine mountains.

His wife's sleepy hello waked him before she turned over and punched him. "Sam. It's that guy, says he's gotta speak to you. Right now."

The clock said three-twenty. Bernie didn't call him in the middle of the night for no reason. Not at home. Bernie hardly ever called him at home.

Can't be good.

Wide awake, he took the receiver. His wife got up, slipped on her house shoes, and went into the bathroom.

"Yeah." His tongue felt thick and furry. His brain was still fried from the trip.

"Call me on a cell."

Nope. Not good. Sam shut off the cordless. *Not good at all.*

He got out a new throwaway cell and crawled back into bed. "Can you give me a minute?" he called to his old lady.

She knew not to come out till he got done.

Bernie was stressed. "You screwed up."

"I scr—? What you frigging talking about? I got it done, didn't I?"

"To the wrong woman."

"The wrong—No way."

"You did. You know who I just got off the line with? Our client. And he's pissed. Real pissed. I don't know who you did but this photog—uh, porn star is back at her place and the bird's people will be home tomorrow and if the woman talks, we'll be hurting."

The wrong woman. What the shit was Bernie talking about?

Bernie got a little shrill. "I've got a plane chartered at the regular place for seven tomorrow morning. Get your ass on it and get back down there and finish the job."

Damn it, Bernie knew how he felt about charters. "I don't like them frigging little planes."

"If this woman puts two and two together, she's liable to mention the stuff. And my client's poured a lot of money into keeping this thing quiet. Listen, we don't want to screw around with this guy, Sammy, believe me, we don't."

Shit, Bernie's frigging terrified. Who's he working for?

Bernie was rushing on. "I arranged for a rental car when you land. You get on that plane tomorrow morning and get down there. Clean it up."

The connection was broken.

Sam turned off the cell and looked at the dark night patterns playing on the ceiling.

The wrong woman.

Who the hell was Bernie's client that had him so scared?

Jeez. All these damned Hispanics running around with the photographer, and the wad of money he was making off this job…

Had to be some of the bad news people from South America. The kind of people what made Sam real nervous.

He had principles, Sam did. He didn't mind doing people who needed it, but this job was beginning to bother him. First Sarita. Okay, maybe she *was* a druggie and a blackmailer. Maybe she *did* enjoy seeing men kill one another over her.

But that voice couldn't be replaced and he'd been the one to mute it.

Now he found out he'd offed some woman he didn't even know.

All for the sake of some Latin gorillas buying a pathway for their drugs. If he'd known that was what was going down, he never woulda taken the contract.

Sam didn't approve of drugs.

But he had taken it.

His wife reappeared from the bathroom. "Did I hear you cussing out here, Sammy?"

"What?" Had he? "Guess I slipped up, Rena. Sorry."

"Hafta watch out in front of the boys. You agreed." She sat on the bed and took off her house shoes. "You gotta leave again? When you just got in?"

"Yeah. Sorry, cupcake." Her disappointment washed over him. It took his mind off dangerous four-seater airplanes and rental cars and having to depend on people he didn't know. He threw back the cover so she could crawl in. "Saved you a warm place. Hey, I'm rested up if you got something good in mind."

Shit, it stunk having to leave when he'd barely got home.

****

ON MONDAY, AS a nervous Sam Bogatti sat bolt upright in the seat of his chartered plane flying toward Atlanta, Autumn and Rennie lay in bed. He was asleep but she was awake, nestled against him when the opal tinge of dawn strengthened into brilliant morning.

She liked being with him as he slept. His chest lay flat and hard beneath her cheek. The muscles in his arm curved as his hand rested on her shoulder. His scent, of sex and vestiges of cedar cologne, suffused her.

How great if she could lie here beside him forever, sated and content, letting her love reach out and enfold the two of them in their own cocoon.

The phone rang.

Oh, no. Not again.

Rennie shifted.

His eyes opened, blinked, found her watching him. A startled look gave way to a sleepy smile. He'd forgotten. He didn't care enough to remember last night.

Don't be so hypersensitive.

He'd been asleep. Sound asleep in a strange place. Of course he wouldn't remember where he was or what had happened right away.

Her cell rang again.

"Why does someone have to call at the worst times?" she murmured.

"Might be something about the fire."

She grimaced—he was conscious of responsibility when she least wanted to be reminded—but answered anyway.

Fran's voice glided out, sultry as drifting smoke. "Good morning, gorgeous. I hoped I'd catch you before you left. Did you see me on TV last night?"

Did the man never drop his seductive charm?

"Fran." She snuggled back against Rennie. His expression revealed nothing but drowsy interest. "I did see you last night. You were wonderful. You did a great job. You actually seemed pretty intelligent. Did you have a script?"

"No script. All me." Fran's chuckle, so like Rennie's, sounded. "And thank you, thank you. All flattery accepted. I thought it went pretty well, too. Listen, I got Dani to wangle us some passes to the High Museum today."

"Passes?" She sat up. *Where the jewelry was. The actual jewelry.* "For the exhibit?"

"Yep. Laney and Norma are taking late lunches and Paul

may come over, too. With John, of course. I hoped you could join us. About two?"

"Two? Sounds good." She looked at Rennie, laid a hand on his chest when she saw the slight downward curving of his inner eyebrows that hinted he was tired. Or displeased. Or maybe not quite awake. "How about Rennie? Got enough tickets for him?"

"Rennie?" Fran's surprise came through the cell, underscored by an instant of silence. "Sure. Is he—did you have plans with Rennie for today?"

"He's going with me to talk to the fire investigators."

"Fire investigators?"

"I guess you haven't heard."

Strangely, losing her studio and possessions didn't seem so devastating this morning. Maybe it was the night spent in Rennie's arms.

She filled Fran in about the fire and listened to his shocked commiseration, saying when he paused, "Yes, well, anyway I'm going over to talk with the investigator on the case this morning and I have no idea how long it'll take. I'd think we should be through by two. If we aren't at your office by then, we'll meet you at the High Museum. How about that?"

Fran hesitated. "Great." His voice deepened. "Rennie isn't coming on to you, is he, Autumn? I noticed in Helen that he was being kind of pushy."

"You're the one who comes on, Fran." She still wasn't sure enough of Rennie's intentions to advertise their new standing. Not to Fran, anyway. "To me and every other female around. Your brother is, and always has been, a perfect gentleman. Unlike some people who beg a cup of coffee after taking me to dinner and end up chasing me around the sofa."

Rennie tensed, and she smothered a laugh. When he opened his mouth, she put a hand over it.

Fran was saying quite enough in her ear.

"Yes, I'm well aware I'm so sexy you can't keep your hands off me."

Rennie gave a rueful shake of his head, amazed.

"And I know you're wild to get me in bed. I'm sure it would be lovely for both of us, but face it, Fran. I'm too timid and you're way too experienced for a shrinking violet like me. You're better off finding somebody with no sexual hang-ups."

"I've got a surefire way to cure hang-ups," Fran said, "but it involves active participation on your part. If you—"

"I've got to go, Fran. We'll meet you. Either your office at two or the High Museum later. Okay?"

"Okay. But—"

She turned off her cell.

He lifted both brows. "You have sexual hang-ups?"

"Sure." She put her arms around his neck. "I don't seem to be able to make it with anyone but you."

That brought on a new round of nuzzling and whispered sweet nothings until she came up for air. "You don't mind us going to the exhibit with Fran, do you?"

That would give her a good chance to look at the necklace and compare it to the one Sarita had worn.

"Going to the exhibit or listening to you bait my poor little brother?"

"Going to the exhibit. And I wasn't baiting Fran. I've told him and told him I wouldn't go to bed with him."

"Why not?" His voice was husky.

She searched for his eyes. "Don't you know? How often do I have to throw myself at you?"

He pulled her down beside him. His lips were soft. The heat rose, diffusing the most responsive parts of her body.

"You can throw yourself at me as often as you like." He was the one to come up for air this time. "We can take this week off and go to Athens later."

"We can?" She laid her face against his shoulder, put her lips against his chest and bit his nipples gently. One and then the other. "Do I get to go with you?"

"Unless you intend to live in Atlanta while I'm in Athens."

Her tongue stopped tormenting his budded nipple. "Do you want me in Athens?"

He shifted restlessly. "I had hoped you'd come with me.

Yes, I know I'm taking a lot for granted, but you told me you loved me, Autumn. That meant something, didn't it?"

"You know it did."

Why did he look so unhappy? "Then sooner or later, we'll have to move on to the next step, won't we?"

Pressing his stomach with her fingers, she nipped his taut nipple. Did he mean what he was implying, or was it simply his morning-after conscience prodding him to hint at something more? She wanted him but not enough to force him into something against his will or halfheartedly. "I'm enjoying this step. I think we should drag it out."

With long lazy motions, she circled his navel, stroked the hairs beneath, stopped short.

His breath caught. He took her hand and moved it down. "I'm enjoying it, too. There. See?"

"Then what's the problem?" The touch of his arousal started excitement sparkling all over again.

She would never get enough of him. Never.

He rasped, "With me in Athens and you in Atlanta, it may be hard to keep in step. Distance does that to people."

He was remembering Jane. Her ardor faltered. This comparison of her to Jane and Jane's choice of career over him meant he was afraid she would make the same choice as Jane.

Maybe she shouldn't be so honest with him. Maybe she should be a little stand-offish.

No. Caution had never got her anywhere. Not until she became reckless enough to risk rejection had Rennie noticed her. Not until she'd turned completely wanton—her face heated as she remembered her blunt confessions, her boldness—did he admit he cared.

"Rennie." She rolled over and sat up on her knees beside him. "Don't you know by now that I'll be as close to you as you'll let me? I'll go wherever you are, stay wherever you stay, for as long as you want me. I have no shame, no pride. Not where you're concerned."

The graveness overlaying his features softened. "I wouldn't let you throw your career away for me."

As Jane had refused to do, floated unsaid.

"I'm not throwing anything away. Athens isn't that far, and besides, one town is as good as another. The studio's reputation pulls clients from all over the state. But if I do decide to throw it away, it's my decision, isn't it? I might like doing watercolors better than erotic photography."

He looked unconvinced.

She shook her head before he could speak, caressed his unruly curls. "Rennie, you are everything to me. Please believe me, darling, you are."

The sweet fool.

She'd give up her studio, cameras, negatives, reputation, everything.

So long as Rennie loved her.

Chapter Sixteen

LATER THAT MORNING, after dragging herself out of bed with Rennie and taking care of the demanding Squeaky, Autumn called Iris.

No answer on the cell, but her receptionist's home phone rang only twice before Iris answered, breathless. "I was walking out the door, headed for work. Is something wrong?"

Iris had spent the weekend with her daughter in Birmingham and knew nothing of the fire. The initial shock was followed by concern for her own welfare.

Autumn soothed her. "Of course I'll need you, Iris. I don't know where we'll be, but I'll find a place as soon as I can."

Even if she lived in Athens with Rennie, she could take appointments here. She'd look for offices on the east side, show up two or three days a week. This might work out very well for Iris since the area she lived in lay on the Athens side of Atlanta. "Once we find a place, it won't take us long to set things back up."

"Won't take long?" Iris wailed. "With all we've lost? Oh, my, the photography records, the outstanding accounts, the customer listings, the bank deposits. How will we ever get them straightened out?"

"We'll manage, Iris."

Iris didn't listen. "Not to mention the books. How will we ever figure up the amount of taxes we owe? The IRS will be after us for sure. What'll we do?"

"I bet they have procedures set up for fires. Don't worry, we'll get through this."

"And our customers. How will they find us? We had a man come in Friday evening at closing. He was anxious to get you to do some of those pictures of his wife, but he'll never be back now."

"Don't be ridiculous. Of course he'll come back. We'll put out ads and let everyone know what happened. You have the studio credit card, so why don't you call the newspapers and get started on that now? Let the radio stations know, too. When we get moved, we'll do some more ads for our new location. Oh, and talk to our computer guy and ask him about file recovery from our backup. He'll need to get started on that right away. And have him find you a laptop to work on at home for the time being."

After a long conversation in which Autumn alternately agonized and comforted and gave Iris instructions about calling the insurance companies and accountant, she put her phone down with a huge sigh of relief.

Rennie, fresh from the shower and smelling of her soap despite wearing yesterday's corduroys and sweater, handed her a steaming cup of coffee. "Sounds like she's taking it hard."

"I've got to keep her busy. Otherwise she's going to worry herself to death. And me along with her."

"You'd think it was her studio, the way she was carrying on."

"Iris has been there for years, since before my grandfather died. She's a good person but she's also a worrywart. Not that I care. I don't care about anything today. I feel wonderful."

Even her appointment with the arson investigator didn't bother her. Not after the past night.

After she bathed and dressed, she and Rennie drove to the Degardoveras so he could change clothes.

Good thing no one was there to remark on her high spirits.

The place was welcoming in its clutter: an afghan on the

sofa pushed back where someone had been lying to watch TV, a newspaper scattered around an easy chair, jackets thrown over chairs. The Degardoveras lived in a home, not a decorator's dream like her aunt and uncle. She'd fled to them when things at her house got too bad. Their chaos still comforted her.

She plucked a magazine off the pile on the floor and thumbed through it till he came out fastening a cuff on his button-down shirt. After he tucked the tails into his jeans, she stood. "Ready for the lions' den?"

His usual sidelong smile seemed abstracted. "It won't be that bad."

"No." Not with him beside her.

He shrugged into his down jacket, pulled out his car keys, took a deep breath. "Ready?"

"Rennie, is something bothering you?"

"Not a thing."

Too shy to delve, she dropped it.

Maybe he was tired. She certainly was. Tired and sore.

That brought on a pleasurable frisson from reliving last night and this morning. The reasons why she was so tired and sore.

Downtown, Captain Cunningham of the Arson Squad waited for them. A petite round-faced woman with cornrows and eyes as brown as Rennie's, the captain exuded a no-nonsense air.

"I appreciate your calling and coming by so promptly." She looked across a cluttered desk at Autumn and Rennie while a portrait of Georgia's current governor beamed down at them from over her shoulder. "Is this your lawyer, Ms. Merriwell?"

"My lawyer?" Autumn caught herself. "No. A friend." She introduced Rennie and waited.

Captain Cunningham was business-like. "As I understand it, Ms. Merriwell, you left for Helen Friday evening. Is that correct?"

"Yes."

Under patient prodding, Autumn told her story. The captain heard it out in its entirety before getting down to detailed questioning that included pinpointing the time Autumn and Rennie had left Atlanta Friday afternoon.

At length, she sat back in her chair. "This was definitely arson, Ms. Merriwell. The ashes aren't yet cool enough for us to dig around in depth, but it was obvious from the way the file cabinets were left open and the different points of combustion."

Rennie, quiet in the background, spoke up, "I think you ought to know that someone tried to stab Autumn Saturday night. And a woman wearing a jacket like hers was murdered at the cabin next to the one we were staying at in Helen. I'm afraid all this, including the fire, may be connected."

Captain Cunningham's eyes popped. She sat up straight. "What?"

Autumn caught his sleeve. "Rennie, we don't know that what happened in Helen has anything to do with the fire."

But she wasn't sure.

The captain took a deep breath. "Tell me about it."

So Autumn had to go into more particulars about the Helen trip.

When she finished, Captain Cunningham turned from the computer where she'd been taking notes and frowned. "It does seem a bit coincidental, doesn't it, Ms. Merriwell? The personal attacks on you after your studio was set afire Friday night. You don't know of any enemies you might have?"

Autumn shook her head. "No."

"No old husbands or boyfriends?"

"No."

The captain cocked her head to one side in mild disbelief. "And no idea why someone would want to hurt you or destroy your property?"

"No. There's no reason anyone would hate me that much."

No reason at all.

****

BY MIDMORNING, LONG after Autumn and Rennie had got up from their well-used bed and left for the arson investigator's office, Sam Bogatti was recovering from his small plane ride.

A nail-biting trip, but with the help of his stress exercises, he'd survived. Even the airsickness was going away.

This was shitty, coming back to stinking Hotlanta.

After stowing his working bag in the back seat of a nondescript rental car, he got in, still steaming but trying to control it. He couldn't let resentment get to him. That was what got you caught, being so mad and uptight you forgot to think.

Finding a busy shopping center en route, he took less than five minutes to switch license tag plates. Soon his rental car blended into the many vehicles clogging Atlanta's expressways as he headed across town toward Autumn Merriwell's condominium.

After he broke open a fresh pack of Juicy Fruit gum, he rolled up a piece but didn't stuff it in his mouth right away.

Bad vibes. This whole deal shouted screw-up. He better be extra careful.

This was the last time he'd take on a job without knowing everything. Like who was behind the contract and why.

****

AS RENNIE DROVE his Lexus toward Gus Huertole's campaign headquarters, Autumn tried to forget her interview with the arson investigator. The captain had been nice enough, but her skepticism showed. The way she said, "Um hum," and the way she sighed and tossed a pen down. Her upraised brows.

A car full of elderly people pulled up beside the Lexus at a red light, laughing uproariously.

Nice someone was enjoying themselves.

She bit a nail. "Captain Cunningham believes I set the fire to collect the insurance."

"Forget her." Rennie touched her thigh. "She isn't worth wrinkling that pretty brow over."

"You heard her asking for the information of my insurance company. And with you bringing up all that stuff that happened in Helen, she probably thinks you're in some kind of scam with me."

"Autumn, don't. If she does suspect you of anything, it won't take long to prove she's wrong. Don't worry about her."

He was right. What difference would worrying make? Rennie loved her.

After all these years, he'd said he loved her. Even if she'd had to push him, he'd said it.

And he knew she wasn't an arsonist, so whatever anyone else thought didn't matter.

She reached across the console and took his hand, comforted by his answering squeeze. She was so happy she even hummed along with the radio.

The country station updated traffic information every few minutes so they were among the first people in Atlanta to hear about Sarita Sartowe's death.

Her mouth dropped.

No, he didn't say Sarita Sartowe. Can't be.

Rennie reached for the radio, turning up the volume.

"—and police are treating it as a homicide. Again, breaking news. Sarita Sartowe's body was found in her family's northeast Atlanta mansion this morning. We'll cut into our programming for more bulletins as they come in."

Rennie pulled over to a side street and found a place to pull out of the traffic. "Did he say homicide?"

They looked at each other in stunned disbelief.

A riot of images raced through Autumn's mind.

Sarita, giggling as she thumbed through the proofs, dancing around the living room, telling Autumn she absolutely positively had to do her concert promotion photos and wouldn't she *please please please* consider moving out to LA.

Rennie broke in on the disjointed memories. "It's got to be connected. Everything that's happened. You and Sarita and everything else. There's got to be some connection, Autumn."

He sounded far away, like a stranger.

Sarita's photographs would have made the studio's

reputation, *her* reputation. But Sarita was dead and there would be no photographs.

This is not a time to be thinking of yourself.

Dead. Sarita was dead.

****

"AUTUMN." RENNIE GRIPPED Autumn's shoulder and willed her to look at him. When she did, he saw she hadn't heard a word he'd said.

Trusting. She was too trusting. Too naïve.

"Rennie, how can Sarita be dead? I saw her Friday and she was fine, she was—"

"Autumn, it's connected." Cold balled up in his stomach. "The fire, Kiki's murder, someone trying to knife you. It's all connected to Sarita. It has to be."

Autumn still wasn't listening. "I took her the proofs and she looked at them and loved them. She was so happy with them and me. She was going to use them for publicity and she said I could choose my customers, that they'd line up at my door. She danced all over the room after she saw them. She was like a kid. Oh Rennie, she was so alive. Who would have done such a thing? Everyone admired Sarita."

"Not everyone," he muttered.

Autumn didn't hear.

Her outer coat of toughness was gone. Her soul was as fragile as he'd suspected. If the police locked onto that vulnerability, they'd split her wide open and leave nothing but the frightened child who'd never trust anyone again.

He had to protect her.

"Autumn, listen to me. We have to make plans. We may have suspected something was wrong before, but now we know. And you're in the center somehow."

She started to shake her head.

"Autumn!"

She stiffened. A magician's hand might have slipped across her, transforming her, calming her. And something else.

Wary. She was wary of him.

The face of his princess. Set against him.

He'd known it would happen.

"Rennie, do you think I had anything to do with Sarita's murder?"

"What? Of course not." He took both her hands. They were freezing. "But her murder must have something to do with the other stuff that's been happening. There's nothing else to explain it."

She started to protest but he tightened his grip. "Be honest. If your butt pack hadn't been in the way, whatever slit it would have slit you."

She shrank back.

He held onto her. "Don't turn away from me, Autumn. This is serious. Kiki Ballencer was murdered. Wearing a jacket like yours. Don't you see? It's all tied together with Sarita. Now Sarita's dead, too."

"But why? Sarita was fine when I left her. She was so sweet to me. So happy. And she was so pleased with the proofs. She was like a little girl."

"The proofs." Rennie had forgotten them. "Autumn, the police will see the proofs, realize you were with Sarita Friday. You have to talk to them."

"The police?" She tugged at her hands. "I don't want to. They already think I set the fire."

He tightened his grip. "I don't want you to have to talk to them either." For his own selfish reasons. "But you have to. The fire's part of it, too. It has to be. This will make them see you had nothing to do with any of this."

But that wasn't true. Someone was trying to implicate her. Or kill her. Because of Sarita.

Francisco. Had his brother met Sarita in the last few weeks? Had he seen her here in Atlanta?

No. Francisco had more sense than to hang around a woman who'd made it plain she was through with him.

But Francisco and Sarita. He'd never seen Francisco so obsessed about any woman.

Autumn wet her lips. "I don't want to get involved."

"I don't think you have a choice."

"I'm afraid, Rennie."

He started to reassure her but couldn't.

"So am I." For his brother; no one could tell what

Francisco might have done if he was somehow involved, if he'd lost his temper. And for himself.

Once the police started sifting through Sarita's background, the ugly details of his involvement would all come out. Autumn would have to know. He ought to confess. Before…

He couldn't. Not now. "I'm afraid, too, Autumn. But you've got to go to the police. Sooner or later they'll see the proofs and be suspicious if you don't tell them."

"All right." She pulled away but covered her eyes. "You're right. I see that now. I can't think straight."

"We'll start with Captain Cunningham. She should be able to advise us." He cranked the Lexus and started back the way they had come.

Francisco couldn't be mixed up in Sarita's murder.

"What about the necklace and other jewelry?" Autumn asked after they rode a few minutes.

The jewelry. Autumn thought the jewelry in Sarita's photos had come from the exhibit.

Francisco was close to the Huertoles. Could he have somehow gotten it and given it to Sarita?

No. Sarita had dropped Francisco months ago. He might have seen her again, but he wouldn't risk his job and reputation by borrowing museum jewelry. Even if he could. Not for Sarita. Not after the malicious way she'd discarded him.

And even if Francisco could have gotten the jewelry, if he'd seen Sarita while she was in Atlanta and she'd talked him into loaning her the jewelry, did that explain the accident to Autumn? Or Kiki's death and the studio fire? What did they have to do with Sarita?

Francisco would never hurt Autumn.

No, his brother couldn't be mixed up in any of this.

"Rennie?"

She was waiting for an answer. What had she asked? The jewelry. "What about it?"

"You know. I told you it looked like that in the exhibition. Do you suppose it's connected to the fire and what happened in Helen?"

"I don't know." He needed to talk to Francisco. He could tell if Fran was implicated in whatever was going on by talking to him, questioning him, watching him. His brother had never been able to lie without a shift of the eye, a twitch of his lip.

But surely Francisco wouldn't have put Autumn in danger. And he couldn't have had any part in borrowing—stealing—priceless jewelry for Sarita. Fran was reckless, but not suicidal.

No, he had to be wrong about his brother fitting into this mess. "The jewelry could be replicas. We don't know that it's the same stuff."

"I have the thumb drive. We could make some more prints and compare the pieces."

"We could." The more he considered, the more he believed the jewelry must be a part of whatever was going on.

That brought it back to Francisco. He was close to the Huertoles and had once been Sarita's lover. Could he have hoped to win her back with the jewelry? If so, it had to be without Danielle Huertole's approval or knowledge.

How could Francisco have been so foolish?

But now the jewelry was back where it belonged. That TV interview last night proved it. And Sarita was dead.

Rennie didn't like what he was thinking.

Francisco was impulsive, given to rash acts later regretted. And Sarita had driven him wild. He had worshiped her.

The Degardoveras didn't know about Francisco and Sarita.

Their mother had jumped on Rennie when he dated her in high school. Fran wouldn't have dared let Reseda know how involved he was with a woman she despised.

But Francisco had been seriously depressed when Sarita dumped him. If he'd thought the jewelry might get her back, would he have risked everything to reclaim her?

No. Impossible.

Rennie would have to confront Francisco. Alone.

As soon as Autumn talked to Captain Cunningham.

****

GETTING INTO THE gated condo complex was a piece of cake. A small car entered, and Sam followed it in.

When he found the photographer's condo number, he parked up the street and looked around. There weren't too many nosy people around these places because most people worked weekdays. The few he saw today seemed engrossed in their own affairs.

Like they should be. Everybody ought to mind their own business. Make the whole world a lot easier to live in.

He got out a new stick of gum. Then he unzipped his bag and pulled out the Ruger and its silencer.

It was messy and loud. But it was also quick and easy.

Final.

Okay, if she answered the door, he'd pop her and push her inside before anyone saw. If she was gone, he'd get in through the garage door and wait.

Drawing on latex gloves, he fiddled in his bag for the garage door code gadget. Then he screwed the silencer on his gun, hid it beneath his coat, and left the car.

He ambled down the empty sidewalk toward Autumn Merriwell's condo. The gum helped his dry mouth.

No one answered the doorbell.

Looked like no alarm system, and a quick gander didn't turn up anybody in view. In less than a minute, his remote retrieved her garage door combination and opened it. Inside sat an old minivan and a neat row of storage shelves.

A switch closed the garage door, a pick opened the inner door lock, and he was in.

An orange cat on the counter raised its head.

Jeez, his stomach tensed like a first-timer. "Nice kitty."

It got up, still watching him. When he neared it, it jumped down and disappeared up the stairs.

Just a cat. He let his heart slow.

Hey, he may've had a run of bad luck on this job, but that didn't mean it was going to last. It had to get better.

Or maybe not. He'd got a weird feeling the moment he saw those photos with the stuff plastered all over Sarita like she was flaunting it for everyone to see. It was like fate was sick and tired of him, and was fooling around, trying to make him shit his pants.

Hell. He was losing it.

About time to get out of this rat race and buy into that motel in Florida like his brother-in-law kept after him to do. Maybe when the kids got out of high school. Except then there'd be college. Both his boys had to go to college, become accountants or doctors or something like that. No lawyers.

Yeah, well, that was for the future. Right now he had to find a way to do the frigging broad.

First the fiasco on the bridge. Then a woman in her coat. Now she wasn't home.

What sour luck. Never been this bad before. He never should've agreed to do Sarita. If he ever got this frigging job finished, he'd go back to the old system. Do the ones who needed doing and damn the money they waved in front of him.

But right now, he'd wait for the photographer and pop her when she walked in. She'd come home sooner or later. She couldn't stay gone forever.

The only question was whether she'd get home before they found Sarita, but he'd worry about that later.

After he made sure nobody besides the cat was around.

He wandered through the living area and curled his lip.

Jeez, this place was like a frigging model house. Personally, he liked books on tables and a few dirty dishes in the sink. Then it looked like somebody's home instead of an ad layout for *House Beautiful*.

But that was him. Different strokes for different folks.

Small, too.

Sarita's house in LA, now. Man, that was a real house. And her mother's place here in Hotlanta was more than okay. But this joint was dinky. The living area, dining area and kitchen all run together with no pitched ceilings, no spectacular window walls, no rock fireplaces taking up one end of the living room.

Just somewhere to hang your hat.

And everything stowed away.

Nobody down here.

Upstairs, her bedroom presented the same order. A neatly made cannonball bed like his grandparents had owned stood on one wall with a chest, top uncluttered and shiny, on another.

No gown hanging from the back of a door like his wife had, no house shoes in the corner, no lipstick and lotion marring the clean surface of the bureau, no laundry hamper.

A rack held magazines and paperbacks while a floral arrangement decorated a small bedside table.

Who the hell was she trying to be? Hazel Housekeeper?

Ah, there. Something out of place.

He turned around a big picture frame on the floor with its face to the wall and grinned.

Some stud. Hanging off the hook above, it woulda faced the bed. Bet the other guy took him down.

They had to be brothers. Both with the pretty photographer? Maybe she favored one over the other. Maybe she'd had a spat with one. Maybe they all got it on together.

She looked kind of prim for a threesome, but the prim ones sometimes surprised you.

Opening the louvered closet doors, he found her clothes sorted by color with shoes and purses stored in boxes. Other accessories draped around different outfits, all ready to wear.

Couldn't help but admire a woman who planned so thoroughly for the future. Too bad she wouldn't have one.

Oooh, his damn tender heart.

The cat peeked out from under the bed. "Good place for you, kitty. Why doncha stay put for a while."

Back downstairs, he picked out a chair in a corner near the front window. One not too comfortable but still easy on the ass. His gum had hardened so he got out a new piece, carefully wrapped the old in the paper for disposal later. Once settled, he laid the silenced gun down and took out the *Readers' Digest* he'd brought from her bedroom.

His cell vibrated.

What now? His luck got shittier and shittier.

He glanced at the message. *Call me.*

Bernie. For a supposedly shrewd lawyer, Bernie sure could pick his moments. What the shit did Bernie want, texting him on his personal cell in the middle of the job?

He looked at the phone on a nearby table, tempted.

No, he wasn't about to be caught like some frigging amateur.

He'd go out, get a throwaway, but not now. Autumn Merriwell might come home any minute.

Frigging Bernie. Sam couldn't run pick up a phone every time Bernie shit. Idiot.

The gloves made it hard to turn the magazine pages, but he managed. He started to read a first-person account of an alligator attack.

Bernie would have to wait.

****

After Rennie and Autumn explained why they thought Sarita Sartowe's death was connected to the fire and events in Helen, Captain Cunningham excused herself.

Autumn could see her through the glass panes of the office wall where she stood at a desk beside a cubicle on the other side of the large outer room. Using the desk phone, she was calling someone while they waited.

The captain carried on a lengthy conversation, then hung up and came back to regard them thoughtfully. "The homicide detective in charge of the case is out of the office, but I left your telephone number and address. He'll be in touch soon." Her eyes shifted to Rennie. "You said your name was Degardovera? Would that be Francisco Degardovera by any chance?"

Beside Autumn, Rennie stiffened. "No. Francisco's my brother."

"I see."

Poor Rennie. He looks like someone put a poker to him. "Do you know Fran, Captain Cunningham?"

"No." The captain didn't look at Autumn. "But I understand he knew Ms. Sartowe."

"My whole family knew Sarita," Rennie said coolly. "She and I went to the same high school. I dated her back then."

"But your brother was intimately involved with Sarita Sartowe this past year. Did you know that, Mr. Degardovera?"

Fran? Autumn managed not to gasp.

"It's Dr. Degardovera. Computer science, not medical. And I did know it." Rennie's hand on her arm was relaxed, but she could feel his tension. "Francisco and Sarita got together while he was in California staying with me. It didn't work out for either of them. His life is here in Atlanta, and her career is—was—across the country. They agreed there was no future for them."

"So they no longer saw each other?"

"They no longer dated," Rennie corrected. "They might see—might have seen—each other occasionally. They are—were—still friends."

"I see." Captain Cunningham transferred her attention back to Autumn. "As I said before, I'd appreciate you not leaving town without letting us know where you're going, Ms. Merriwell. And you, too, Mr.—*Dr.* Degardovera." Her caramel face remained neutral. "Purely a matter of routine."

"I'm sure it is," Rennie answered before Autumn could. "Ms. Merriwell may be staying with my family for the next few days. I assume that's all right, since you have my telephone number and address there?"

His courtesy did nothing to soften Captain Cunningham. "Do you have cells? Mind leaving me those numbers as well?"

Autumn reeled hers off by rote.

What was going on? She was a suspect in arson and maybe in Sarita's death. Now Fran was somehow being brought into it.

And Rennie… Something was off with Rennie, too.

That suspicion stayed with her when they went outside into the bright day.

The sun, since it neared noon, streamed down on the sidewalk despite the tall buildings around them. After the grim office and the suspicious Captain Cunningham, the cheerful light was disconcerting but welcome.

Rennie took her arm as they started toward the parking

lot. After several silent minutes, she said, "I didn't know Fran dated Sarita."

"A while back. One of those things. Does it matter? You said you and he were just friends."

"We are." Surely Rennie didn't believe she was jealous of Fran. "I don't care that they had an affair, but I'm surprised."

He was preoccupied. "Why? Francisco's every woman's dream lover and Sarita is, or was, every man's fantasy. What's so strange about the two of them getting together?"

Every man's fantasy? Was Sarita Rennie's fantasy, too? Somehow she couldn't imagine Rennie yearning over a sex symbol the way a lot of men did.

But Sarita… Sarita would be a temptation. "Fran never said anything to me and he always talked about his women."

"If he'd told you or any of our sisters about her, you'd have told Mom and Mom wouldn't have approved. Sarita's not the type Mom wants in the family. Wasn't the type."

Something knotted up inside her. The light reflecting from the sidewalk hurt her eyes. "Like I'm not your type?"

He stopped short on the sidewalk and turned, gripping both her upper arms like he could shake her. "You're putting words in my mouth again. Damn it, all you do is put words in my mouth. I've warned you and warned you we aren't the same kind of people, that you'll be disappointed in the end. If you regret our—"

"No." Tears pricked but she blinked them back. "I'll never regret loving you. Never."

"Ah, Autumn. What am I going to do with you?"

Her chuckle sounded watery. "I thought you'd already done it."

He turned away, taking her arm so she had to fall into step with him. "Mom didn't like Sarita for a couple of reasons. Sarita wasn't a one-man woman. Ever. And Mom doesn't approve of promiscuity. For another thing, Sarita's black. Mom's prejudiced. We know that and accept it as part of her. But the prejudice is definitely there. She's never been like your people."

"Uncle Parnell despised Republicans."

"It's not the same and you know it."

She wouldn't admit it. Reseda had never said anything in front of Autumn, but she'd been aware, maybe, in the back of her mind that Reseda didn't approve of everyone.

And not just Sarita. Reseda wanted her children to marry within the Hispanic community. When Laney started going with John Kinsellen, Reseda had made unreasonable objections. He was uptight. He was stuffy. He was a workaholic.

The week before the wedding, she'd entered the hospital for diagnostic tests in hopes, Laney confided later, of sabotaging the nuptials.

Even now, though Reseda was reconciled to her Anglo son-in-law, she still exuded a faint disappointment every time she saw him.

No, Reseda would not have approved of Fran dating Sarita.

And Reseda might not approve of Autumn and Rennie.

She wouldn't think of that, nor about Rennie's continued warnings. He loved her and that was all that mattered.

"Fran could have told me about him and Sarita. I wouldn't have said anything to Reseda if he'd asked me not to." A thought struck her. "Was that who those photos were for, those nudes I took of him? For Sarita?"

"I'd say so."

"Well, pooh. He should have told me."

Rennie chuckled.

"What's so funny?"

The creases in his forehead were deeper. "You. Francisco wouldn't have told you or anyone else, Autumn. Sarita was a lot different from his other flings. She was experienced, famous, accustomed to having men at her feet. Francisco was wild about her. He usually gets the women he wants, but he didn't get Sarita."

"Nor me," she said automatically.

"No. But Sarita... Things worked out fine for him because when it was over, you were there to pick up the pieces. You might not have been so accommodating had you known he was carrying the torch for her."

She put up her chin. "I was his friend and not a consolation prize. I'm still his friend."

He traced her jaw with his knuckles. "I know that, but I'm not so sure he does."

They reached his Lexus, and he opened the door for her. Miffed, she flounced in.

One more thing she'd been left out of. Fran could have told her. Rennie knew, and she bet Laney and Norma knew, too. Maybe not. Neither of them could keep something like that to herself.

Darn Rennie. He had no business laughing at her as if she were a naïve schoolgirl.

When he put the key in the ignition, she said, "If Fran and Sarita agreed to call it off like you told Captain Cunningham, why was Fran so upset? He was depressed for the longest time. We were worried he was going to do something—"

Rennie's hand clamped down on her wrist.

"Don't say that. Please don't ever say that to anyone, Autumn. Not now."

"What? Oh. I see." She couldn't. It would give Fran a kind of motive, however farfetched, for killing Sarita.

"You understand?" His hand tightened until her wrist hurt. "Promise."

How unfair. He wouldn't confide in her that he was afraid Fran could have killed Sarita in a jealous rage, but he still expected her to help protect Fran. He was closing her out like she was as hostile as Captain Cunningham.

Desolation swelled.

She'd never be a real part of his family. No matter how much she loved him or how often and how tenderly he made love to her, he would never accept her. She would be shut out just like always.

Understanding led to conscious acceptance.

It didn't matter. She took a deep breath. "You know I won't say anything, Rennie. I'd never get Fran into trouble."

He released her wrist, touched her cheek. "I know you wouldn't intentionally." The Rennie she knew was back again. "I also know it's easy to get tripped up when you're trying to cover for someone. Especially when you aren't used to it."

"Like you are?"

He flinched.

Uh oh. She'd struck a nerve. He looked like a man caught in a lie.

Something else he was keeping from her. She swallowed. "Okay. So you're afraid those pictures I took of Sarita might somehow implicate Fran."

"They might. We need photos to compare with that jewelry exhibit."

"Let's get the thumb drive and have them printed up."

"Autumn, the police will take it as evidence."

"No!" She hadn't thought about that. "I can't lose them. Even if Sarita's dead, they… I need to make a copy of the drive. I can copy it and print them out before I give them to the police."

In half an hour, after she'd called a photographer friend who agreed to let her use his equipment, they were at her condo to get the memory stick from the van.

While Rennie sat in the Lexus, Autumn hopped out and opened the garage door. "Is the thumb drive all I need? You don't want to come in and have a sandwich?"

"No. We'll pick up a hamburger on the way. Hurry."

He left the motor running.

Chapter Seventeen

DESPITE THE CLOSED windows, Sam Bogatti heard the car pull up in front of the condo.

He threw down the magazine, gripped his gun.

A peek through the window blinds showed the Hispanic's Lexus in front of the garage and the photographer emerging with a remote aimed toward the garage door.

The man didn't get out.

Bingo.

Lady Luck was back. He'd do her, wait for the man to leave or, if Romeo came inside, escape out the front.

As the automatic door whirred, he went to the kitchen and took a stance where he could see the door, gun poised. Some muffled movements inside the garage. A car door opened, then slammed.

Was she getting into her van? Leaving?

No sound of an engine cranking.

He gripped the Ruger, eyes glued to the kitchen door, and slid toward it.

The garage door whirred again.

What the shit?

A car door slammed outside.

He rushed back to the front window in time to see the Lexus pull out with the photographer in the passenger seat.

"I don't believe this. I frigging don't believe this."

Nobody had this kind of luck.

Nobody.

He sank down in the chair and dropped his head into his hands.

The stress was getting to him. Some manic malevolent force was buffeting him back and forth and laughing like a frigging hyena.

"This is the last time," he muttered. "I swear on the Bible, this is the last job for Bernie. Let me get finished with this one contract and no more. I'm outta the business for good."

Since it was doubtful the photographer was coming back any time soon, he left to get a throwaway.

He might as well call Bernie and see what the dumbass wanted.

A half hour later, after talking to Bernie, Sam felt a helluva lot better.

Things weren't so bad. He'd have to rearrange his schedule, but he could still finish the job today.

Checking his phone GPS, he found the location of the High Museum and started driving.

Jeez, things had to get better.

He'd never had this kind of rotten luck in his whole frigging career.

****

AT THE PHOTO shop near Perimeter Mall, Rennie watched as Autumn picked up her last photograph.

She had, with her usual dispatch, lined up use of a processing lab that belonged to one of her contacts. Once they got there, she'd plugged in her stick, copied it to another, then sent her shots to the printer.

Efficient and capable.

Not that he would have expected anything less from his accomplished princess.

The lab owner was busy with some customers when she finished. They gathered up the prints. She waved and thanked him before they left. He waved back, incurious.

In the car, she pulled one out. "There. That's the necklace."

"Dios mio, Autumn." Rennie was struck by the photo, by the composition and attention to detail, but mostly by the sheer eroticism. "You've turned her into someone, something bigger than life."

She stiffened. "You don't like it?"

"It's wonderful. No, it's more than wonderful, it's magnificent, a masterpiece. I've never seen anything like it."

At his blunt admiration, she relaxed. "I was right, though. It is the same necklace, isn't it?"

"We'll have to compare it to the one in the Museum to be sure, but yes, you're right. It does look like the same one."

She frowned. "I knew it. Do you think the police will realize from the proofs where the jewelry came from?"

"I don't know."

"I'll have to tell them, won't I?"

He wanted to say no. "Yes."

"Rennie, do you think there's any chance Fran borrowed it for her?" she asked hesitantly. "He and Dani Huertole are on good terms."

"No." Jolted back to reality, he glanced at his watch. He had to talk to his brother about that very real fear Autumn was voicing. "Certainly not. Don't mention anything like that to anyone. It'll give them the wrong ideas about Francisco. Listen, Autumn, we need to go. It's one thirty and Fran's expecting us at his office."

She didn't believe him. Her eyes gave her away. She knew Francisco could have borrowed the jewelry for Sarita, but being Autumn, she didn't call him a liar. "Fran will have heard about Sarita."

He turned the key. "Yes."

"I still can't get over how closemouthed he was about her."

Except to him.

Sarita had told Francisco about every detail of her affair with Rennie, but she'd also told him she'd dumped Rennie.

So Francisco made sure that Rennie knew he was bedding Sarita.

Anything big brother could do, little brother could do and better. That had been Fran's philosophy since grade school.

Rennie hadn't bothered to enlighten Francisco about his and Sarita's relationship because Fran wouldn't have believed him. And he hadn't told his brother about Sarita's appalling appetites because Fran would find out soon enough.

He *had* advised Francisco not to get emotionally involved.

Fran hadn't listened. Francisco never listened to anybody.

****

RENNIE OPENED THE door for Autumn and followed her slim figure into Agustin Huertole's campaign headquarters.

Downtown on Peachtree Street, the office took up space that had been, successively during the past twenty years, a shoe shop, a music store, a deli, and a pub. Desks and work tables lined the front lobby area where several volunteers huddled round a television. The mansion where Sarita had been found flashed on its screen.

Autumn flinched. She must be remembering. He touched her arm and called to his brother in the rear of the group. "Francisco."

Francisco, pinched and pale, broke away. "Autumn." He hugged her and turned to Rennie. "You know about Sarita?"

"Yes, we've heard."

"I can't believe it." Francisco ran a hand through his hair, further mussing curls that were normally arranged just so.

He couldn't have anything to do with Sarita's death. He was annoying sometimes, but he wasn't a criminal. If he'd somehow got hold of that jewelry and let Sarita use it…

Hold off accusing anybody. The jewelry might not be the same. And Francisco and Sarita's affair had been over long before Autumn took those pictures.

Francisco cleared his throat. "We've been trying to find out more ever since Gus called and told us about her."

Gus Huertole. Here was another man close to Dani.

Hope flared, unreasoning and anxious.

Francisco wasn't the only man devoured by Sarita. Gus

Huertole could easily have been hooked in, and he would have had as good an opportunity as Fran to borrow the jewelry. A better opportunity since his wife was custodian.

Yes, Huertole was, all around, a better candidate than Francisco. He was an attractive, powerful man. And Sarita specialized in attractive, powerful people.

Rennie didn't know how afraid he was till his guts relaxed like a thousand pounds had been lifted. "Did Gus know Sarita?"

Francisco's nostrils flared. "Gus had met her. Come back to my office."

Someone flung open the front door. Frigid cold swept the office.

Danielle Huertole burst in, breathless and hair wild from the December winds. She ignored everyone except Francisco. She grabbed his arm. "Where's Gus? I have to see him."

She looked ill, more so than at the pizza restaurant the past Saturday. The sculpted planes of her face were gaunt beneath the skin while the fine eyes were recessed and red-rimmed. Her skirt was wrinkled, her scarf askew, its blue-green dapples clashing with a navy blouse far too dressy for the maroon knit suit.

Like she'd climbed out of bed and thrown on the first things to hand.

Francisco pried off her fingers, patted her shoulder. "Gus isn't here, Dani. He's meeting us at the museum around two thirty, don't you remember? What's wrong?"

Her shoulders slumped. "Nothing," she muttered. "Nothing that can be fixed now. Late. It's too late, all too late." She turned and flew out the door without looking back, leaving astonished workers staring after her.

"Is she all right?" Autumn asked, at the same time Rennie asked, "What's wrong with her?"

Francisco wiped a hand over his eyes. "Who knows? She's been uptight this past week. I guess with the exhibit opening and Gus's announcing for Governor and everything else going on, it's been too much. She and Gus had a big fight this morning. When he called to tell me he'd be late and would meet us at the museum, I could hear her screaming in the background. It's got me worried. Gus's campaign won't get off the ground if he and Dani can't pull it together before the real pressure starts."

As if remembering his position as Gus Huertole's head cheerleader, he glanced toward the people still clustered in front of the TV.

Rennie read his anxiety. "They didn't hear you."

"Good." Francisco jerked his head toward the back. "Come on into my office."

What did the Huertoles have to argue about? Sarita?

Maybe his theory wasn't so farfetched. Implicating Gus Huertole would absolve Francisco. Besides Autumn's safety, his brother was his most pressing concern.

"Have they said anything else about Sarita on the news?" Autumn asked as they headed toward the back. "How she died or why?"

Francisco shook his head. "Her mother and stepfather were in the Bahamas for the week. They came back and found her strangled."

"They don't know when it happened?" Rennie asked.

"She'd been dead several days, according to one report."

"She was alive Friday." Autumn shuddered. "I saw her, Fran. When I took the proofs out to her Friday morning. She was so bright and happy. The whole thing's so terrible."

Francisco stopped short at an office door. "You didn't— she didn't say anything?"

Autumn looked at him blankly. "What about?"

Francisco motioned her to go in before him. "I don't know. Meeting someone, maybe. Being threatened by anyone."

"No, she was bubbling over, so pleased with the proofs, so full of plans. I can hardly believe she's dead."

"If she's been dead several days, Autumn may be one of the last people to see her alive," Rennie said. "She's already talked to the police. They're supposed to interview her in depth tomorrow."

Francisco looked at Autumn with sharpened interest, wheels churning behind his handsome features.

Rennie's fears returned.

Whether Francisco had taken that jewelry for the photo shoot or whether it was Gus Huertole, he would be scurrying big time trying to cover his butt or his employer's.

No matter which, Rennie wasn't about to let Francisco embroil Autumn to save himself or Gus. She was an innocent, caught up accidently in something to do with Sarita's murder.

Francisco, whether he took or helped Gus take the jewelry, was no innocent. He knew the risks.

And if he left them in the dark, deliberately exposing Autumn to danger...

Rennie's hands bunched. *I'll beat that good-looking face to a pulp.* He loosened his fists. *Come on, man. You don't know anything for sure.*

Fears for Autumn were overwhelming his common sense. He had to get hold of himself.

The first thing was to find out what Francisco knew, what he'd done. And he would have to dig for it without Autumn. Keeping her safe didn't mean betraying Francisco. Not unless he had to give up his brother to protect her.

Okay, if he had to, he would. Francisco and Sarita's parting had been stormy. She'd ended the affair in a humiliating way that had devastated Francisco, but he still couldn't see Francisco murdering Sarita.

No matter. If Francisco knew anything at all about Sarita's murder or the jewelry, he would have to tell.

"I can't find out anything about what happened to Sarita except what's on the news," Francisco was saying as he paced the small office. "Our usual sources have dried up. I've tried Victoria, but she doesn't know anything either."

Boxes of literature and envelopes took up most of the space, while a battered desk covered with a tangle of phones and three poured plastic chairs took up the rest. Francisco stopped to push a chair aside. "God, this is so unbelievable."

"To all of us." Autumn sat down in one of the uncomfortable chairs.

John Kinsellen stuck his head in. "Say, Fran, do you

have a minute? Oh, sorry. Didn't realize you had company."
He recognized Rennie and Autumn. "Hi guys. Some week,
huh?"

"Have you heard anything else about Sarita, John?"
Francisco asked.

"Nope. Police are being real closemouthed."

"Yeah, I'll bet," Francisco muttered. "This is one case
they won't want to botch."

"I dropped by to see you about these new ads. Gus
thinks they need to accentuate his family life more. Can you
spare a couple of minutes?"

Francisco hesitated. "Sure." He started to the door. "I'll
be right back, people. Oh, before I forget, Autumn, Iris
called here looking for you. Something about insurance
papers you have to sign. She sounded hysterical. I told her
we'd be at the High Museum after two so she's going to try
to catch you there."

"Poor Iris. I've had my cell off. Thanks, Fran. She's
speedy. I only spoke to her this morning."

"You're lucky to have her to chase all that around for
you," Rennie said absently.

He wanted to be upfront with Francisco but that might
not work. Might be better to dance around, start with the
photographs and go from there.

"I'm sure Iris is anxious to get back to a regular job,"
Autumn said.

"And you, too."

She breathed deeply. Her eyes crinkled. "Maybe."

He perched on the edge of Fran's desk. The cold
weather had put color in her usually pale cheeks, and she
looked so happy and fragile it hurt.

Was it a dream? Had he spent last night and this
morning in bed with her? Had she taken him into her body,
made him soar until he thought he would die from rapture?

Warmth filled him.

That wouldn't do. He swallowed. "Autumn, would you
mind if I spoke to Francisco alone for a moment?"

Quicksilver surprise told him she wanted to refuse, but
being Autumn, she agreed with a smile. "I'll get a fresh cup

of coffee when he comes back and try to call Iris. How's that?"

He wished he could express how glad he was that she was so uncomplaining. When she realized he could never live up to her standards, she was going to be hurt and maybe angry.

And maybe gone. An outcome too terrible to think about.

He got up and went over and brushed her forehead with his lips. "I love you."

She flashed her wonderful smile. "Don't forget it."

When Francisco returned, she left with a murmured excuse.

Rennie closed the door behind her.

How to begin? In the end, he plunged in. "The police know about you and Sarita, Francisco."

His brother's face emptied. "Did you tell them?"

Rennie couldn't read any shock or fear. "I didn't have to tell them anything. The investigator we spoke to this morning asked if I was related to you. So they've started digging into her past. They're bound to find out about you mouthing off when she gave you the brush-off."

Francisco's muscles tensed. He swallowed nervously.

So he wasn't as unconcerned as he seemed.

"How'd you hear about that? My mouthing off, I mean?"

"Sarita. She told me you said you'd like to see her dead."

The blankness transformed into anger. For big brother's benefit?

"Christ, Rennie, I never said that. Oh, when we broke up. I was so damned mad that I may have said some things she took that way. But I didn't mean them. I was upset because of what she did. You didn't tell the police, did you? I don't want them getting the wrong idea."

"Tell the police? You think I'd do that to you?"

The anger went out of Francisco. He sat down, put his head in his hands. "I could feel it coming. Sarita dumping me, I mean. It happened when I went with the Huertoles down to the Islands. Not long after I got the job with Gus. Sarita's stepfather has a house down there so she flew in for a week of pattycake. I knew something was wrong soon after she got there. Sure enough, the night before we came back she ended it."

Rennie already knew what had happened. Sarita had gotten Francisco in bed, caressed and seduced him until he was out of his mind, then called in her airplane pilot and made Fran watch as she mounted him.

She'd enjoyed telling Rennie about that, explaining piously how she'd thought Fran should learn from a real man what a woman likes. She'd intended for Rennie to share his brother's pain and humiliation, but he'd learned Sarita's tricks long ago.

Francisco hadn't.

He'd ached for Fran. Still did.

And Sarita had known he would, damn her.

He cleared his throat.

What happened between Francisco and Sarita, or him and Sarita didn't matter. Francisco had to protect himself.

"Listen, Francisco. You didn't care when Sarita dumped you. You knew from the beginning it wouldn't last."

"That isn't true." Fran sat up, his eyes bleary. "I did care, Rennie. I thought we had something more than sex going. Oh, yeah, maybe I subconsciously knew, but it was still..." Dull red blotched his complexion. "Out of the blue, she ended it. She up and ended it without even telling me why."

Would he have to spell it out? Was Francisco still so hung up on Sarita he didn't realize he was in trouble?

Rennie moved in, gripped his brother's shoulder. "You and she both knew it wouldn't last." He pronounced each word precisely, drilling it in. "You may have said a few things but there was absolutely no bitterness afterward. It was expedient for both of you to call it quits."

"Expedient? What do you mean?" Understanding sunk in. Francisco went pale. "They won't think I... Oh."

The brothers stared at one another before Francisco jumped up. "You don't think I'd hurt Sarita, do you?"

"It doesn't matter what I think. The police are the ones who matter. There were no hard feelings between you and Sarita," Rennie said doggedly.

Francisco licked his lip, finally looking as scared as Rennie felt. "We tried, but in the end we both decided it wouldn't work," he said slowly. "We didn't quarrel, if that's what you're asking. I may have said a few things, but she was pretty snide about my bed manners, calling me a two-bit Romeo without the equipment to back it up."

So Sarita's words still rankled.

"Forget what she said. Just remember you got over the break-up. You and she were still on good terms."

"All right." Francisco straightened his hair. "Besides, she said those things so I'd lose my temper and give her an excuse to break it off. I cooled off fast once I realized that."

"I'm not asking you to tell me anything about what was said." He knew too much already.

Sarita, gleeful at how she'd cut Francisco down, had repeated everything she'd said, every sneering innuendo, every hateful taunt about his masculinity. She had loved describing how Francisco cried when he watched her screwing another man, how he'd fought the pilot afterward.

Yeah, Rennie could imagine how it had gone. He'd seen her manipulate men until they exploded. The blood and violence turned her on.

Francisco hadn't known that. Afterward she'd sought out Rennie and pretended she wanted him to tell Francisco she was sorry, that she'd been carried away in the heat of the moment and hadn't meant her cruel words.

But Rennie was wise to Sarita and her ways.

The real reason Sarita had told Rennie about the breakup was to let Rennie know that Francisco was in love with her, and that she had destroyed him.

Francisco had been her payback for Rennie walking out on her.

Rennie shivered. Sarita had led him a long way down the path to hell. He'd wanted to help her, show her she was better than what she'd become, encourage her to change. Instead, he'd ended up in her cozy little sexual carousals. He was the one who'd changed.

At first, he'd assumed her self-esteem was the big problem. Sarita, darling of the critics and adored by the public, wanted everyone to love her. All her life, she'd wanted everyone to love her and couldn't stand it when someone held out. She'd do anything to make sure he fell into line.

But her low self-esteem was a symptom. One morning Rennie woke up to the stench of several sweaty bodies still hung over from alcohol and drugs, and wondered what he was doing. Sarita couldn't change because she didn't want to change. He didn't like her or himself any more. He left and never went back.

But Sarita didn't forgive slights. She'd taken Rennie's defection out on Francisco.

Back to what was important. "You and Sarita broke up by a mutual decision, Francisco. No hard feelings, no leftover grudges. That's all I know about it, all I want to know."

Francisco nodded, eyes darting back and forth. "That's what I'll tell the police if they ask."

"Yes. You do that. And Francisco."

Francisco had turned away but looked back. "What?"

"Something else. When Autumn made Sarita's photographs, Sarita was wearing some jewelry. Some jewelry that looks like that in the French exhibit at the High."

"Dani's exhibit?" Francisco's brow furrowed. "Sarita?"

If Francisco had expected the question, he would be careful to show surprise, but Rennie would stake his life his brother knew nothing. "Is there any way she could have gotten hold of it?"

"I wouldn't think so. I'm not privy to their security arrangement, but I'd guess Dani and her people never let that stuff out of their sight."

"Not even if a close friend asked to borrow it for some photo shots?"

Francisco's eyes widened and his mouth gaped. He laid a hand on a stack of boxes to steady himself. "Are you accusing me of taking it for Sarita?"

"No." The word exploded in the air. Quick. Too quick. "Not at all. But let me know if you think of any way Sarita could have got access to it, okay?"

"Sure." Francisco rubbed a hand over his eyes, like he was gauging what Rennie meant.

Better let him know Autumn was involved, too. "I think Autumn's tied into it because she photographed Sarita in the jewelry."

"Autumn did what?" Again the surprise wasn't feigned.

Rennie explained about the butt bag being slit and why he thought the fall was connected. "So Autumn's going to stay with us for a while."

Francisco, stunned, didn't even leer. "Yeah. Okay. I guess that... Autumn... I can't believe this."

He looked frightened, but who could tell what was going through Francisco's mind?

Rennie wasn't sure he wanted to know.

Chapter Eighteen

AT THE RECEPTION desk of Gus Huertole's campaign headquarters, Autumn waited patiently for Rennie.

So her feelings were hurt. So what? After all these years, she was used to being excluded.

I'm just being hyper-sensitive.

Not that telling herself that helped, not even after the past night when he had told her he loved her and proved it so sweetly. She'd assumed, in her happiness, his loving her meant the two of them would share everything, that she would never again feel like a child looking into a candy store window.

Nope. She was still the odd man out.

That's what gnawed at her gut, that unhappy awareness of being a stranger looking on while the other kids had fun.

Once when she was ten, playing dolls at the Degardovera home with Laney and Norma, Reseda had stormed in after someone broke a porcelain Madonna that normally sat on a shelf in the hallway. Reseda demanded to know who'd done it.

Norma said, "Probably the dog, Mom," without looking up from dressing her Barbie.

"Yes, Chief was in there earlier, Mom," Laney added, busy arranging her own doll's hair.

From across the room where Fran and some of his friends were watching television, he called, "Chief wouldn't mean to, Mom. You know how his tail catches things."

Autumn knew Fran and his friends were the cause of the

broken statue because she'd seen them roughhousing with a football in the hall when she first got there. But she sat quiet as a mouse while the Degardoveras perjured themselves. None of them asked her to keep quiet, but she still didn't say anything.

She had rationalized that she wasn't lying, that she would be truthful if Reseda specifically asked her whether she knew anything about what had happened.

But the rest of the Degardovera children, including Norma and Laney, had known and covered up. When they never spoke of the broken statue again, she realized they wouldn't even admit to her who'd broken it.

However much she loved the Degardoveras, she would never be one of them. No matter much how she wanted to be.

Except Rennie had admitted he loved her. That ought to count for something, shouldn't it? She should automatically become part of the tacit conspiracy of trust the Degardoveras shared.

At least where Rennie was concerned.

Guess she was wrong.

The Degardoveras closed ranks whenever outside forces threatened one of them. Closed ranks as Rennie and Fran did now, coming out from the back office and standing together in a solid front against the world and everyone else, including her.

That was what hurt.

The men's grave faces made them seem more alike than ever.

"It'll work out," Rennie was saying, "I'm going to take Autumn by her place and let her get some clothes. She's going to stay at Mom's house for a few days."

"No, I'm not." She would learn to live with exclusion from their councils and get over smarting because she was still an outsider. No matter how she felt about Rennie, she was responsible for herself and could still make her own decisions. "I'll be as safe at my condo as I would at Reseda's."

So there.

"Autumn, we all agree these things are connected, that someone may be…" Rennie hesitated. "Someone may be after you. Maybe whoever it is thinks Sarita told you something. Or maybe you saw something you don't realize you saw."

"She didn't, and I didn't." She looked at her watch. "I thought we were going to the exhibit."

"Oh, damn." Eschewing his usual care, Fran ran his fingers through his curls without noticing he'd mussed them. "I forgot about it. Laney and Norma will be waiting for us."

"Then we'd better go," Autumn said with false cheer.

Rennie looked at her a long moment before his lazy grin hit her, warmed her despite her disillusionment. "Whatever the lady wants." He picked up her hand, held it.

She let him.

She loved him.

Even though she was an interloper. Even though she was an outsider. Rennie had made love to her so beautifully that she had forgotten for a while he would never treat her as one of the Degardoveras, never turn to her as he did his family.

He loves me, she told herself fiercely. *He said he loves me. And I know I love him.*

When she held his hand to her cheek, Fran's brows rose. He launched a darkening stare at her and then at Rennie. "So that's the way things are heading, huh? Big brother moved in on you while I was looking the other way? Kind of fast, wasn't it?"

She shouldn't have been so blatant, but it was hard to hide her feelings for Rennie. "You make it sound like Rennie's a trespasser."

"I thought you and I had an understanding." Fran pushed his bottom lip out in a gesture he'd long grown out of. "I guess I was wrong."

"Now, Fran. Don't pout." She tried to tease him out of his ill humor. "I was a shoulder to cry on. We both know I've never been your type."

"I didn't think you were Rennie's type, either." Fran's

eyes moved from her to his brother. "Or is it retaliation? Is that what it is, Rennie? Are you using Autumn to pay me back for Sarita? Because I dared go where big brother couldn't make it? Because I went where you'd already gone and failed, right between Sarita Sartowe's thighs? Is that it?"

Shocked, Autumn at first didn't understand Fran's crudity, then when she did, she uttered a little cry, though it must have been in her mind for neither of the men looked at her.

"Don't be foolish, Fran," Rennie said wearily.

The blood roared in Autumn's ears.

She had accepted Jane's existence as a part of Rennie's life. Jane didn't matter after Rennie said he loved her.

But Sarita? What had he called her? Every man's fantasy.

Rennie and Sarita? She didn't want to imagine them together.

Fran's hands clenched. "I took Sarita away from you so now you take Autumn away from me. What's the old saying, sauce for the goose, sauce for the gander? Is that what you're thinking?"

"Sarita was never mine for you to take." Rennie's voice was deathly quiet. "No one ever owned Sarita."

"No, but you would have liked to, wouldn't you?" Fran's voice was rising. "She told me how you begged, pleaded with her when she got sick and tired of you and your scruples. She bragged about you calling her on the phone, sending her flowers, trying to get her back after she dropped you."

Rennie and Sarita.

Autumn wanted to ask, to break in and demand Rennie tell her it wasn't true, that he hadn't done what Fran said he'd done.

But he had. She could look at his face and see.

I don't believe it. Answer him, Rennie. Tell him he doesn't know what he's talking about. Tell him you didn't love Sarita.

Instead, Rennie shook his head. "Don't do this to our friendship, Francisco. Don't do this to yourself. You're worth a dozen Saritas, can't you see that? She was a cheat and a liar. She was a waste of your time and mine."

Fran jerked as if yanked by a string attached to his body. Pain, pure, jagged, white-hot pain showed before he turned away. Pain that she understood and empathized with. When he turned back, bleakness remained. "You shouldn't use Autumn to get back at me for Sarita, Rennie."

"Francisco. Don't you know me better than that? I love Autumn. I hope she'll marry me."

The unsolicited, clear declaration that once would have given her everything she desired, filtered through her mind and heart.

This is what I wanted. I should be happy. I am happy.

Fran swung toward her. "Is that true?"

I am happy. She hadn't waited all these years, longed for Rennie all this time, dreamed of him all those lonely nights, to turn his proposal down. No matter how forced it was.

She loved him and wouldn't throw away her opportunity to have him. No matter how numb her heart had become after imagining him with Sarita, she still loved him. "If that was a proposal, Rennie, I accept. Yes, Fran, I love him."

Strange how calm she sounded. No one could tell her heart was broken.

Fran didn't want to believe her. "Even if he's using you?"

Strength returned. She could overlook anything. Jane, Sarita, however many women Rennie had known in the past.

She didn't care. She was his lover now and that was all that mattered.

But the image of him and Sarita together still cut through her. Why hadn't he told her?

Because she was an outsider, because she would never be the one he turned to with his intimate sorrows and joys. Because she was and would ever remain on the outside.

"Even if he's using you, Autumn?" Fran persisted.

She glanced at Rennie. A melancholy hinted at the faint unhappiness she had suspected before.

That shadow isn't there because he's thinking of Sarita. He's upset because of what Fran is saying. He's worried about Fran.

She clung to that belief.

Rennie spoke to his brother, but his words were for her. "I'm not using Autumn, Francisco. I would never use Autumn."

"Nobody's using me for anything, Fran." Her voice was her own, clear and prosaic despite how disembodied she felt, how separate from everything around her. *Sarita and Rennie.* "I'm surprised you'd say such a thing about your brother. He's right. You should know him better than that."

"Should I?" Fran's teeth flashed but his grin was mirthless. He didn't take his eyes off Rennie, but Rennie didn't flinch. "If you're not trying to get back at me, then you're using Autumn to take your mind off somebody you can't have. Either way, it's wrong."

Autumn's gut clenched. At some point Rennie had loosed her fingers or she had pulled away from him. Her hands hurt. She was gripping them together too tightly.

"I wouldn't do anything like that to Autumn, Francisco. Not to anyone, but especially not to Autumn. And I can't believe you'd think that." Rennie's voice was quieter than before. The skin over his cheeks and around his eyes was so tight she could see his bones. "I care too much for her. I hope she knows that."

"Of course I do." That was her own voice so calm, so reassuring, so matter-of-fact.

Rennie's tightness relaxed. He pried her clenched hands apart and tucked one through his arm. "Isn't it time we left to meet the others at the High? They'll be wondering where we are."

Outside, the day was bright, with blue skies and fleecy white clouds and fifty degree temperatures better suited to March than December. The building shadows remained minimal, allowing the sun leeway to fall on parked cars and pedestrians alike.

The exceptional weather was wasted on Autumn. The ten minute walk to the High Museum between the two men was interminable, with Fran stiff and removed on one side of her while Rennie's fingers entwined with hers on the other. No joy bubbled up as it should from Rennie's proposal.

She wouldn't cry, no matter how she felt like it.

****

THE BUILDING HOUSING the High Museum of Arts rises like a modern fortress at Peachtree and Sixteenth Street. Its poured concrete seems to be all circles and squares and glass. Large white porcelain tiles frame and protect the sides, and give it a dazzling pristine appearance. Designed by architect Richard Meier, the striking edifice houses Atlanta's art treasures and hosts visiting exhibits from around the world. Atlantans take great pride in the High.

As Autumn and the two brothers approached the ramp, she ignored the large and hideous modern sculpture that towered over the grounds beyond. Even the graceful statue in the Rodin tradition that surveyed the sidewalk from their left barely warranted a glance. The tension between Rennie and Fran consumed her. She ought to do something but she didn't know what.

Their feet clomped on the walk as they went toward the curved underbelly of the building that housed the entrance. Two hardy souls ate lunch beside a merrily playing fountain below them, but the usual lines of impatient school kids were absent.

Good. She didn't think she could stand the noise. Not with the headache forming in her right temple.

Inside the lobby, Norma and Laney chatted with a security man and the admittance attendant until Laney caught sight of them. "Oh, there they are! Come on, Norma. Autumn, we heard about the fire. What happened? Did anything get saved?"

In the light-filled atrium, Rennie dropped her arm as the sisters threw question after question at her. In the flurry of answers and explanations and exclamations, Fran's tightlipped silence went unnoticed along with Autumn's tension.

She was grateful Rennie sensed her confusion and had stepped aside so that he wouldn't subject her to more of his sisters' scrutiny. After Fran's attack, she couldn't deal with Laney's excitement and Norma's squeals if they realized what was going on between her and Rennie.

Or worse, their censure. They had matched Rennie up with Victoria Montezela and might disapprove of Autumn's horning in.

One other thing to worry about. *Oh, my head.*

Before they started up the ramp to the exhibit on the third floor, John appeared. In the flurry of Laney's affectionate greetings, Fran tried to excuse himself from the tour. "I don't need to be wasting time here." His glance challenged Rennie and rebuked Autumn.

"Not a waste of time," said John. "Good PR."

With that, and in the face of his two sisters' annoyed indignation, Fran sulkily agreed to stay a few minutes, but strode on toward the elevators without waiting for anyone.

On the third floor, *Ornaments for the Human Body* was being presented. The spectacular jewelry lay behind sparkling glass, in high and low cases, and throughout different galleries. Viewers wandered at leisure, pausing to admire and rave to bystanders.

John and Fran fell back, surveying the crowds while Laney dragged Autumn to the first case. Norma, who had quarreled with Paul, tagged along with her sister and Autumn, anxious to confide details. "Then I told him if he couldn't come today after Dani had gone to the trouble to get us passes, not to bother coming over tonight. Can you blame me?"

Autumn's head throbbed. Rennie moved up beside her to stare at a sumptuous jeweled tiara.

Laney, attention torn away from the tiara to counsel her sister, groaned. "Norma, do you like Paul?"

"Of course I like him."

"Well, you act like you're trying to drive him away. You can't expect a man to take criticism all the time and still hang around."

"I don't criticize him. But I'm not going to be a doormat either."

Norma would never let a man, any man, walk all over her. Not like Autumn.

She put two fingers to her aching temple.

As the sisters moved away, arguing the merits of playing

hard-to-get versus ready-to-fall, John and Fran strolled up discussing campaign issues.

Fran hadn't said one word to Autumn or Rennie on the way to the museum or after entering.

Good grief, if she wasn't careful, she would alienate the entire Degardovera family.

As if reading her mind, Rennie took her arm and led her to the next case, where they stopped and pretended to be looking inside at the glitter of precious gems and metals.

She couldn't focus.

After an awkward silence, he said, "About Sarita and me."

"You don't owe me an explanation, Rennie." She didn't want to hear what he had to say, not here in the museum after their confrontation with Fran, when her defenses were down and she was so miserable. She wasn't sure she ever wanted to hear anything about Sarita from him.

He put a hand against the glass protecting items worn centuries before. "When I first went out to Los Angeles, Sarita looked me up. Mom had told her mother that I was out there, and her mother told her. You know we were in high school together. We'd worked on projects and gone to the prom and done other things together. She was a different person then. Still promiscuous, but I liked her sense of humor. Her optimism. She was always upbeat. And she was fun. When she called, I was glad to hear from her."

"It doesn't matter, Rennie." Her stomach twisted. "I don't need to hear this."

She had fought her personal demons concerning Rennie's relationship with Jane and had put them aside when he'd said he didn't miss Jane anymore and that he loved her, Autumn.

But an affair with Sarita was different.

Rennie himself had described Sarita as every man's fantasy. She'd wondered if he fantasized about Sarita, longed for her like other men, but until today she hadn't let herself be tormented by it.

To discover he actually had fantasized about Sarita, gone further...

Rennie and Sarita had been lovers.

There, she'd faced it. There was something else she had to face. Could any ordinary woman live up to Sarita's memory? After having been with Sarita, would Rennie be satisfied with a nonentity like Autumn?

Her heart felt as if it weighed ten tons.

Rennie's hand dropped from the glass. His shoulder touched hers as they stared at some sort of jade pendant collection that she later remembered little about except that it lay on cream colored velveteen.

"Come over here so we can talk."

She didn't want to talk, but he pulled her to a side corner. So close his breath warmed her ear, he said, "Autumn, I never loved Sarita. Not like I love you, not even like I loved Jane. Sarita came to see me and she looked lost, like… And I was homesick as anything, out there by myself with no friends, no family, not much money. She was just starting to make it. Having someone like her interested in me was flattering. And she seemed as glad to see me as I was to see someone from home."

"Rennie, you don't have to tell me this." *I don't want to know.*

"I do have to tell you, Autumn. You've entitled to know what I am. With Sarita, I thought I was helping her. Then I got sucked in and… I told myself I loved her. But it wasn't love. It was something else. Sex. Weakness. I don't know. By the time I realized what she was, I was in real deep."

He kept his mouth at her ear, not looking at her. "She liked to take men and wrap them up in knots. One man died because she set him against his friend. Oh, she liked kinky sex and group sex and whatever else was in fashion. Designer drugs, too. But she really got off on getting men to fight over her. The blood, the idea that they were ready to kill each other over her… It jacked her up like… I woke up one morning and realized I hated myself and had to get out. I told her I had to concentrate on my studies. And I did."

She could imagine the scene. He'd had plenty of experience at telling a lovesick female he would be her friend but not her lover, that she'd find someone else. He'd make it seem so logical, be so reasonable.

She knew firsthand how smooth he could make it.

"Was she upset?" How could she sound so calm?

"Upset? You could say that." Rennie gave something like a chuckle. A bitter chuckle. "I don't know why. I was simply another man to her. I sent her flowers like Francisco said, but it was to soften my leaving. Not in hopes of making up with her. I had no intentions of getting involved with her again. Ever."

"Did you continue to see her?" *Go ahead, turn the knife.*

"We kept in touch. I wish we hadn't. She met Francisco through me. When he stayed with me last year, we ran into her and," he made a wry face, "given the two of them and their appetites, it wasn't long before the inevitable occurred. I liked her, Autumn, at least the person she could have been. She was so damned cheerful, so full of energy and ambition. I kept waiting for her to change, but she couldn't. Or wouldn't. I never loved her. I don't think I've loved anyone like I love you."

People kept sliding by their corner, chatting and laughing like everything was normal. Normal like last week before…

She wanted to believe Rennie, wanted to ignore the sick jealousy rushing through her, but what if he was mistaken? What if someone like Sarita was what he wanted deep down in those hidden depths he guarded so closely?

Something like weariness touched his eyes. "I told you." He lowered his voice further as a jabbering group of pubescent females rushed past. "I told you you'd be disappointed in me if you ever came to know me, but you didn't believe me. You and I don't share the same background, the same ideas. Now do you understand what I was trying to say? I've done things I'm not proud of. Things you'd never understand or approve of."

He waited but she couldn't speak.

When he threw his hands out and turned away, she forgot her headache.

She was losing him. She would lose him if she didn't do something.

Like stamp her foot. "Now who's putting words in whose mouth!"

He jumped, turned back at her show of temper.

She didn't retreat. "Yes, I mean it. You keep accusing me of putting words in your mouth when you're as bad as I am. If I'm disappointed in anything, Rennie, it's that you don't trust me enough to tell me these things, that you let them come up and slap me in the face when I'm not expecting them."

"Autumn." He looked around as a crowd came toward them, led her into a mercifully empty showcase on the balcony. "It isn't that I don't trust you. You must know I trust you."

She pushed him away. "I don't know anything of the kind. Keeping secrets about Fran and Sarita, about you and Sarita. Kicking me out when you and Fran were discussing whatever it was you were discussing this afternoon. Does that look like you trust me?"

When he would have spoken, she shook her finger at him. "Don't think I don't know you're afraid I'll tell whoever it is whatever it is you're scared Fran's done. Do you think I can't see what's going on?"

"What?" His brow wrinkled.

Gibberish. She'd spouted off gibberish.

She hit her forehead. "I know you don't trust me. But I won't tell anyone anything about Fran. Why won't you trust me?"

"It isn't that I don't trust you. I don't want you to get involved in something that's not your fault." He licked his lips. "I should never have gotten sucked in by Sarita. I knew it was wrong, but I rationalized it because I wanted to. That's the kind of man you think you're in love with. Someone who can't stick to his principles."

"Damn your principles." Tears prickled, but she never cried.

She turned to hide them and found they had wandered over to the balcony railing.

A long ramp curved down to the atrium. Inside it, a man dressed in a business overcoat with a red and green scarf entered, stopped, and surveyed his surroundings. When he looked up, she recognized the symmetrical face and thick brows.

An ordinary man. A man that could show up anywhere.

Something about the confidence in the mouth and chin made him a likely subject for a portrait.

She'd seen him someplace, but couldn't recall where.

Not that it mattered. She was too close to losing Rennie. If she didn't do something, say something, he'd leave her.

And she couldn't bear it. If he had sex with every woman he met and would always keep his heart locked away from hers, she would learn to live with it. She was his, and had been from the time she was five years old, when hiding behind Reseda's cushiony hip, she had peeked out to see him smiling at her and decided that maybe life wasn't so bad.

She could have Rennie or lose him. It was that simple.

Gripping the metal railing of the balcony, she used a long, shuddering breath to compose herself. "So you made a mistake when you were young and homesick and lonely, and let yourself be seduced into a life of evil by a glamorous actress. So what? Big deal. I don't care."

"You say that now but—"

"I mean it. I don't care about your principles, or about your girlfriends or about whatever secrets you want to keep from me. I love you and I want to marry you and if you've gone to bed with a hundred Saritas, I still wouldn't care. You can't back out, it's too late. You proposed to me in front of Fran."

He stood for a long moment. Then he reached out to touch her hair. Tenderly, wearily. "I won't back out."

Fear and anger fled. Relief flooded her. "Good. Let's go look at the rest of the exhibit."

"I'm at your disposal. Now and forever."

She turned and gripped the railing to hide her misting eyes.

Down below, in the airy atrium, the man in the holiday scarf she almost but not quite recognized, crossed the lobby.

Forgotten scents of pizza and wood ashes and beer swept through her memory.

Helen. That's where she'd seen him.

"Rennie. That man down there by the far column." She leaned over the railing. "He was in Helen."

"Which man?"

"The one in the overcoat and scarf. He's headed back toward the offices now."

"He was in Helen? Are you sure?"

"Yes. I saw him in the pizza place and then in the elevator when we took Laney and John's suitcase up to their room. I remember thinking he had such an ordinary face, it would be hard to do a portrait. Except for the chin and jaw. That made me wonder how to catch him in the right light to…"

They looked at each other. "Laney said there was a gun," she said slowly. Where did that come from?

Rennie understood. Without a word, he took off.

What if the man was dangerous?

"Rennie!"

He didn't stop.

She began to run, too, getting to the entrance of the three story ramp as he started down, then brushing past climbers and nearly running over a man in a wheelchair as she hurried to catch up.

Chapter Nineteen

SAM BOGATTI HAD found her office earlier, but it was empty. Now she was there, but she had company.

He listened outside the door. Shit, who was she railing at like that? Classy dame like that shouldn't know such words, much less repeat them. Today's women were bad as men.

"You were responsible! You cheating, lying sonofabitch! I trusted you, like you said, I trusted you and you feed me this crap!"

"Dani, calm down. For chrissake, there's no use in bringing the entire staff in here." The man's voice was deep, modulated. An orator's voice. Soothing, rational.

Unlike Dani Huertole's.

"Why?" she asked plaintively. "Why did you do it? I would have worked my fingers to the bone for you. I would have campaigned, talked you up, done whatever you wanted. I would have looked the other way whenever you pulled off your dirty little deals. All I asked was one tiny favor."

"I love you, Dani, and I tried."

"If you loved me, you'd never have done this to me!"

"It wasn't my fault. I swear it wasn't my fault. Think about it. You'll realize I couldn't have helped it."

"Then whose fault was it?" Her voice had quieted, but something in its steely control alarmed Sam. "Who will you blame it on, Gus?"

Sam was used to hysterical females and angry men, but he didn't like this false calm.

This broad's frigging crazy-mad and ready to blow.

"Dani, you haven't thought this out." The man remained reasonable. "There was no other way. If there had been any other way out, I would have found it."

"I loved her."

"I'm sorry, but you'll get over it. After you think about the choices." The modulated voice broke, rose. "What are you doing with—Dani, don't—Wait!"

The air exploded. Once.

And again.

Sam knew then. "Shit!" He wrenched open the door.

Two more shots filled the air.

Gus Huertole lay on his back behind a heavy desk, eyes staring upward at the tiled ceiling and mouth open as a stream of blood colored his shirtfront.

"Holy shit!"

Sam's exclamation jerked Dani Huertole around, gun still clutched in her hand. Eyes were wild, face contorted in fury. Too frightening for him to approach. No time to rush her.

"Get back," she snarled.

Oh shit. Her gun swung up. Toward him.

His mouth dried. His wife. His boys.

Holding up his hands, he stood still. "It's okay."

The Ruger was in the back of his belt. Why the shit hadn't he taken it out before he went in?

Something had told him he shoulda dropped the job. He shoulda listened.

His heart hammered in his ears. He took a step back.

A sudden jerk of her hand put the barrel into her mouth. Before he could do anything, say anything, she fired.

Blood and brains spattered the wall. Her body slumped against the desk. Gore everywhere.

Her head fell over, away from him.

Lucky he didn't shit his pants.

Light from outside streamed through the windows, touching each detail, brightening Huertole's white shirt against the redness, turning the navy of Dani's blouse to bright blue, bringing out the red glints in the cherry desk, turning the gray of the gun beneath still fingers to silver.

Highlighting the bloody pulp in her hair and on the walls.

Someone behind him whimpered. He whirled, saw the photographer frozen behind her boyfriend. Both stared past him with wide horrified eyes.

The Merriwell woman was the whimperer.

He moved for the door, but something in her heartbroken face touched him.

"It'll be okay. Some people don't know when they got it good, do they?" He patted her kindly on the shoulder as he went past. "You oughta be thankful it wasn't you. It coulda been, you know."

He brushed by. They stood unmoving, her and her man. Still stunned. Them kind of people weren't used to death like this.

Escaping, he felt tons lighter.

The wacko dame had done his job for him. Unbelievable.

"Forget the photographer for now," Bernie had said. "We got bigger problems. Take care of Huertole's wife. We got the jewelry back to her in time, but she's still a loose cannon waiting to go off. If she does, Huertole's chances for winning are slim and none. Nobody's going to vote for a man whose wife's having an affair with another woman."

So Dani Huertole had taken care of herself. But she'd also taken with her the candidate that Bernie's client had spent so much money to protect.

Bernie's client was going to be one pissed hombre.

What the shit. This was looking more and more like a good time to quit the business.

In the rental car, Sam popped a fresh piece of gum into his mouth and started toward the airport.

The trip home on the small airplane decided him. Actually, an air pocket over Kentucky where he spewed the enchilada he'd had for lunch decided him.

This is it, he promised. For sure they'd find his body parts strewed over the frigging mountain peaks.

No more jobs involving nice people who didn't deserve to be hit. No more rides in frigging little planes that could crash at any time. No more getting calls in the middle of the night and having to take off when the kid had a big game the next day.

He'd got enough money socked away. His wife was a frugal woman, not like some of the bimbos Bernie took up with.

If he bought into that motel like her brother wanted him to do, they could manage real good. Even with the costs of college for two boys. Especially if they could get hockey scholarships.

Yeah man, I'm quitting.

In a small airport outside Chicago, Sam reached his own car and opened a new piece of gum to celebrate his deliverance from the big hand of the sky.

That's all she wrote, folks.

Kinda nice he hadn't had to off the photographer.

She and the big guy made a good-looking couple.

****

SOME DAYS AFTER the tragedy at the High Museum, Autumn worked in her condo while Rennie hung out. She was studying real estate specifications for an office in a new building near Lawrenceville when Rennie's cell rang.

After he hung up he relayed an invitation. Laney wanted him and Autumn to come to her house for dinner the following evening.

"Mom got in, and she and the rest of the family will be there. I think the idea's to throw a kind of engagement party for us."

Autumn dropped her papers. "Your mother knows? Who told her? What did she say?"

Rennie, his back to her as he searched for the remote control, shrugged. "I don't know. I haven't seen her or talked to her."

"Well, what did Laney say she said? She doesn't approve, does she? Of you and me, I mean. That's why Laney's having us over to her house instead of us going to Reseda's."

"Don't be silly." Rennie turned, remote in hand. "I imagine Laney's having us over to help cheer up John.

From what she says, he's pretty concerned about the hearing coming up."

"But John didn't know about Gus's connection to that drug cartel. He's an innocent victim. He and Fran both."

Rennie sat down beside her. "The government lawyers may not believe that. He and Francisco will both have to answer some pretty hard questions. But they'll be all right."

She sighed, went back to her own personal worries. "So what did Reseda say when she found out about us? Laney must have said something."

He shrugged. "That she's a little disappointed because she had you and Francisco paired up, but that as long as one of us had the good sense to get you in the family, she's okay with it."

"She didn't say that. You made that up."

Rennie chuckled. "She's thrilled, absolutely thrilled according to Laney. I can't tell you her exact words. I told you, I haven't talked to her."

"Then you'd better pick up the phone, don't you think?"

He cut his eyes at her and made a sound of disgust. "There's a program on Georgia football about to come on. It's a preview of their bowl game."

She handed him the phone.

Reseda was volubly thrilled.

****

A SMELL OF RICE and beans and roast pork met them as they entered Laney's apartment. They had come early, and no one else was there. A normal family evening except that everyone was still trying to make sense out of what had happened with the Huertoles.

"Dani's letter told everything," John said.

He had taken the Huertoles' deaths hard. He'd been close to both Gus and Dani for years.

"She told about Gus's connections to the cartel from South America, how he promised if they helped him get elected, he'd ease off enforcement so they could transport the drugs through Georgia, how long he'd been working with them. I can't believe I never guessed where his money was coming from."

"How could you?" Laney asked. "You were busy finding political agendas that would get him elected, making sure he kept appointments with the right people, keeping track of the paperwork. You had nothing to do with whatever deals he made with those people."

"I hope the investigators see it like that," he muttered.

"Of course they will. You had nothing to do with Gus Huertole's bad decisions." Autumn reinforced Laney's reassurances. "But what about Sarita? How did Dani get involved with her?"

"The Huertoles met Sarita last spring, when they were at the Islands. Sarita had come down to be with Fran, but she and Dani struck it off right away. Evidently it was love at first sight." John looked perplexed. "I would never have thought Dani Huertole was a lesbian."

"Sarita swung both ways," Rennie said tonelessly. "I learned that in California."

"Dani must have been latent. All those years I saw her with Gus, I knew they weren't overly affectionate, but they got along." John was still bewildered. "They were so suited to each other. It's just so hard to believe."

"So Dani borrowed the jewelry for Sarita?" Autumn asked. "How could she get away with it?"

"She was in charge of security arrangements. She had her own keys. The pieces arrived in Atlanta ten days before the exhibit was to open, and she was the one to check them out, make sure they'd arrived unharmed, then put them in the safe. The security folks witnessed it. Nobody thought about her taking them out again. Since they weren't going into their cases till the day before the exhibition, she figured Sarita would have them back."

"So she loaned them to Sarita," Rennie murmured.

"That's what she said."

"Because of the photo session," Autumn said sadly. "Sarita was pleased with the jewelry, but I never guessed it was from the exhibition. I just took pictures of her in it."

John nodded. "Then Sarita took them with her to LA. Dani had to tell Gus. He hit the roof. He knew if the story broke, he'd never get elected. I imagine he was running scared, because the cartel wouldn't like investing all that money and time for nothing. So he used them to get the jewelry back."

"Which they did, but they also killed Sarita," Rennie said. "After Autumn had taken the photos with her wearing the jewelry."

"It's all so horrible." Laney shuddered.

John took his wife's hand. "They think Gus didn't know about the pictures. When his backers found out, they were the ones who decided Autumn had to go, too."

"So that guy with the gun I saw in Helen was real after all." Laney smirked. "Even though my husband refused—"

"Laney, I've apologized and apologized for making fun of you. What do you want? Blood?"

"I have something much better in mind," Laney said demurely.

"But it didn't matter in the end," Autumn interrupted the marital mending of fences. "When Dani heard about Sarita's murder, she knew Gus and his friends were behind it."

John sighed. "She called Gus, hysterical. Fran said she was upset, but he didn't know what about. When she came into the office looking for him, she looked wild. Well, you saw her. But still, I would never have guessed she meant to kill him."

Autumn shivered, remembering Gus Huertole's terror-filled scream and the shots that followed. "No one ever knows what goes on in a marriage."

"No one ever knows what goes on between two people," Rennie said. "Except for the people involved."

We'll share that. Rennie and I will know and everyone else can guess but we'll stand up and face the world side by side. And I won't be shut out any more. I'll have him.

It was a nice vision, her and Rennie making their way through life together.

The doorbell rang and Norma came in followed by a lively Reseda, an older version of Laney. "Autumn!" She hugged and kissing her on both cheeks. "Sweet, sweet Autumn, you don' know how happy I am. I was so scared some insensitive arrogant person like that Victoria whatshername that Laney brought home would catch Rennie."

Her daughters' mouths dropped open. "Mom! Victoria is a perfectly nice person."

Reseda ignored them and turned to Rennie. "And you. *Mi nino retrasado.*" She playfully patted his cheek. "It took you long enough to see what was right under your nose, didn't it? I could have had grandchildren by now." She glared at Laney and Norma. "Maybe the only ones I will ever have if I leave it to my daughters."

Norma huffed. "I'm not even married."

Laney opened her mouth and snapped it shut. If she were a teapot, steam would be pouring out of her ears.

Rennie distracted his mother from her daughters' shortfalls. "So I'm slow, Mom." He put one arm around her and the other around Autumn. "You'll have to bear that in mind."

"So long as you make up for it." Reseda beamed. "You are not getting any younger." She frowned at her daughters. "Any of you."

Laney rolled her eyes.

Norma sighed.

Autumn looked at Rennie.

Rennie flicked his trademark glance toward her, and her heart swelled.

She'd love to photograph that slanting glance. Have him face his computer, but turn his eyes toward the camera. With that same laidback smile.

Had she ever been this happy? If she had, she couldn't remember. Maybe she'd never be so happy again. This moment deserved to be packed away in silver wrapping along with that of their first night together.

Reseda plumped herself down and took Autumn's hand in both hers. "So tell me, *chica dulce*," she murmured, "do you think you and Rennie will be starting your family right away?"

"No," Autumn said promptly. "We have to get married first. We're thinking about five years or so for an engagement period. What do you think?"

After her shriek, Reseda told them what she thought. At great length.

The End

If you enjoyed this book, please consider leaving a review to help others discover it. Several sites offer places for reader reviews including

Amazon at:

http://www.amazon.com/Intimate-Portraits-Cheryl-B-Dale-ebook/dp/B00B35SWCY/ref=la_B007L4NVD6_1_4?s=books&ie=UTF8&qid=1383949469&sr=1-4

and Barnes and Noble at:

http://www.barnesandnoble.com/w/intimate-portraits-cheryl-dale/1116291943?ean=2940148511915

If you do have the time to leave a review, please accept my sincere appreciation and thanks.

LOSING DAVID by Cheryl B. Dale

A vintage mystery with suspense and romance, inspired by tobacco heir R.J. Reynolds' Sapelo Island.

1962. An era of rotary phones and clacking typewriters. Sleepy southern towns cling to tradition while determined blacks and soft-spoken women want change. Still, one constant remains: respectable people, like elderly attorney Lawrence Wykerton, prize integrity above everything.

All his life, Lawrence distinguishes right from wrong so confidently, a close friend called him the only honest lawyer in Georgia. Sadly, that same man died before a son/heir David vanished at sea in a boating accident.

For sixteen years, sole trustee Lawrence has safeguarded his friend's estate. Now he must turn it over to a dilettante, a man who'll dismantle and sell businesses. His friend would never have approved the destruction of the local economy, but Lawrence will do his duty however unpalatable. Until he learns the man murdered David.

His ethics fray. When he finds an unsavory actor who resembles David, they completely snap. He hires the actor to resurrect David, trap the killer, and save his friend's legacy.

But David's childhood playmate, as moral as Lawrence once was, appears. If she exposes the truth, Lawrence will forfeit everything—his career, his reputation, even his freedom. And David's murderer will go unpunished.

Available 2014 at Amazon and other booksellers

"If *Losing David* were a film, it would blend parts of *Charade* and *To Catch a Thief* into an *Anastasia* set on a fictional barrier island off the southern coast."

LOSING DAVID

AVAILABLE 2014

Excerpt from *LOSING DAVID*
by
Cheryl B. Dale

PROLOGUE

"Temptation"
As Performed by Perry Como (1945)
Music by Nacio Herb Brown
Lyrics by Arthur Freed

Harmony Island, Coastal Georgia
June, 1946

THERE WASN'T A damn thing personal about it. He didn't hate the boys. Okay, Robby was a sour-faced brat, but David was okay. He liked David.

Didn't matter now. They were in his way so they had to go.

This isn't real. I can't be doing this. Not Theodore Rhodes Pack. Factory manager, ex-army lieutenant, Vandy almost-grad. He couldn't be toting a drugged kid. Not him. No sir.

Theo seemed to float far above, spying on an anonymous man slogging toward the dock. Wreathed in flimsy night clouds, he could see David bob on the other man's shoulders. Watch David's legs dangle, head loll. Hear some man who wasn't Theo grunt under David's weight.

The crunch of the shelled path banished frivolous imaginings. The two Theos melded.

Hallucinations, that's all. Tricks of the mind.

Spanish moss streamed from the great live oaks to block all but the most obstinate moonbeam, but no matter. He knew the way by heart.

Not much farther. Getting hard to breathe. Good thing he was fit. Who'd think a skinny sixteen-year-old kid would be so heavy? If the boys had agreed to a moonlight cruise like he'd suggested, he could've slipped them the mickeys on board. Saved himself this nightmare.

No nightmare. James was really dead. *Screw you, James.*

James Harmony, richer than the Rockefellers. His larger-than-life cousin who overshadowed celebrities, bested government auditors, trampled competitors. Trampled *him*.

He was too winded to laugh. Not like when Sondra's secretary had phoned earlier to tell him James had died. He'd almost sniggered. Lucky his legs buckled and plopped him down on the gossip bench. When she asked him to break the news to the boys, he'd dredged up the proper gravitas. "Yes. Of course I will."

Good thing he'd chosen his words. David, croquet mallet in hand and curious—the phone seldom rang when James was off the island—materialized as he hung up. "Who was that?"

He'd improvised. "A friend in trouble but I can't help him."

"Gee, that's too bad." David took after his mother. Softhearted. Gullible. Not like James. "Feel like a quick game while it's still light out?"

"Sure thing."

Theo, mind on other things, had lost.

His toe caught a root and he staggered. The kid slipped. "Shit!" He got a better grip.

A rustle in the bushes. *What was that?*

Nothing. A rabbit or squirrel maybe. No need to be so damn jittery. The staff were away or in homes scattered over the island except for the doddery watchman who spent most of the time playing solitaire.

Once David was aboard, Robby'd be a piece of cake. Then the boys would be fishbait.

Bile roiled. *I can't do this.*

He gulped. Yes, he could. And he would.

Waves soughed through pilings. Nearly there.

He stopped, breathing hard, at the woods' edge where croaks of tree frogs and crickets overlaid marshy odors of decayed creatures and moldy reeds. Among glittering pinpoints, the crescent moon flirted with a wispy cloud. Moonlit boats at anchor rocked, silhouetted masts naked and jutting.

No late fisherman or crabbers. Safe to leave the shadows, move to the ramp.

SCREEECH!

"What the hell!" *Just that rusty hinge. Get a grip.*

On the dock, the cabin cruiser's metal rail glinted. He kicked aside a stack of tarpaulins and threw David over onto the cruiser. After wiping sweaty eyes, he rotated cramped shoulders.

Supposing the watchman gets up off his ass and makes a round, spots the kid? Better stash him inside the hold.

A hand on the rail, a quick spring, and he landed on the deck. The cruiser bobbed with his weight. "Okay, kid. Moving you one last time."

When he heaved David into the inky cabin, memories flooded.

Him teaching David how to shoot a thirty aught six rifle. Him helping David land a seven foot swordfish. Him and David hanging off the side of the catamaran, laughing like maniacs as the wind whipped them with saltwater and they skimmed across the whitecaps like masters of the sea. David looking to him...

A twinge of regret, then: *I can't think of that.* A live David meant no future for him. No future with Sondra.

Hells bells, the thought of her in James's bed twisted his guts.

Can't think of her either. I'm not half done.

Waves lapped against boats and pilings. A loon's mournful warble added to insect clatter.

Still alone. Still safe. Hurrying back, he stumbled over the root again and swore.

In the kitchen, fluorescents glared at the counter where he doctored a glass of milk.

Upstairs, Robby, in shorts but scrawny chest bare under the lazy ceiling fan, worked on a model airplane. A cabinet for his 78 records stood beside the desk. A foot below the ceiling, a wall shelf circled the room, holding a track for the Lionel model train.

Little hotshot collected stamps, too.

Theo held up the glass. "Brought you some milk, sport."

Robby didn't look up. "I don't want any."

"It's chocolate milk." *With a little something extra.*

"I don't care." Brusque, like James.

Christ, his mouth was parched. Everything seemed weird. Was he really doing this? Yes. Too late to back out. "I made it how you like it, with lots of Hershey's syrup."

Robby had this coming. Only twelve but blasé about luxuries most adults couldn't afford. His own bathroom with tub and shower. An RCA radio/phonograph playing in the corner.

"Go away." Robby laid down a glue tube and picked up the plane. "David thinks you're swell. Hang out with him. Daddy may pay you to stay with us while he and Sondra are gone, but you aren't my nanny."

Arrogant little shit. Just like James. Theo's hand clenched the glass. *Relax. Don't lose your head. Too much is riding on this.* "Aw, come on. You didn't eat much supper."

"I ate plenty."

"I really want you to drink this, Robby."

"Go jump in the ocean. And I told you, stop calling me Robby. It's Robert. Jeez, if you weren't kin, Dad wouldn't put up with your bunk for one minute, much less give you a job."

A red haze. His ears roared. Snotty Robby was all that stood between him and Sondra.

I'll show you. He calmly set the milk down. Then he jerked Robby up and ripped away the airplane. It sailed through the air.

Robby's eyes widened. "What're y—?"

Theo used a chokehold. "Shut up, you crummy, sniveling brat. You're not going to fuck this up for me."

He tried to force the milk down, but Robby twisted. His head bent back.

Theo pressed harder. A bone cracked. Breath whooshed. Robby sagged.

Oh shit oh shit oh shit! I broke his neck.

He let go. Robby thumped onto the bare waxed floor. The red haze faded, but the room blurred. Theo swayed, rubbed his eyes till they could focus on Robby's crumpled form.

Was the kid still alive?

He bent down.

Oh God. He was dead.

Like James. He couldn't breathe. *This can't be happening. Not here. I need air.*

That detached person who wasn't Theo took over. *Get a grip, pal. So Robby's dead. He had to die anyway. Does it matter where?*

No. Theo inhaled, licked his lips, pushed his hair back. *Stupid brat should've drunk the milk.*

He straightened the chair, laid the stupid airplane on the desk and stuck a pin in the cement tube. Then he picked up the needle to silence the stupid Andrews Sisters wailing about rum and Coca Cola, sleeved the record, and put it away.

All stuff finicky Robby would have done before bedtime.

Dead, the kid looked small and defenseless.

Nausea swelled. *No getting sick. Pretend it's that last buck you shot. No difference.*

Yes, it was. That waxy flesh creeped him out, made him feel...

He wrapped the kid in a blanket. "Okay, sport. Going for one of the midnight boat rides with your brother your father always fusses about." *Fussed about.*

This time, when he trudged through the live oaks, he sidestepped the root. At the cruiser, a tarp spilling from the pile tripped him, made him drop Robby. The blanket parted. Robby's head, eyes staring, bounced on the dock's weathered boards.

He recoiled, caught himself. No time to be squeamish. Robby couldn't feel anything. Get him aboard and into the cabin. "Join your brother, sport."

The dory fit between the cruiser seats. The motor and oars went inside.

Ready to put out to sea. Soon he would have everything. As the boat cut through dark water, he mapped out his future to take his mind off what he was doing. What he'd done.

He'd keep the island that his ancestors had settled. But forget that 1942 Buick; he'd buy a new sports car. And the yacht James had scoffed at? His now. Along with hunting lodges, polo ponies, airplanes. And a Girard-Perregaux watch like his fraternity brother flaunted.

My great-grandfather's ring! David's still wearing the druid's ring.

The wheel veered. His hand straightened it automatically.

The other Theo—the detached one, the clever one— surfaced. *You can't keep it. It's unique. Someone might see it and guess what you did. Don't be stupid.*

But a kid like David had no business with an heirloom like that. The ring should have been his to start with. His grandfather was the oldest son, not James's. So what if he couldn't wear it in public? He'd still own it. Along with everything else. James's money. The island.

Sondra.

Seductive, beautiful, passionate. He was risking everything for her but Christ, how he loved her. He'd been a goner the first time he saw her, an angel in her nurse's white, all big eyes and sultry smile. He could've killed James for taking her away.

Forget it. James was dead. She'd be his soon enough.

On the open sea, mist rose. Occasional boat lights diffused into hazy glimmerings and faded before he cut the engines. Should he throw out life preservers? Yeah. If they were picked up, the *Harmony Island* logo would confirm the boys' deaths.

Anything else?

No. Launch the dory and get in. Then light the slow fuse.

Mulrennon would never miss a few sticks of dynamite from the farm shed.

By the time the distant boom came and night skies blazed out at sea, he was at the mansion's inlet. He collapsed over the tiller, shaking all over but unable to stop grinning.

He'd done it. The boys were ashes. The mickeys could have been too weak, the dynamite too old, the fuse bad. But everything had worked. He might have been screwed once by Lady Luck—orphaned, left dependent on James's charity—but no more. *Stay with me, baby!*

His hands were steady by the time he moored the dory.

At the house, he bounded upstairs and poured Robby's untouched milk down the bathroom sink. One last check to make sure nothing was out of place, then back down to wash out telltale traces in the boys' glasses before leaving them in the dishwasher.

There. Chores done.

He needed a belt. Bad. No reason to squander the pitcher of martinis.

The alcohol should have helped him sleep, but it didn't. This night had been a dream. It was like someone else had carried David, choked Robby, set the dynamite. Not him.

And the strange hush now that it was over. Like the house knew. Creepy.

He plumped his pillow. Shit, he hated killing the boys. Even runty Robby. *I had no choice. Not when it came down to them or Sondra.*

Sondra. Christ, her moist lips. Her breasts ripe for a man's hands. How he loved her. He'd do anything for her.

No. I've done it.

And she was worth it.

Along with the money.

Chapter 1

"My Buddy"
As Performed by Henry Burr (1922)
Music by Walter Donaldson
Lyrics by Gus Kahn

Coastal Georgia
May, 1962

FOR SIXTEEN YEARS attorney Lawrence Wykerton had dealt with Theodore Pack. For almost that long, he had absolutely despised the man.

A weakness that went against every principle instilled by his father.

"Give a person the benefit of the doubt," his father had preached. "Everyone has some good inside." "Be fair; consider all viewpoints." "Always, always do what is right."

The younger generation might sneer, but the old platitudes had served Lawrence faithfully for nearly seventy years. He could have gone through life never doubting their worth.

Except for Theo Pack.

That's why, when his secretary buzzed to say Theo was on the line, Lawrence almost instructed her to say he was out. She might bustle in to see if he was ill, but he didn't care.

He knew exactly what Theo wanted.

Confound it. He shouldn't have let his hopes rise when

the Packs' current island sojourn brought no new demands. But he had. After all, they were flying out today. Perhaps they wouldn't ask for an advance. Perhaps this time they'd make it till the quarter.

The cursed phone call brought him to his senses. He should have known better. The Packs were always short of money.

Botheration. He did not want to deal with Theo. How tempting to say he was busy.

Oh dear, oh dear. What to do, what to do.

As if he had a choice. He squared his shoulders and, ruing his father's training, picked up the phone. "Hello, Theo."

Theo didn't hem or haw. "We need an advance, Lawrence."

No apologies, no excuses, no polite "please." Their turbulent history precluded warmth, but that didn't mean common courtesies couldn't be observed.

He picked up the pen from the Harmony Trust folder, open to where he'd been ticking off deceased beneficiaries. The clack of typewriters filtered in from the clerks' room next to him.

"Lawrence? Are you there? Did you hear me?"

He swallowed a sharp retort—Lord knew he'd had enough practice—and managed his normal neutral tone. "Yes, I'm here, Theo. How much?"

Theo told him.

"Goodness gracious." He jotted down the amount. Ridiculous. "I'll send what's available to the usual account."

They'd gone through the drill often enough. If he came up with part of what Theo wanted, Theo would bluster and sulk but manage till next quarter. The boy had finally realized accusations and lawsuits would get him nowhere.

Boy. Humph. Theo was thirty-eight. Long past being a boy, no matter how pigheaded and extravagant he'd turned out.

After hanging up, Lawrence played with his pen and watched dust motes dance in sunshine streaming through a large bow window onto shelves of law books.

The advance posed no real problem; the Packs always overspent their income so he always budgeted a reserve. The problem was protecting the Harmony Trust. He could only do that till next year when the Packs would get control. Then...

Hard to think of what would happen without gagging.

The pen stopped twirling.

That was neither here nor there.

He looked at the amount again—outrageous!—and flung the pen down. Then he ran a hand through his hair. "Damn Theo."

Unbelievable that a dilettante like Theo Pack could be related to a great man like James.

Ah, James, my friend, my friend. How I miss you still.

At noon Lawrence, somewhat calmed, arrived for his weekly Rotary meeting at the Blue Crab Diner across from the city pier. While he sought his panama, his driver opened the car door.

Pungent odors drifted over from the inland river. An unhurried shrimper, nets raised but followed by gulls hopeful of scavenging thrown-back fish, glided by the pier on its way to the marina. Against a cloudless blue sky, boat and birds stood out in stark relief.

He laboriously swung out his legs. "I must have left my hat at the office, Curtis. Seems like I forget everything nowadays."

"It's right here, Mr. Lawrence. I'll get it." Part of Curtis's summer intern duties involved chauffeuring The Old Man.

Ah yes. Lawrence knew exactly what his coworkers called him behind his back. His father had once earned the same soubriquet, and his grandfather before that.

Both fine men, but sometimes hard to live up to.

While Curtis retrieved his hat, Lawrence dragged himself out. A speck marred his linen suit sleeve. He flicked it off as the boy, smoothing the panama's brim, reappeared. "Here you go, Mr. Lawrence. Let me help you up on the curb."

Lawrence snatched his hat and shook off the proffered hand. "No, thank you, Curtis. I'm not in my dotage yet."

Mollycoddling him like he was an old man. Sixty-eight

was not old, no matter what a rising college senior might think.

"Course not, Mr. Lawrence." Curtis, straight and muscular, the grandson of Lawrence's housekeeper, tilted his head. "Thing is, Mam said she'd whup me if I don't watch out for you. And'f she thinks I'm not, she will, too. I'll pick you up at one."

Blast him. The boy was way too uppity.

Not that he didn't have cause. One of James Harmony's more controversial endowments provided a college education to any high school graduate in the county who passed entrance exams and maintained passing grades. White or Negro. After his junior year at Morehouse in Atlanta, Curtis held a three point eight average with ambitions centered on Yale Law School.

If necessary, he would call in markers to get the boy in. But fondness for Curtis didn't mean he'd stand for any guff. "I'll tell Mam about your backtalk."

"Yessir." Black coffee eyes in a *café au lait* face feigned meekness even as Curtis called his bluff. "You do that."

Curtis knew perfectly well he wasn't the only one his grandmother bossed around.

Lawrence gathered his dignity. "Don't bother coming back. I'll walk." He slapped his hat on his head and marched off.

"It's pretty warm, sir. Mam says you shouldn't be—"

"It's not that hot."

"But Mam—"

"Three blocks isn't far. I'll walk. Do not come back."

So there. He strutted away. Nobody, including Mam via her grandson, would tell him what to do.

Inside the cafe, she-crab soup, sweet local shrimp, and regular camaraderie swept umbrage aside. By the time the speaker finished tearing apart Kennedy's botched foreign policies and outlandish domestic strategies, Lawrence's stomach was full and his equanimity restored.

Then the banker, gray suit snug on his stout frame, tugged at him while he shook hands with the Baptist preacher. "Got a minute, Lawrence?"

Berriman, the youngest brother of a man Lawrence had started first grade with, handled part of the Harmony monies. Lawrence knew at once what he wanted. The Packs. Always the Packs. Packs meaning Theo. "I do. Needed to talk to you anyway. D'you have a pen?"

After Berriman scribbled notes on a business card about drafting money to Theo's New York account, he launched into why he'd detained Lawrence. His bank had received credit inquiries. Theo was pricing yachts. Expensive yachts.

Careful not to show annoyance, Lawrence listened. *So that's what the rascal's up to. He just bought one, what? Six, seven years ago?*

When Berriman asked whether to approve Theo's loan, Lawrence shrugged. "Might help you hang on to the accounts next year."

"You think Theo'll move them when they inherit?"

"A good possibility. He and Sondra aren't down here that much."

Was Berriman always so thick? Of course Theo would move them. Theo would have shifted everything to one of his dubious cronies years ago except for Lawrence.

Berriman, jowly face troubled, chitchatted about whether the Packs' banking business might end up in New York or Palm Beach or, God forbid, Europe.

Lawrence heard him out, ire dwindling. Berriman was worried, not thick. He was like the other locals: unwilling to believe the Packs would destroy the local economy. It would be cruel to disillusion him so Lawrence put on a noncommittal front till he could escape, fuming.

No Town Car in sight. Good. He needed to get hold of himself.

On the horizon, far beyond the outskirts of town, smoke puffed from a Harmony plant. Its steel had helped build Liberty Ships during World War II, and booming automobile sales kept it profitable. Theo, the fool, was already mouthing off about selling it and other lucrative holdings next year when the Trust ended.

Lawrence had pored over every phrase, every word, every comma in James's will, seeking a loophole. But everything depended on that one damning sentence James had insisted on inserting: "The Trust shall be disbursed on October 2, 1963."

No ifs, ands, or buts to be misconstrued. That was the date Robby would have turned thirty, but James didn't specify his son's birthday. Only the date. The courts would do nothing.

Lawrence couldn't complain. That sentence had saved the estate from Theo's depredations so far. But that same sentence would soon end Lawrence's stewardship, allowing Theo to liquidate companies, leave employees jobless, and squander the proceeds.

Everything James had achieved for the region, for the state, for an entire country at war, would be lost and forgotten.

"I've failed you, James." There should be something he could do, but he couldn't see what. He'd sounded out Sondra Pack, but she, foolish woman, thought Theo hung the moon.

Heartsick, he strolled the avenue of century-old coastal homes until he came to three small girls in shorts and flip-flops, playing in puddles of sunshine filtered through oaks. His appearance halted their squeals and chalking of squares on the sidewalk.

Then one recognized him. "Hello, Mr. Wykerton. Be careful of our hopscotch."

He tipped his panama. "Of course, ladies."

As they watched mistrustfully, he avoided wobbly lines before proceeding.

A chorus of "thank you" followed. Someone had taught them manners.

Beads of sweat on his upper lip made him dig for his handkerchief. So hot. He envied the girls their indifference to the weather. Curtis would give him that "I told you so" look.

He inhaled deeply.

Ah, it wasn't that bad. Not really. A river breeze, carrying scents of sunshine on water, half-heartedly tempered the sticky Lowland heat. Why, some Junes were scorching, dry enough to wither the resurrection ferns lining the live oak trunks.

No, today wasn't bad at all.

He should have let Curtis come back for him.

Oh, well. Not far now.

He trudged on, the old days filling his mind. How often had James laid an arm across his shoulders to say, "You can handle it, Whitey. You're the only *honest* attorney I know," then squeeze while that unforgettable laugh boomed out. "Personally, that is."

Their private joke.

"No handling it this time. I'm sorry, James."

If only you had gone to the doctor as Sondra begged. If only the boys hadn't taken the boat out that night. If only one of them had survived.

"Stop your whining, old man."

Be grateful James had been spared knowing his sons' fate.

Lawrence's childhood home, a Victorian now housing the law firm of Wykerton Perth and Ross, came into view. Pink camellias beloved by his mother still lined the front walk. The azaleas and daffodils were long done, but gardenias and plate-sized magnolia blossoms diffused cloying fragrances.

As he plodded down the broad brick walkway, the oval-glassed door sprang open. Clerks in spike heels and summer dresses exited in a flurry of squeals and splash of white petticoats.

He paused. "What's wrong?"

"Rats!" The new receptionist nearly knocked him down. "We have rats!"

"Nonsense." He should have known better than to hire a flighty young female.

He reached the veranda steps in time to be shoved aside when his own secretary burst out. Blue shirtwaist dress flapped and sturdy walking heels thudded, but tightly permed hair didn't bounce a lick. "A rat in the office!"

"Come now." Such an uproar. He'd thought better of her.

Inside, he caught several attorneys hanging back as

Curtis hit out at something small and furry. It scurried across the floor. "Here, here, Curtis!"

Then Megan Mulrennon, navy skirt and white blouse businesslike but copper chignon falling apart, appeared. "Don't hurt it, Curtis. Wait. It's behind the wastebasket."

She grabbed a sweater off his secretary's chair and with two steps, threw it over the creature and scooped it up. "Ground squirrel. Must have sneaked in through that open kitchen window." She brushed by to release the creature outside.

Short in stature, she had a face that would appear youthful even when she had gray hair. Her nose turned up, and her upper lip was slightly longer than the bottom, suggesting a melancholic disposition. The dancing eyes, when she came back inside, dispelled the notion. "I'll have to wash Miss Ruby's sweater for her."

Levelheaded child. Never moody or prone to tears. He'd watched her grow from a tomboy shadowing the lively David, to a shy teenager working afternoons in his office, to a law school graduate taking on a man's job. She was capable. He'd never doubted her ability else he wouldn't have brought her into the firm no matter how fond he was of her and her mother.

If this new law Kennedy was pushing got passed, it would mean her salary would have to be adjusted so the firm wouldn't save as much money. But no matter. She'd soon leave, anyway, with her engagement to that Atlantan. Marriage was inevitable, even for plainer girls than Megan, but her move would sever one more link to the past. He'd miss her.

Though not as much as the attorneys whose work she helped with.

Speaking of which... Ah, things were getting back to normal. The male spectators had returned to their offices while the runaway women were sheepishly filing back inside. He held the door for them. "Goodness gracious, ladies. Perhaps I'll start skipping Rotary. Things are much more exciting around here than at our stodgy lunches."

In his office, he called Theo's New York banker about

the forthcoming draft. Then he opened a law volume, only to slump and push it aside. No use. He couldn't concentrate.

Taking off his glasses, he rubbed his eyes.

Each time Theo had sued for control of the estate, the courts had ruled Lawrence had absolute discretion. An unwanted obligation, but when James remarried and changed his will, he'd asked Lawrence to be sole trustee and guardian for his sons.

How could he refuse? Especially when James confessed that he might have been a wee bit hasty in trying to give the boys a mother figure so soon after being widowed.

Humph. James had glossed over his own appetites, but it would have taken a colder man than James to resist Sondra. Nor had age dimmed her allure, as witness Lawrence's own son who should have long ago outgrown mooning after Sondra but hadn't, more was the pity.

A bigger pity Sondra and Theo would get the bulk of James's estate.

Lawrence massaged a temple. If life were perfect, Theo would break his neck skiing. Or get shot in a hunting accident. Or fall off a yacht and drown. Or crash his plane into a mountain.

Theo and his set drank heavily. Flying while intoxicated might induce a fatal error that...

"Tsk, tsk. You should be ashamed of yourself." One did not hope for a man's death simply to protect a friend's legacy.

But there had to be some way to save it. Lawrence had studied James's will for sixteen years; there was nothing there to help. Maybe a closer look at James's other papers would yield something—a word, a phrase, anything—he could use to stop Theo's dismantling everything .

One couldn't hope for Theo to die, but one could dream of fate intervening in other ways. Would that be so terrible?

He sighed. If only the boys had survived.

Chapter 2

"I've Got the World on a String"
As Performed by Frank Sinatra (1953)
Music by Harold Arlen
Lyrics by Ted Koehler

South of France
July, 1962

SONDRA SELLIN HARMONY Pack, clutching her tennis racket and wearing her favorite Tinling tennis dress with the red embroidered flowers on the skirt lining, sauntered to the hotel elevator and pushed the up button.

Its bell dinged and gleaming doors opened to discharge two men in casual shirts and slacks, one of whom caught Sondra straightening her panties. She flashed a *so-what* smile.

A double take, a quick intake of breath, and his hand shot out to hold the elevator for her.

Oh yeah. Talk about it. A flutter of lashes could still stop them in their tracks.

Inside the elevator, she used her key for the penthouse, then turned to catch him admiring her legs before coming back to her face. She'd got her own eyeful by then.

Uh huh, a stiffie. Those tight stylish pants showed it all.

The doors whispered shut. Grinning, she took off the headband.

Nice to know she hadn't lost it. She might not be

twenty-one anymore, but she could still get men going. Not that she'd ever follow through. She had Theo.

Peering into the side mirror with a pout worthy of Brigitte, she searched for wrinkles.

Nope. Nary a one, thanks to Dr. Hamm.

Only lush lips, smooth forehead, and eyes so blue they seemed purple. Elizabeth Taylor eyes, everyone said. A poet had written verses about them. A shame nobody had ever heard of him.

Only three more days till Theo would be back. Christ, she missed him. She'd known from the beginning she'd have to share him with his silly sports, but keeping him happy was worth an occasional separation.

A wise woman gave her man plenty of space.

The elevator opened to huge windows hung with burgundy silk draperies that overlooked the blue Mediterranean. Below, the yellow sunshine she adored drenched sunbathers littering a sparkling pebbly beach. Here and there, bright umbrellas protected the sun-dodgers.

She never tired of this place. It was tangible proof that she'd pulled herself out of a two-room shack in Mississippi to the world of millionaires and celebrities.

Too bad they didn't have their own house here. Hotels, no matter how plush, got old. But when they first married, Theo had wanted an African hunting lodge, and everyone who was anybody simply had to have a place in New York. Lawrence Wykerton, stingy thing, had docked their income to make up for those purchases. That was the first time they'd butted heads.

Next year the old fart would be history.

Peachie came out yipping happily. She picked up the tiny poodle and crooned, "Is Mama's baby glad to see her? Has her been a good girl?"

The heavy fragrance engulfed her before she saw them.

Scarlet masses, everywhere.

She set Peachie down. Admirers sent her flowers all the time, but this... This was a garden of red roses brought indoors. One huge vase loomed over the foyer console. In the living room, blooms blanketed a sofa table, a cocktail table, and side tables while the mantel held two smaller vases. Even the dining room across the hall was stuffed.

"Christ, Janie," she said when her maid appeared to take charge of her tennis racket and headband. "There are enough roses here to open a flower stand. Who sent them?"

Janie rounded her eyes. "Aren't they something? Miss Linda took the card."

"I wonder who they're from."

Not Theo. He was in the North Sea on his annual sailing trip with his male clique. The straitlaced German she played bridge with? Not a chance. Had to be the British MP who monopolized her every chance he got. He was besotted and yeah, maybe she *had* led him on.

Her secretary appeared. "The card's right here."

"Thanks, Linda." Sondra took the sealed envelope. "How are the invitations coming?"

"Addressed and ready to go."

"You're the best." Sondra had agreed to co-hostess a charity ball with an Italian contessa of some notoriety. She loved lending her name and Linda's services for these events as long as they were splashy with an abundant attendance of the celebrities in residence.

This affair promised to be both. Yves Montand and that Greek millionaire and some of the Kennedy clan were coming. Not the President or Jackie, but there was always a chance the invitees might later offer access to the glittering couple themselves.

That's how she and Theo had met the luscious Frank Sinatra. And Princess Margaret; the bitch had snubbed them but then she snubbed everyone. And they barely knew the Frenchman who'd introduced them to the Duke and Duchess of Windsor at a garden party.

Theo called the former king a fairy, but she thought he was absolutely charming. And oh, the Duchess's jewelry! Fantabulous.

Like these roses. She held one to her nose. "Mmmm."

"Yummy, aren't they? Thirty dozen. Janie counted. They have to be from the MP." Linda's guess echoed Sondra's.

She put the rose back. "A cliché, so many, but what can

you expect from an uptight English politician whose wife keeps him on a short leash?"

Clichéd or not, so many were good for her ego. She might have hit forty—not that she'd admit it—but they proved she was still in the game.

As a phone rang, Linda rushed to answer and Sondra ripped into the envelope.

There wasn't a card. Only a folded newspaper section.

What in the world was this?

She spread out a clipped photograph to see a man posed with his fists on his hips. The article caption read: "Downing's Richard III Wows Hardened London Critics."

She froze, but not because of the headline.

The grainy face of the actor had been circled in red ink. To the side, heavily underscored, block letters in the same ink shouted: "DAVID HARMONY'S COMING HOME!"

Her eardrums pounded. "No." *No, no, hell no!*

Christ. Good thing nobody was around. She pulled herself together as Linda returned.

"A few problems with the wines but everything's copacetic." Her secretary frowned. "Are you okay? You're white as a ghost."

"Yes." Sondra crumpled the clipping. "I'm fine. Where did the roses come from?"

"I don't know. Janie took the delivery. Are they from the MP?"

Sondra went in search of her maid.

Janie, cleaning Sondra's black *peau de soie* heels for a soiree that night, knew exactly where the flowers had originated. "The shop in the hotel. Is something wrong?"

"No." Sondra wet her lips. "I need to change. I want to, uh, to walk in the gardens. Lay out the white capri pants and the pink top with the ruffles."

"Don't forget your massage and hair color appointments."

"I have an hour yet." The words came automatically, evenly.

Damn good thing she'd never been one to panic. As a nurse in Cherbourg during the war, she'd learned iron self-control. It had come in handy when she had to watch James die in such agony. She would have broken then if she hadn't been so tough.

No, she wouldn't think of James's suffering. Or the wounded soldiers. Or the dead captain she'd hoped to marry. The terrible parts of her life were over.

Think about how wonderful everything is now. Think about Theo. Think about your homes, your clothes, your jewels, the parties. You're somebody *now. You're part of the jet set.*

Once changed, she told Janie, "I won't be long. Keep Peachie here, will you?"

Once outside, away from her staff's curiosity, on a secluded path that meandered away from the beach, she pulled out a lighter and lit a cigarette. The brilliant sun and azure sea held no pleasure anymore. A private bench nestled within towering shrubbery offered a haven where she could unfold the clipping and soak in every word about stage actor Nick Downing.

The article lauded his performances but mostly gushed about the man himself and his captivating personality. After a second reading, Sondra took one last drag on her cigarette.

What shitass had sent this? And why?

Once she ground the stub into the gravel path, she pulled out her lighter, set fire to the clipping, and held a corner till the last vestige turned black and disintegrated. With steady hands, she lit a new cigarette and inhaled.

Bees buzzed nearby. The midday sun touched flowering shrubs. Her favorite fountain, featuring a large Adonis and Aphrodite—who everyone agreed looked remarkably like her— trickled merrily. A couple holding hands appeared on one of the trails that dotted the gardens.

A perfect spot to relax except for that pissy clipping.

Another crackpot, that's all. Over the years, such notes had appeared constantly. Addressed to her, to Theo, to their attorneys, to the newspapers. Even to Lawrence. Christ, she was tired of them. Why wouldn't these assholes leave it alone?

Someone was jealous. Jealous that the daughter of an

illiterate Alabama sharecropper had walked off with the Harmony fortune.

Shitasses.

Was it her fault she was smart as well as beautiful? When they'd advertised for nurses during the war, she had jumped at the chance to escape the cotton fields.

They didn't tell her what she was in for. The bullets, the blood, the terror. But she'd kept her bargain, hadn't she? More than kept it.

And it was worth it. Some dumb clerk had misspelled *Sandra* on her birth certificate, but not till the army changed little Sandra Lynn Sellin to the impressive Second Lieutenant Sondra L. Sellin did she realize how lucky she was.

No more country bumpkin *Sandra*.

She was the exotic Sondra, who did her job when the artillery shook buildings they operated in. Who soothed the faceless, armless, legless remnants of men. Who watched a fellow nurse die from shrapnel as they helped evacuate wounded. Who saw the artillery captain she'd planned to marry with his brains splattered.

She shuddered.

No, forget that. Forget all the bad memories. Think of the good things.

Like after the war. When she'd heard James Harmony needed a nurse, she'd gone straight to his dying wife because no sensible woman would let her husband hire a beautiful woman.

Her strategy had worked. Kindhearted Livvy had chosen her though James, he'd laughingly admitted after their marriage, had lobbied for the daughter of an old friend.

How clever she'd been to approach Livvy first.

Her self-congratulatory glow faded.

David Harmony's coming home.

By God, she'd earned her position. She deserved every bit of this fabulous life.

And nobody—nobody!—had any right to send her ugly newspaper clippings.

She didn't know who the hell Nick Downing was, but

she did know one thing. David was as dead as his father and brother, and had been for sixteen years.

Next year the Trust would wind up—finally—and she and Theo would get it all. Envious assholes could send her a hundred newspaper articles and they would change nothing.

Nothing!

She had a good mind to see who'd sent those frigging roses. Throwing down the unfinished cigarette, she got up and brushed off the seat of her capris. She'd end this right now.

The order had come by mail, the haughty Frenchwoman presiding over the flower shop informed her. "With a large banknote to defray the cost, *madame*."

"Was there a letter or card?"

Appraising eyes frosted. "A typed letter with the order specifics came to us. The missive included a sealed envelope for inclusion with the flowers. *We* do not open such cards, *madame*."

The envelope bore no return address but may have come from Paris. Or perhaps London. Or Rome or New York. The saleslady shrugged bony shoulders. "*Qui sait?*" Who knows?

Though quick to palm proffered franc notes, the blackclad bitch evinced smug regret that the postmarked envelope with its instructions had been discarded and was irretrievable.

As Sondra left the shop, the sharp aroma of chrysanthemums brought images of James's funeral where monstrous wreaths had sapped the island chapel air and turned her faint. That in turn evoked hazy images of James's sons.

The face in the clipping did resemble David's. The actor wasn't David. Not a chance. But if David had lived, he might have looked like this Nick Downing.

A chill touched her. What if this was some kind of omen? They'd waited so long.

Don't be such a lamebrain.

Theo would be back this weekend. Once he got over his

irritation at another anonymous letter, he would mock her premonitions and laugh at her for imagining David could be alive. He would tease her out of her funk and make her scream when she came.

Christ, she missed him.

That night, after the soiree in a luxurious villa where liquor flowed and women glittered with jewels and laughter floated overhead on the high hill looking down on the Mediterranean, Sondra arrived home pleasantly buzzed.

An unwelcome message waited. Theo's group had decided to extend their Scandinavian sailing trip.

Never would she let Janie see her upset, but after stripping off her Givenchy dress and donning a silk nightgown and climbing into the opulent bed, she cuddled Peachie and lay awake. She'd counted on Theo. She needed to run her hands over his body, feel him against her, in her.

She needed a good screw, dammit.

Sometimes she wished she didn't love him so much.

But she did. Despite the faint thickening of his body and the sun creases on his face, despite his occasional moods and the niggling signs his drinking might be getting out of hand.

Okay. Intimacy sooner or later led to aggravations, but they were minor. Theo was her life. She hated being weak but where he was concerned, she was pathetic.

Oh Theo, what would I do without you?

That damned newspaper clipping hung in the back of her mind as she cried in the darkness before she fell asleep, the first time she'd cried in a long time.

Peachie, sweet baby, licked at her tears.

Losing David

Available 2014

from

Amazon, Barnes and Noble and other
booksellers

www.ingramcontent.com/pod-product-compliance
Lightning Source LLC
Chambersburg PA
CBHW071129200626
46817CB00018B/2493